Hearts *racing*.
Blood *pumping*.
Pulses *accelerating*.

Falling in love can be a blur...
especially at 180 mph!

So if you crave the thrill of the chase—on and off the track—you'll love

BACK ON TRACK
by Abby Gaines!

"I don't want you here and, trust me, that means you don't want to be here," Trent said.

"I'm not quitting. I've been offered a job and I accepted it. I'm certain you'll soon see the value of my assistance."

"So certain that you'd bet on it? You say I need you, I say I don't. I'll give you a week to convince me. If you fail, you quit."

"Why would I agree to that? Chad hired me for the rest of the series."

"You can babysit me for six months and I'll tell the media exactly what I think of your half-baked psychology. Or you can persuade me you have something to offer and everyone will know you're a key part of the team when I win the NASCAR NEXTEL Cup Series Championship. Which I will do. Do we have a deal?"

She didn't doubt that if she refused his offer, he would figure out some way to get her off the team.

"Deal," Kelly said.

Dear Reader,

I love the way whole families get involved in NASCAR, at all levels of the sport—fans, crew members, drivers. It's a heritage thing, a shared passion that binds us when our differences might otherwise drive us apart. In *Back on Track*, you'll meet the Matheson family—three brothers bonded by NASCAR, with the blood of champions in their veins. The winningest Matheson of all is the youngest—Trent Matheson, gorgeous and charming, almost unbeatable on the track.

When Trent's racing hits a glitch, sport psychologist Kelly Greenwood is certain she can figure out what's wrong, whether Trent wants her help or not. She has something to prove to her own family, and falling for the "irresistible" Trent Matheson isn't on her agenda. When two such determined, strong-willed people come together, you can bet the sparks will fly.

I'd love to know if you enjoy Trent and Kelly's story—please e-mail me at abby@abbygaines.com.

Sincerely,

Abby Gaines

|||||| NASCAR®

BACK ON TRACK
Abby Gaines

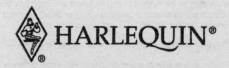

HARLEQUIN®

TORONTO • NEW YORK • LONDON
AMSTERDAM • PARIS • SYDNEY • HAMBURG
STOCKHOLM • ATHENS • TOKYO • MILAN • MADRID
PRAGUE • WARSAW • BUDAPEST • AUCKLAND

ISBN-13: 978-0-373-21775-5
ISBN-10:   0-373-21775-7

BACK ON TRACK

Copyright © 2007 by Harlequin Books S.A.

Abbie Gaines is acknowledged as the author of this work.

NASCAR® and the NASCAR Library Collection are registered trademarks of the National Association for Stock Car Auto Racing, Inc.

www.eHarlequin.com

Printed in U.S.A.

ABBY GAINES

Like some of her favorite NASCAR drivers, Abby Gaines's first love was open-wheel dirt track racing. But the lure of NASCAR—the speed, the power, the awesome scale—proved irresistible, just as it did for those drivers. Now Abby's two-timing the dirt, and absolutely thrilled to be combining her love of NASCAR with her love of writing.

When she's not writing NASCAR romance novels for the Harlequin series and for Harlequin Superromance, Abby works as editor of a speedway magazine. She lives with her husband and three children on an olive grove. It's every bit as peaceful as it sounds...except on Saturday nights, when the roar of engines warming up at the local speedway drifts across the river and sets Abby's heart thumping—and has the family piling into the car for a night at the racetrack.

Visit Abby at www.abbygaines.com, or e-mail her, abby@abbygaines.com.

For Dave Stewart and Bill Buckley.
Thanks for the in-at-the-deep-end introduction to
speedway, and for the most fun job I ever had.

Huge thanks to Ant Williams, sport psychologist
extraordinaire, for his insights into the racing mind.

Thanks also to Jamie Rodway at Roush Racing
for his time and assistance.

CHAPTER ONE

"HEY, TRENT, you're on TV."

Trent Matheson didn't look up from his laptop computer. "Am I with a blonde?"

He didn't know how the media managed to get so many different shots of him with so many different blondes. At the very least, it seemed like discrimination against brunettes. Trent had dated a brunette a couple of months back, he was certain. Almost certain.

The regular sounds of Matheson Racing's race car preparation—the clang of metal on metal, the hiss of the air guns, the whine of the welding torch—ceased as everyone except Trent looked up at the TV. Then Rod Sutton, Trent's crew chief, said, "She's blond, for sure. But not your kind of blond."

Trent hit the Send button that would transmit his e-mail newsletter to thousands of NASCAR fans all over America, then checked out the TV high on the wall at the far end of the workshop. The sound was off, but sure enough there he was, his face blown up large behind the woman. Like Rod said, she was blond. Pretty, but awkward-looking. The on-screen caption read Kelly Greenwood, Sport Psychology Consultant.

"Not another one," he muttered. Another expert with an opinion on what made Trent Matheson a winner. He shook his head—he'd rather spend his time answering the dozens of fan e-mails that had come in today than listen to what other people said about him. Then a picture of Danny Cruise flashed up on the screen alongside Trent's face. Cruise was his number-one rival for the NASCAR NEXTEL Cup Series.

"Turn up the sound, will you?" Trent called to Rod.

When the volume came up, the camera had panned back to show the TV network's traveling prerace studio. Kelly Greenwood was one of four guests being interviewed by host Chris Spires. Trent recognized the other three: a regular race analyst, a former Cup champion who wasn't racing this year and a retired crew chief. All male.

"Okay, folks, let's have your picks," Chris Spires said. "Trent Matheson won last week's NASCAR race here in Charlotte—can he do it again this Sunday?"

The analyst spoke up first. "Cruise is good, but I'm picking Trent Matheson."

"Matheson, without a doubt," the retired driver agreed.

A cheer went up around the Matheson Racing workshop. Trent flashed a grin to his team. "Smart guys, huh?"

The ex-crew chief took a little longer to make up his mind. He sounded reluctant when he said, "It'll go down to the wire, but Matheson will win it."

A grumble ran around the workshop, but Trent waved it away with good humor. He knew the ex-chief's reluctance stemmed from the fact that Trent had dated his daughter, then ended it when she refused to accept what he'd told her all along, that he wasn't after a serious relationship. The old guy just plain didn't like him. But he couldn't deny Trent was the standout driver in this year's field.

"What about you, Kelly?" Chris Spires turned a smile on the blonde.

For a bare second, she froze. Then her tongue came out to moisten her lips, and she cleared her throat. She lifted a hand to push a stray strand of hair behind her ear, but her watch tangled in the cord of the microphone clipped to her shirt. There was a brief, inelegant tussle that had the guys in the workshop sniggering. Trent smiled, too—Kelly Greenwood didn't look as if she'd been on TV before. She was blinking too often and, going by her flushed cheeks, the heat of the studio lights was getting to her.

At last she got her watch free, tucked the hair out of the way and gathered a sufficient grip on herself to say, "Trent Matheson is brilliant…."

A ragged cheer went around the crew and surprisingly— because this woman's opinion meant nothing to him—Trent's grin widened into his trademark cocky smile, the one that had proved all-too-elusive lately.

Kelly Greenwood added, "But totally unreliable."

"What the—?" Trent snapped to attention, made an impatient shushing motion to quiet the hisses and boos that bounced off the concrete floor and walls of the workshop.

The blond shrink continued, "So, will Trent Matheson win tomorrow? Not a chance." Then she had the nerve to beam at the shell-shocked interviewer as if she'd won first prize in the "Big Mouth of the Year" contest.

"But Matheson finished in the top three the last two weeks," the former champion, sounding miffed at having been contradicted, pointed out.

The blonde nodded. "But he crashed out the two weeks before that at Richmond and Talladega. It's a pattern I've noticed with him." She sounded more confident now.

"So…Sunday's race?" Chris Spires prompted her. "Matheson typically does well on the high-banked turns here in Charlotte."

She spread her hands as if in sympathy for the totally unreliable Trent Matheson. "He'll be lucky to last beyond lap two hundred. My money's on Danny Cruise—for tomorrow's Cup race and for the whole—"

Trent got to the TV and hit the off button before she could finish her sentence. He turned to the assembled company.

"What say we invite her to join me in Victory Lane after I win tomorrow?"

There was a chorus of support from every corner except the one that mattered. Chad Matheson, who sometimes forgot he'd been Trent's older brother for thirty-one years and his boss for just five, was rubbing his chin as if he actually lent some credence to the garbage that woman had spouted. Chad said, "She's right, you did crash out twice in a row."

"Eight million Americans could have told you that," Trent snapped. *Thanks for the vote of confidence, bro.*

"You did that last season," Chad said. "You won two, lost two, won two, lost two."

Deliberately, Trent stayed where he was, next to the life-size poster of himself pinned to the wall below the TV set. They'd sold thousands of those posters when Trent won the NASCAR Busch Series. He'd autographed so many, he'd practically gotten carpal tunnel syndrome. "I finished top-three the next five after that, and I won the Busch series. For the second time," he reminded his brother. He knew what Chad would say to that.

"The Cup is different."

Bingo.

Chad continued, "There's more pressure, you don't have the same experience in the series."

So what if Trent had been the highest-performing rookie in the history of the NASCAR NEXTEL Cup Series on his debut two years ago? So what if last year he'd set the fastest lap time more often than any other driver and had finished fifth in the series, leaving everyone to predict another quantum leap in his performance this season? Chad wouldn't be confident of victory until he was standing next to Trent in Victory Lane, helping hold up that coveted sterling silver trophy.

"I'm ready for this," Trent told his brother. The two men locked glares for several long seconds. Chad looked away first, and it was as if a spell had been broken, freeing the crew to return to their work of setting up the Number 186 car for Sunday's race.

Trent let a confident swagger into his walk as he did the rounds of the workshop, checking on the cars, cracking jokes and giving the guys the encouragement that helped bond them into an unbeatable team.

He planned to win on Sunday. No sport psychologist was going to tell him otherwise.

KELLY GREENWOOD popped the top of her soda and set the can down on the coffee table. She sank into the comfort of her leather couch. What more could a girl want than a Sunday spent watching the most exciting motor racing in the world? Even better, it counted as work.

She switched on the TV just as the NASCAR theme music played. Along with the 170,000-odd people at the track, she closed her eyes for the invocation, then sang along to the national anthem. And when the grand marshal said those time-honored words, "Gentlemen, start your engines," she felt the familiar lurch in the pit of her stomach. Who needed to go to the race, when watching it at home was as good as being there?

Who am I kidding? She'd have loved to be at the race track, rather than sitting here in the condo she'd rented for the duration of the NASCAR NEXTEL Cup Series. But insulting Charlotte's favorite homegrown race driver had made her Public Enemy Number One. Who knew Trent Matheson had so many fans? And who knew one little TV interview would make Kelly instantly recognizable to the complete strangers who'd upbraided her this morning at the mall, at the park, even in church?

Turning up at today's race might start a riot. She should never have been so rash as to predict Trent Matheson wouldn't go more than half of today's four hundred laps.

I'm a psychologist, not a psychic.

Kelly huffed out an anxious breath that lifted the bangs off her forehead. Maybe she'd gone too far. But Suze, her friend who was a production assistant on the network's NASCAR show, had warned her to make the most of this opportunity to stand in for Don Carson, motor racing's foremost sport psychologist, after he had a minor car accident.

"Don't say 'uh.' Don't fiddle with your hair. Smile. Talk in sound bites." Suze had fired instructions at Kelly as an assistant applied makeup that felt heavier than normal, but would apparently come out okay on TV. "Whatever you do, don't go along with everyone else—say something different."

Which sounded fine, until Kelly heard who the other guests were.

"Those guys have a combined experience of about a thousand years in NASCAR," she said, horrified. How could she, a longtime fan but with zero professional involvement, contradict them?

When they all picked Trent Matheson to win, that's exactly what she had to do. If a snappy sound bite would help establish her as a sport psychology consultant in NASCAR…well, she wasn't about to blow it. She'd been knocking on the doors of the top racing teams for months, getting only dumb jokes about shrinks and offers of driver autographs for her trouble. No use at all to a woman who had to resurrect her career before her family discovered just how badly she'd failed.

She'd done what she had to.

Trent Matheson is a casualty of my ambition. Kelly chewed on the thought then spat it out. Matheson was the poster boy of this year's NASCAR NEXTEL Cup Series. Never without a pretty blond girl, always with a charming smile on his lips— maybe he'd spent a fortune on dentistry and didn't want to waste the results—Matheson had the ego of a champion.

And the brain of a…well, put it this way: Trent Matheson wasn't the sharpest tool in the box.

She could tell from the way he gave long consideration to the most inane of the journalists' questions, always delivering his eventual answer in a drawl punctuated by "uh's" and "huh's."

Kelly's comment would have slid off him like a race car off a wet track.

She watched as the cars circled the track in their starting order. In any case, she was probably about to be proved completely wrong. Matheson was starting this race in pole position, thanks to an outstanding performance in Friday's qualifying, and he had a record of being hard to catch off the pole.

Kelly winced as they showed once more that clip of her saying "not a chance" and predicting Trent wouldn't last two hundred laps. Couldn't they just start the darned race?

Suze had assured her after the interview that it didn't matter if she was wrong. Viewers had been phoning and e-mailing the station, some to agree with her, more to disagree. "We love that," Suze said. "I'm certain you'll be invited back."

"Which means," Kelly told herself aloud now, "it's fine by me if Trent Matheson runs all four hundred laps without a problem." *But if something goes wrong...nothing that might hurt him, just a moment's inattention that lets fifteen cars get past him...then they'll see I know my stuff....* The stray thought shocked her, and she turned up the volume on her TV to drown its seductive clamor.

TRENT GOT AHEAD of his front-row rival within a quarter lap of the fall of the green flag. He didn't for one second relax the grip of his gloved hands on the steering wheel, but he was aware of an easing in his gut, and the message being transmitted to his brain that now he could move into race mode—the space in his head where he was focused on nothing but the win.

Today, he had trouble finding that space. Thanks to that TV shrink and her dire predictions. Also, Chad had been wound up before the start—Trent wasn't the only one with something to prove to Dad—and that had translated to Trent. He blew out a breath and relaxed the jaw he'd clenched. Tense didn't win races. He won by going into his zone. A zone where the comments of people like Kelly Greenwood were no more than a meaningless buzz.

Damn, he still couldn't get there. By predicting he'd fall out by lap two hundred she'd made him too aware of everything going on around him.

"Number 53 behind." Trent's spotter conveyed the information through his radio that NASCAR ace Tony Stevens had worked his way up from fifth on the starting grid to run second behind Trent. And it was only lap six.

"Got it." You didn't beat a guy like Stevens when you were distracted by some woman and her kooky crystal ball. Trent tried again to get into the zone, and this time, he found it. His breathing evened out as everything else disappeared, leaving nothing but the car, two straightaways, four turns and six hundred miles of pavement to conquer.

TONY STEVENS passed him on lap 143, two laps out of Trent's third pit stop. Trent didn't let it faze him, he kept in the zone, and on lap 150 he stole the pass on Stevens. Once again, he was out in front.

"Clear," the spotter told him.

"So there, Kelly Greenwood." A chuckle over the radio told him he'd said that out loud.

On 180, Stevens got past him again, and a lap later so did Danny Cruise.

"You're too slow," Chad said over the radio.

Chad would hit the roof if Trent told him that was deliberate. But with the Greenwood woman predicting his downfall about now, it didn't hurt to get through these midrace laps without taking too many risks—much as that went against Trent's instincts.

"I'll catch them," Trent said. "And we're faster in the pits." He reckoned Stevens was maybe three seconds ahead of him, Cruise about one point two.

Lap two hundred. He'd done it!

Right away, a burden heavier than Trent knew he'd been carrying lifted. He began to close on Cruise, aiming at the narrow gap between the other driver and the wall that ran around the top of the track.

"Hold fire." Chad warned him to wait for a bigger gap.

Trent's brother was conservative like that. He'd raced the NASCAR Craftsman Truck Series for a few years, but he'd never had the instinct for taking those risks that made the difference between winning big and being an also-ran.

"I could drive a semitrailer through that gap," Trent told Chad. He squeezed through, catching a rude gesture from the other driver out of the corner of his eye. "So long, sucker."

But before the spotter could tell him he was clear, the back of Trent's car clipped the wall. He shot across the pavement, mercifully in front of the car he'd just passed rather than over the top of it. Trent fought to get his car under control at 180 miles an hour.

He almost made it.

Then the rookie in the Number 63 car, running around the bottom in lapped traffic, saw Trent's semicontrolled slide across the track and panicked. He spun with a squeal of tires that Trent could hear over the noise of his own engine. Trent managed to steer away from him, but the car he'd just passed crunched into his back bumper, pushed him back into the rookie and the two cars spun onto the infield.

KELLY SPURTED her soda halfway across the room. Trent Matheson had clipped the wall, gotten tangled up with a rookie and was out of the race.

On lap 201.

She was still coughing and blowing soda out of her nose when the phone rang. It was Suze, ecstatic with the news that the network's NASCAR commentator, Mick Jay, wanted to interview Kelly right now, live on the phone.

"I won't know what to say," Kelly protested. "That accident was a fluke."

"Same as yesterday." Suze rushed the words out. "Sound bites, keep it controversial. Three seconds delay on transmission so we can bleep out any curse words."

What about any sheer stupidity?

"Do this right, hon, and the NASCAR world will be your oyster," Suze said.

Kelly had never liked oysters.

She didn't have time to argue further. On her TV screen, Mick Jay said from the booth, "We're going to talk to Kelly Greenwood, the sport psychologist who yesterday predicted Trent Matheson's exit from this race." Her face flashed up on the screen, a still shot from yesterday's broadcast with her name beneath it.

As Kelly stood up to shake herself out of couch-potato mode, she bumped her leg on the coffee table. She was still rubbing her shin through her sweatpants when she heard Mick on the line. Hastily, she muted her television set.

"Kelly, you were dead right—Trent Matheson bombed out of the race, just when you said he would," the announcer said. "How did you know?"

"It's not rocket science, Mick." She hoped that sounded like nonchalant confidence rather than utter astonishment. "In the last two weeks, NASCAR fans have seen Trent signing autographs, partying hard and taking a midweek vacation. What they haven't seen is any kind of focus on his racing."

"You're saying Matheson doesn't have his mind on the job?"

She nodded, then remembered the guy couldn't see her.

"That's exactly what NASCAR is, Mick—a job. To get the kind of consistency that wins the series, you have to take that job seriously. Trent Matheson gives the sport a bad name. The guy's an airhead." Yikes, she'd gone too far. "No, that's not it," she babbled. "I mean his attitude—"

She realized the line had gone dead. Oh, heck. Heart in her mouth, she unmuted the TV. The three-second delay had her still talking. "…a bad name," her voice, sounding more nasal than she thought she did, said. "The guy's an airhead."

Then she was cut off. The network had its sound bite.

Kelly sagged onto the couch, still holding the phone, four fingers spread across her mouth as if she could bar it from slinging any more outrageous insults at NASCAR stars. *Too late.*

A muffled ringing had her staring at the phone in bemusement. Then she realized the sound was her cell phone, wedged down behind the cushion of the couch.

She dragged it out. The number on the display meant nothing to her. She pressed the answer button and put it to her ear.

"Kelly Greenwood?" The voice was male, not unfriendly. In the background she could hear…was that the race track?

"Ye-es."

"This is Chad Matheson. Trent Matheson's brother. I heard you on TV just now."

She squeezed her eyes shut in mortification. "They cut me off, I was trying to tell them I didn't really—"

"Ms. Greenwood—Kelly." He interrupted her and she realized with a shock there was a smile in his voice—the last thing she expected from a team owner whose star driver she'd just dissed on national TV. "I want you to work for Matheson Racing."

No, *that* was the last thing she'd expected from a team owner whose star driver she'd just dissed on national TV. "Work? For you?" The words came out a squeak. Kelly cleared her throat. "What sort of work?" She envisaged herself washing dishes in the team cafeteria for the rest of her natural life. Without pay.

Chad Matheson's voice turned grim. "I want you to knock some sense into the airhead."

CHAPTER TWO

IT'S JUST A MEETING, Kelly told herself on Thursday morning as she parked outside the Matheson Racing team headquarters, two miles from the race track. *I'm good at meetings.*

Admittedly she was going into this one with the teeny disadvantage of having labeled her new client an airhead in front of millions of television viewers. But nothing was insurmountable. She could get this job, and by the time her folks— or anyone else—learned of the mess she'd made in her last job, she'd have a track record of success in her new field.

Apologize, then empathize. She repeated her new mantra as she crossed the parking lot on shaky legs.

As she approached, the automatic doors of the glitzy glass-and-concrete complex swished open.

"Kelly Greenwood for Trent Matheson," she told the receptionist with a level of enthusiasm usually reserved for root canal surgery.

She pinned a belated smile on her face. She had to meet the guy and that was that. She and Chad had all but agreed on the terms of her employment over the phone last Sunday. Elation had surged through Kelly when he approved the program she outlined and didn't quibble at her fee. But just as she was about to put the phone down and whoop for joy, he burst her bubble with an atomic-strength missile.

"We'll sign the contract just as soon as you convince Trent

he needs you." He added blandly, "His first instinct might be to reject your help."

Might be? Kelly paced the foyer, too tense to take a seat while the receptionist phoned through. Surely Trent Matheson would rather drink unadulterated engine oil than work with her?

Chad had resisted Kelly's suggestion that he should be the one to convince his brother. "Trent's gotten used to people sucking up to him and telling him he's the greatest. If you're as blunt with him as you were on TV, you'll cut through all that and get his attention. Just don't let him distract you."

It figured she was on her own with this. All her life, she'd been forced to carve her own path. "Why should it be any different now," she murmured, "just because I'm desperate?"

The receptionist gave her an odd look as she put down the phone. "You can go on in." She pointed at a set of double doors beyond the reception area.

Kelly clipped the visitor pass the woman gave her to her jacket. She smoothed her skirt, taking the opportunity to dry her damp palms. Then she pushed open the doors to the airhead's den.

The dominant impression of the workshop was of a cavernous space, barely diminished by several race cars in various stages of preparation. High-set windows let in sunlight while keeping Matheson Racing's secrets beyond the reach of prying eyes. At ground level, Kelly counted maybe a dozen guys working on the cars, the hum of good-natured conversation competing with the clatter of tools and the rumble of a Craftsman truck engine, louder than normal because of the open hood. Where was Trent?

THROUGH THE OPEN DOOR of his office, Trent heard the buzz of activity fizzle to a gradual silence. He looked up from the performance statistics he and Chad were studying and scanned the workshop through the glass wall.

A woman—blond, dressed in a suit—headed toward the office. It took all of two seconds for Trent to clue in.

"What's *she* doing here?" He got to his feet, ready to sling Kelly Greenwood out of the building.

"I invited her." Chad's words stayed him.

Trent glared at his brother. "I told you I didn't want to meet her." Normally when Trent dug his heels in Chad accepted it, even though as Trent's boss he had the final say. Their brand of give-and-take—Chad gave orders and Trent chose whether or not to take them—was the key to their normally functional working relationship. But they were both under extra pressure this year, thanks to Dad, and Chad was getting high-handed.

The thought put a sour taste in Trent's mouth. "I won't work with her."

"Because she had the nerve to tell the truth?" Chad demanded.

Trent growled. Okay, his focus had been off lately. But Chad had no idea what the real distraction was—the girls and the sponsors had nothing to do with it. Kelly Greenwood could only make things worse.

One of the crew pointed in the direction of Trent's office. The clacking progress of her heels drew and held the attention of every man there. Trent wanted to believe their stares were born of resentment over what she'd said on TV. But he suspected the men's preoccupation owed more to Kelly's appearance. Even if her tailored suit and crisp, high-necked blouse hadn't looked totally out of place, the woman would still have turned heads. She wasn't gorgeous—not in the obvious way that Trent liked, the way that made the to-date-or-not-to-date decision a snap.

But she carried herself with a straight-backed determination that emphasized the high, full curves where her jacket parted and the sway of her hips in the tight skirt, short enough to reveal shapely calves. A leather belt with a fancy silver buckle drew attention to her slim waist. Trent doubted she intended sexiness with her conservative clothing. That lack of intention was what might turn a guy on.

Another guy, not him.

Chad's fraternal radar jumped into action with its usual irritating accuracy. "Admit it, you think she's cute," he said.

"You think she's cuter." Though Trent couldn't be sure about that—lately, Chad seemed to have lost his appreciation for the fairer sex.

But right now cuteness was irrelevant, so Trent concentrated on giving Kelly the evil eye. When she saw him her gaze locked on his. No smile, no discernible excitement at meeting the man named NASCAR's most eligible bachelor in a recent issue of a women's magazine.

But then, she'd already told the world what she thought of him. Thanks to her big mouth, Trent had lost a key race—sure, it was his own fault for allowing her to distract him, but still... And instead of spending the last few days on the research that would help him make some headway with Dad, Trent had been forced to meet with his sponsors to convince them he didn't give NASCAR a bad name and that his irresistible charm wasn't pure airheadedness.

Kelly Greenwood had been nothing but trouble. But no doubt Chad wanted to feel like he was still in charge, so Trent would let her waste ten minutes of her time meeting with him. He wasn't, however, about to risk having her snooping into his life. She was expecting an airhead, and that's exactly what she would get. He'd behave just badly enough to make her wish she'd never heard of Trent Matheson—subtly, of course, so Chad wouldn't catch on—then he'd whisk her pretty little butt out of here.

He pasted on his best airhead smile, concealing every scrap of his resentment.

Only to find she was no longer focused on him. She'd seen Trent's Number 186 car to her left.

She stopped, took one step toward it, then another. She walked the length of the car, trailing a finger along the gleaming scarlet bodywork. Then she stood in front of it, her gaze devouring Trent's racing machine with the kind of hunger women usually reserved for him.

"Ms. Greenwood," he said.

She didn't hear him. Now she was peering through the windshield, her fingers doubtless leaving smudges on the supertough plastic.

"Hey," he said sharply, and she jumped. When she looked at Trent, the longing fled her tawny brown eyes. The color was unexpected, given her blond hair and fair skin. Apprehension flickered in her gaze, and was in turn masked by cool purpose.

She was right to worry. Trent stretched the airhead smile until his mouth hurt and stuck out a hand. She stepped away from the car with evident reluctance.

"Hello." She began to walk toward him. "It's nice to meet—"

Before he could warn her to watch her step, she tripped on a power cord that snaked across the floor. Her greeting rose to a yelp of alarm as she crashed into the trolley jack stationed next to the car. The jack moved forward on its wheels, taking Kelly with it. Arms flailing, she grabbed for the nearest solid object. The car.

She clamped both hands over the driver-side window opening. Momentum swung her body against the car and her high heels slid out from under her.

Sccrrrk.

There was no mistaking the sound of a scratch being put into the bright red paint. Kelly's eyes widened as she struggled to get back onto her feet.

Trent stepped over to help her, grabbing hold of her upper arms and tugging her away from the car. He caught the clean scent of her hair—jasmine and apples.

She stiffened in his grasp, her arms rigid at her sides, definitely not taking advantage of being this close to Charlotte's favorite NASCAR driver, and began to pull away. "If you could just let me...I'm fine now...thank you."

Trent took his time letting her go, his attention preoccupied by the jagged mark left on his car by her fancy belt buckle. "You scratched my car," he accused her. "The guys just finished the new paint job last night."

Kelly wrested herself out of Trent's grip and stumbled back. She pressed her palms to her hot cheeks. She'd scratched that beautiful, perfect car. Could this meeting get any worse?

"I'm sorry." Her voice quivered. "I tripped."

It was far removed from her planned, power-packed opening line. Although she might be back on her feet physically, the inner balance she worked so hard to maintain, the equilibrium that allowed her to tackle obstacles with calm self-reliance, now had the consistency of a bowl of Jell-O left in the sun, thanks to those few seconds spent in Trent Matheson's arms.

Then he was giving her the trademark Trent Matheson smile, the one that sold magazines by the hundreds of thousands, as he ran a hand through his thick, dark hair. The left side of his mouth quirked slightly higher than the right, lending a wry, self-deprecating edge to the killer charm. The smile said, "Sure I'm gorgeous, but it's not my fault. I've just gotta go with it."

This close, with the strength of his shoulders just a hand's reach away, with the imprint of his fingers still sizzling on her arms, with his blue, blue eyes gleaming in laughing awareness of her discomfort, she almost believed it.

The man blazed with charisma on a scale that Kelly, who'd met more than her share of sports celebrities, had never encountered.

Then he said, "Mighty pleased to meet you, Ms. Greenwood," in a lazy drawl that glided over her like hot wax. "I loved your interview on TV last weekend."

Her first thought was, *He really is a half-wit.* But convenient though that would be, no one was dumb enough not to be offended by her airhead comment. And that voice was too drawly, that attitude too I'll-be-with-you-just-as-soon-as-I'm-done-chewing-on-this-hayseed. From her research she knew Trent was Charlotte born and bred. And though he hadn't gone to college, she suspected he had plenty of street smarts.

Which meant he was toying with her, just as Chad had suggested he would.

"Why don't we go into my office, sugar, give you a chance to recover from your little tumble?" His amused voice was gravelly in a way that prickled at her nape.

"Fine." Her fingers clenched around the handle of her briefcase as she followed him into the glass-walled office. This might be a game to him, but it was her future. He did not get to charm his way through this meeting and get her out of here in five minutes flat.

Another man stood as they entered. Taller than Trent, good-looking but not as dazzling as his younger brother, Chad Matheson made the inside pages of the motor sports magazines often enough for Kelly to recognize him. Grateful to have an ally in the room, she shook his hand.

But her relief proved momentary. Chad said, "I'm here as an observer, I'll leave the talking to you, Kelly."

Overheated by her stumble and the ensuing panic—nothing else—she shrugged out of her jacket and draped it over the back of her chair. Trent looked her up and down in a leisurely, entirely unsubtle inspection. Then he had the nerve to incline his head slightly, as if in approval.

Kelly didn't know what was worse about that approving gesture—that it was wholly inappropriate for a business meeting or that it was fake. This man could have any woman he wanted, so he wasn't eyeing her for any reason other than to make her even more uncomfortable. She wasn't about to give him that satisfaction. Rather than rushing into her seat to escape his searching gaze, she sat down slowly.

She was used to people resisting the idea of using a consultant in sport psychology. That was why she had a perfectly prepared spiel and a polished résumé. She launched right into her pitch, touching on her experience and her observations of his racing.

Ten minutes later she concluded, "I would like to work with you to, uh, smooth out the irregularities in your recent performances. You'll see I'm eminently qualified for the job." She slid her résumé across the table.

Trent didn't pick it up. He said in that smooth drawl, "I struggle with these fancy documents, so why don't you just tell me what it says?"

No matter that his demeanor was all innocent inquiry, Kelly didn't miss the flash of blue steel in his eyes. She realized she still hadn't cleared the air between them about the TV show.

"Trent, I'm sorry I—"

"Scratched my car," he finished for her. "You said that already, sugar. I want to know what's in here." He tapped the résumé.

Kelly kept her voice even. "I have a master's degree in sport psychology. But I'm not a certified psychologist. I blend psychology with life coaching in what I think is a more holistic approach to athletes' problems. After I graduated I worked with Bob Stein—" recognition of the top football coach's name flashed in Trent's eyes "—and I recently returned from a year in New Zealand, coaching the captain of the national rugby team. In my spare time I worked with a couple of speedway drivers down there. One of them won their national series and gave me the credit. You'll see I've listed him as a reference."

"New Zealand," he drawled, wide-eyed with spurious fascination. "That's near…no, don't tell me, I know, it's near…" The silence stretched out to painful dimensions as Trent squinted and cocked his head this way and that, apparently struggling to recall the exact location of New Zealand. Torn between the urge to leap in with the answer and the desire to slap him, Kelly gritted her teeth. "Near Australia," Trent produced triumphantly.

Kelly released the breath she'd been holding and said brightly, "That's right." She cringed as she realized she sounded like a kindergarten teacher congratulating a five-year-old on his finger painting. Going by the flattening of his mouth, he'd noticed. "Trent," she said, "I'm sorry I—"

"Why did you come back to the States?" he asked.

"I missed home." Which wasn't a lie. It was just some way short of the whole truth. She didn't want to go any further down that track. "What I really want to say is I'm sorry about calling you—"

"Do you know much about sports, Ms. Greenwood?" Trent leaned back in his chair and rested one foot on the other knee, a pose that could have been laconic but which reminded Kelly of a lion stretching out in the sun while it waited for its chosen prey to fall behind the herd. "I'm not talking about your psychiatry…."

"Psychology," she corrected him.

Airily, he waved a hand. "They're both big words, both tough to spell. I mean, do you know what it's like to be a professional sportsman, other than what people have told you when they're lying on your couch?"

"I don't use a couch," she said shortly. "I work on a consultative basis that emphasizes a collegial relationship between me and my client."

Trent yawned.

"I understand the pressures of professional sports at more than a theoretical level," she snapped.

The glint in his eyes mocked her loss of control. But how could she *apologize, then empathize* if he wouldn't let her say she was sorry? Telling herself she should be grateful he was showing some interest in her ability to do her job, she added more calmly, "I attended college on a sports scholarship."

She'd surprised him. He leaned forward, those hands that had steadied her earlier splayed on the table. His fingers looked strong and controlled, the nails clipped short. "What sport?"

"Excuse me?" As if she didn't know what he meant.

"In what sport," he enunciated slowly, as if she were the airhead around here, "did you attain your scholarship?"

"That's not relevant."

"But I'd like to know." He smiled pleasantly, drawled the words. "Because if I'm going to work with a psychotic—"

"Psychologist," she corrected him. She ploughed on, unwilling to further undermine her own credibility, already as flaky as a bad case of dandruff in his eyes. "In addition to my own sports background, I'm from a family of sports professionals—that gives me an even broader appreciation of the psychological aspects of competition." Most of the time, her talented family registered on her emotional balance sheet as a liability. No matter how much she loved them and they loved her, their abilities emphasized her own shortcomings. She relished this rare opportunity to use her nearest and dearest as an asset.

"Greenwood," Trent said, as she knew he would. "There's a Josh Greenwood running in the NASCAR Busch Series."

"My younger brother."

Trent thought again. "Dave Greenwood?"

"He's the oldest. He's been one of the top players in the NFL the last five years."

"Anyone else?" he asked.

She cleared her throat. "My big sister, Stacey."

"The only woman playing in the PGA this season," Trent said. He obviously watched a lot of sports on TV.

"Uh-huh. She's always been handy with a golf club."

He cocked an eyebrow. "That's quite a lineage. Do your siblings employ your psychology skills?"

How could she tell him they thought even less of her abilities than he did?

"Before we go any further," she said, "I'm sorry I called you—" She broke off as he glanced at the gold Gucci watch he sported on one tanned wrist. Through clenched teeth she said, "Am I keeping you from something more important than your racing career? A facial, perhaps?"

Next to Trent, Chad rubbed his chin in a way that concealed his mouth. But not before Kelly saw the smile there.

Trent shook his head in mild disapproval. "You haven't answered my question about your siblings. And that comment about a facial was just plain not nice, Ms. Greenwood."

The time for niceness was long past. Kelly laced her fingers on the table in front of her and looked him in the eye. "It makes a lot of sense that you're treating this meeting as a joke, Trent," she said. "Because right now, your driving is a joke."

The sharp intake of breath she heard was Chad's. Trent's face was impassive, which meant she'd at least wiped away that idiotic smile. Maybe now he would listen.

"Thanks to my background, NASCAR drivers with giant egos don't faze me." She wasn't sure if the strangled, snorting sound came from him or Chad. "If you could focus for one second, you'll learn that I've identified some areas where you can improve your performance. I have the qualifications and the experience you need." Kelly ticked off her points on her fingers. "Your brother thinks I'm the right person for the job. And I can start tomorrow."

For a moment she thought she'd got through to him. His eyes glinted with what might have been admiration for her pitch, but what was more likely the intention to climb into his Number 186 car and run her over as she left the building.

She didn't mind that. Anger was good, anger provoked change—some of the best work she'd done was with clients who'd had to get mad before they let her help them.

Trent's mouth tightened, then relaxed again into a jovial smile. "That's kind of you, Ms. Greenwood, but I don't think—"

She slammed her hand down on the table and had the satisfaction of seeing him jump. "Drop the Forrest Gump act, Trent. I'm sorry I called you an airhead. It was inexcusable."

"Does that mean you'll go on TV and retract it?"

She opened her mouth, but no words came out.

"I thought not." His smile widened, but nowhere near enough to reach his eyes. "You said what you think. I appreciate honesty." He leaned forward. "I'm going to be honest with you right now, Kelly." It was the first time he'd called her by her name, and it sounded like a caress—the silken caress of a spider's web as it tightened around a ladybug.

Kelly sucked in her cheeks so her mouth wouldn't tremble. No matter how bad it looked right now, she was close to getting this job, she could feel it. She just had to say the right thing.

Trent said, "I'm not in the market for a shrink." His tone said, *Subject closed.*

And I'm not in the market for another failure. Kelly racked her brains for the perfect line that would clinch the job.

Before she could speak, he said, "I know how I win races. I have a strategy, and most of the time it delivers the right result." Although a smile still curved his lips, his voice was so cold and hard that Kelly couldn't imagine how she'd ever dreamed he might agree to work with her.

"So you're telling me," she said almost as frostily, "that you know why you tangled with Danny Cruise at Daytona, why you lost control on a dry track on the last lap at Atlanta, and why you blew a pole start at Phoenix."

She heard a muffled snort from Chad, but she didn't let it distract her from meeting Trent's glare full-on. *This is it.* "Your strategy," she continued, "wouldn't happen to involve wishing upon a star and rubbing a lucky rabbit's foot, would it?"

Chad's laugh cracked the thunderous silence. Trent's eyes chilled to arctic blue. Kelly took that as progress and pressed her advantage. She said with a loftiness she didn't feel, "Winning races is a science. There's luck involved, but winners use science to harness their good luck and minimize the bad."

She sensed Trent reining in his anger before he spoke. "Winning the NASCAR NEXTEL Cup Series is about brilliance." He folded his arms across his chest and lifted his chin with an arrogance at once infuriating and entirely justified. "It just so happens, *I* am brilliant."

They stared at each other across the table. Kelly tried hard not to blink.

Chad spoke. "I've changed my mind."

That startled her into breaking the eye contact. Just like that, she'd lost the job? When she'd been this close? She ran her fingers through her bangs. "If you'll just give me a chance, I'll—"

Chad quieted her with an impatient shake of the head and turned to his brother. "You have to agree, Trent, you've spent too much time thinking about other things recently."

Kelly suspected Chad meant blond things. Bare-midriffed, curvy things. Starstruck things.

Trent gave a curt nod—he was still glaring at Kelly. Could he see she wanted to cry? Wanted to, not would. She could still rescue this. Somehow.

"That's settled then," Chad said with weary satisfaction. Kelly's mind raced. Had she missed something?

"What is?" Trent demanded.

"Sorry, little brother, but this time I'm pulling rank. I really believe Kelly's the right person to help you. I want to expand her job description."

Her heart leapt. "To what, exactly?"

Chad said, "It won't be pleasant, but I'll double your money. From now on, you're not just Trent's adviser. You're his minder."

CHAPTER THREE

TRENT SHOVED HIS CHAIR back from the table. "I don't need a shrink and I don't need a minder. And if I did, *she*—" he jerked his thumb at Kelly "—is the last one I'd want."

Chad's mouth set in the line that when they were kids had meant Trent would soon be on the ground wrestling his big brother off him. These days, Chad was a little more subtle. "You need to focus, Trent. You're going to blow the Cup."

Not fooled for a second by his brother's mild tone, Trent snarled, "The hell I will."

Chad's chair scraped on the floor as he stood up. "If you don't at least come close to winning the series, Energy Oil won't sign with us next year. Every other team in NASCAR is courting them." Trent might have predicted Chad would start name-dropping their primary sponsor. "If they dump us, Dad's joint venture with Energy will likely collapse. You don't want that, do you?" Chad gave him a tight smile, an ironic blend of sympathy and frustration.

Oh, yeah, play the Dad card. But Chad was right, dammit, though he didn't know the real reason.

Trent wanted to take over as head of Matheson Performance Industries, the family engine-building business, when Dad retired.

Winning the NASCAR NEXTEL Cup Series would show Dad Trent could be trusted to deliver results. Of course, Dad would give Chad, as team owner, just as much credit as he gave Trent for the win. And Chad wanted that job every bit as much as Trent did. With his college degree and business experience, Chad was Dad's logical successor.

One step at a time, Trent reminded himself. The last thing he needed was for his father to think he was unreliable or uncommitted, in his racing or in anything else. If showing Dad he was willing to work on his "focus problem" meant agreeing to have Kelly Greenwood around... He expelled a noisy breath that told Chad he'd won. His brother's expression lightened, as much in relief as in triumph.

"Kelly, you'll be with us pretty much 24/7 through to the Chase," Chad said, businesslike now he'd gotten his way. "Until Trent's ready to take some serious advice from you, your job is to keep his more ardent fans at bay and to help him put limits on the work he does for sponsors without offending anyone or breaching his contract. Anything that'll improve his focus."

Chad issued a few more instructions before he left the room. Trent, busy thinking about how he could get rid of Kelly while appearing to cooperate, barely noticed his departure.

Kelly Greenwood would ruin everything. Not because of the grief she'd already caused, although that was reason enough to want her out of here. Chad was paying her to keep tabs on him—and she looked to be the sort of woman who took her duties seriously.

"We don't need to wait until tomorrow. I can start today," she said, confirming his estimation.

How long before she found out what Trent was really up to and reported it to Chad? When that happened, the harmony they needed in order to produce a NASCAR NEXTEL Cup Series-winning effort would be shot to pieces.

Trent couldn't afford that.

So he would appear to accept Kelly as his minder, for

Chad's peace of mind, and Dad's. Then he would convince her to quit. Of her own free will. Soon.

Doubtless Kelly thought she was as determined to practice her psychology skills on Trent as he was to get rid of her. But that's where he had a natural advantage. Until you'd been a rookie up against the world's best race drivers, you didn't know what determination was.

"We can start planning our time together now." She glanced down at the notebook she'd been writing in ever since she got there, holding it close to her like a teenage girl's diary. "We have a lot of work ahead of us." She closed the notebook, put it on the table and pulled a bulky day planner from her briefcase.

Didn't she know he was a two-time NASCAR Busch Series champion who had delivered brilliant results, time after time? *A lot of work ahead of us? I don't think so.* Taking advantage of her inattention, Trent reached for her notebook.

"Give that back!" She jumped to her feet and started around the table.

He flicked rapidly through to the last page she'd written on. For someone so neat of appearance, her writing was a mess. He could only just make out the words *sibling rivalry* and, farther down the page, the scribbled question, *Insecure?*

He was so shocked, he didn't resist when she snatched the book from him. "Those are my private case notes," she said.

"I'm not a case. And I'm not insecure." He grabbed her hand, the one that held the notebook. "I want you to cross that out." Great, now she had grounds to add *childish* to her list.

"You know what they say about eavesdroppers," she said snootily.

Her hand twitched beneath his as she tried to extract it. He would have put that down to annoyance, except she was blushing and her breath was coming faster than it had a moment ago.

It was the same kind of physical reaction she'd had when

he'd helped her up from that fall earlier. He wasn't exactly unaware of her, either—her skin felt like warm silk under his fingers—but he wasn't as transparent.

Ms. Kelly Greenwood looked as uncomfortable as if she'd sat on a pincushion. Uncomfortable enough to quit?

Trent increased the pressure on her hand and moved his thumb across that silken skin. Her hand trembled. He pasted on his cute smile, ramped up the playboy charm, and said, "I've never had a minder before, let alone a girl one. The situation seems full of—" he dropped his voice half an octave "—possibilities."

The idea was she would dissolve into a pool of longing and realize they couldn't work together. Instead, she gave a mighty tug that got her hand free. She shook it as if ridding herself of something unpleasant, and said, "Surely you can be professional about this."

Trent persevered, stretching his arms to clasp them behind his head and leaning back in his chair so she could get a good look at his torso in his fitted T-shirt. Women had been known to swoon when he did that. "How about we add massage to your list of duties?"

Her gaze didn't even flicker below his neck. "You mean massaging your ego?"

Okay, so she wasn't about to dissolve, swoon or in any other way fall for him. He should have guessed from the way she'd lambasted him earlier that she preferred the direct approach. Trent could be as direct as the next guy. He leaned forward and fixed her with a hard gaze.

"I don't want you here and, trust me, that means you don't want to be here," he said. "Why don't you quit right now, go find a driver who needs you?" He paused. "Try Danny Cruise."

"Danny doesn't need me," she said. "He's going to win the Cup."

Anger hit him like a fist in the chest.

"Which he deserves to do," she continued. "Not only is he a great driver, but he's a nice guy. And smart."

That statement showed how genuine her apology hadn't been. "Where do you get off with this airhead thing?" he demanded.

"Uh, well, I guess, uh, Trent…" Her imitation of his usual post-race interview technique was so accurate that Trent had to fight off a smile. She scratched her head. "It was, um, let me see, I guess it was around…"

"Can it," he growled, annoyed her rotten opinion of him had wormed under his skin. If she couldn't see he played dumb in order to lull his rivals into a false sense of security, that said more about her intelligence than his.

She folded her arms and gave him a supercilious look.

"In my experience—" damn, he couldn't resist the urge to defend himself "—the more a driver insists publicly that NASCAR is a head game, the less likely it is he possesses the brainpower to win."

She shrugged. "If you say so."

"I let my results speak for themselves." He ran a hand through his hair. "There must be someone else you can work for. Hasn't anyone showed an interest?"

"Bobby Merino," she admitted.

"There you go." He sat back, beaming. "If you can help Bobby finish anywhere above last in the series, you'll convince everyone you're a miracle worker."

"I want to work for a high-profile driver," she said.

"How much is Chad paying you?"

She named a sum so outrageous Trent had to clamp his mouth shut. "Are you sleeping with him?"

Two furious spots of color in her cheeks flagged her anger. "That includes the double for minding you, which is probably danger money."

"So you don't deny you're sleeping with him?" That was just to provoke her. Kelly was attractive and she was his brother's type, but Chad seemed to have sworn off women, though he denied it every time Trent teased him about it.

"Of course I'm not!"

Trent shrugged. "So I can pay you what he's paying you, and you can quit tomorrow."

Now she looked mad enough to burst a blood vessel. "I'm not quitting. I've been offered a job and I accepted it. Matheson Racing is the perfect place to start my NASCAR career."

"Why NASCAR?" he demanded. "Why don't you go back to rugby?"

Kelly dropped her eyes lest he saw the panic there. *Because I burned my bridges so badly, there's no going back.* "I…" She struggled for an answer that wouldn't sound desperate. "I know NASCAR, I love it, it's the logical choice." She looked him in the eye again and managed a degree of calmness. "I'm certain you'll soon see the value of my assistance."

"How certain?" He snapped the question out so fast that she had to regroup her thoughts.

"Er…very certain?" She winced. Once again, he'd thrown her off balance.

"So certain that you'd bet on it?"

Kelly blinked. "*Bet* on it?"

He leaned forward, the smile on his lips positively devilish. She shivered.

"I'm suggesting a bet that will be to our mutual advantage."

"That doesn't surprise me," she said disdainfully. "This whole season has been a gamble for you. One with very long odds."

He frowned. "I take calculated risks. That's not gambling."

She sniffed.

"Here's the bet," he said. "You say I need you, I say I don't. I'll give you a week to convince me. If you fail, you quit."

He said "quit" with a finality that brought the panic flooding back. "Why would I agree to that? Chad hired me for the rest of the series."

"I'm not planning to let you advise me, so that leaves you as nothing more than my minder," Trent said. "You get to scare away my fans, drink beer with my sponsors and be nagged by my overbearing brother."

"That would be the overbearing brother who's signing my paycheck?"

"Your *inflated* paycheck," he corrected her. "Chad expects value for money. He might be on your side now, but if you don't make progress with me, and soon, he'll get mean. Very mean."

Kelly swallowed. Chad Matheson didn't exactly look mean, but there was a contained ruthlessness about him.

"Think about it," Trent said. "You can babysit me for six months and I'll tell the media exactly what I think of your half-baked psychology. Or you can persuade me you have something to offer, work with me, and everyone will know you're a key part of the team when I win the Cup. Which I will do."

He was so convincing, the hairs on Kelly's arms stood up and saluted.

Then logic reasserted itself. So he believed he could win—that was a good start. But he wouldn't win the way he was driving now. Trent needed her every bit as much as she needed the association with him. "If you're going to win anyway, what's the harm in having me on board?" Because it didn't make sense that he should be so determined to get rid of her.

"That's not relevant." He parroted the answer she'd given when he asked about her college sport. "Just accept that I don't want you here."

"You just said if I can convince you, I can stay."

"But I don't believe you can convince me."

One thing Kelly knew for sure, she was very persuasive when given a fair chance. She squared her shoulders and hardened her voice. "I can."

His eyes lit with a mix of triumph and annoyance. "So, the bet's on?"

"It's on," she agreed. A thrill coursed through her, excitement and fear, as if she'd just boarded a roller coaster blindfolded.

Trent's smile was unsettlingly like that of a man who knew every twist and turn of that roller-coaster ride. "Tell you what, I'm feeling generous. You can have until the day after the race in Pennsylvania—that's nearer two weeks. Between now and then you get to say whatever you like about my racing. But if I haven't said 'I need you, Kelly' by then, you have to quit." He paused. "Without telling Chad about our bet."

"This really is not a professional way to work," she reproved him.

"It's *my* way. And if you want my cooperation, it's the only way." He stood. "Do we have a deal?"

She shouldn't agree. Of course she shouldn't. But what was more important here? That she did things by the book, or that Trent got the help he needed to win the NASCAR NEXTEL Cup Series? She didn't doubt that if she refused his offer, he would figure out some way to get her off the team.

"Deal," she said.

Yes! Trent barely restrained himself from punching the air in triumph. Just like that, he'd all but gotten rid of her. Because no way would the words *I need you, Kelly* ever cross his lips.

He settled for shaking her hand to seal the deal. When she pulled her hand back, she rubbed it against her skirt as if it tingled the same way his did. "I'm feeling generous, too," she said, slightly breathless. "I'm willing to apologize on TV for calling you an airhead."

This was getting better and better. Maybe Kelly wasn't the kind of woman to respond overtly to his charm, but obviously he'd gotten to her. Trent chucked her under the chin. "That's real good of you, sugar."

She flashed him the first real smile he'd seen from her. It put a mischievous curve in her lips and warmed her tawny brown eyes. "I'll do it right after you win the Cup."

As Kelly left the building, it was hard not to break into a skip—once she was certain Trent wasn't waiting to run her over. Okay, so he wouldn't be the easiest of clients. But she could make something of this. She already had. By offering to apologize on TV, she'd laid the seeds of a challenge that a guy like Trent Matheson couldn't ignore. *I'm messing with his mind and he doesn't even know it.*

CHAPTER FOUR

KELLY WAS COUNTING ON Trent crashing out at Dover three days later, in keeping with his "win two, lose two" pattern. Then he would concede he needed her.

But he confounded her—and his rivals—with a win so convincing, so graceful despite the bumpiness of Dover's concrete track, it was poetry in motion. And she couldn't take a scrap of credit. Not because she hadn't been feeding him suggestions. Because he'd totally ignored her and gone on to win anyway.

As soon as he climbed out of the car in Victory Lane, he disappeared in a sea of congratulations.

Kelly had no hope of keeping the adoring fans and sponsors away from him at the party that night in Energy Oil's hospitality suite. The party was one of Trent's prearranged sponsor appearances, to which Energy had invited its VIP clients. Trent was determined to fulfill his obligations, and the fact that he'd won the race added a special edge to the occasion.

She chatted to Trent's crew, most of whom didn't like her after that TV interview, which meant conversation soon dried up. Kelly moved on to rehash the day's race with Chad, then introduced herself to as many NASCAR people as she could, so that when she lost this job she would have contacts to call. Unlike the last time she'd lost her job.

Around one in the morning Trent emerged from the dancing, partying crowd with a beer in one hand and two blondes in the other.

"Kelly, sugar." The wink that accompanied his customary grin suggested he'd had a few of those beers. "What did you think of today's performance?"

"Brilliant," she said.

He stilled, as if her unqualified approval surprised him. Then he tilted his beer bottle in a toast.

"Truest thing you ever said." There was a faint slur in his voice.

One of the blondes giggled.

"Looks like you've had enough," Kelly said. "Shall I take you home?" Chad would doubtless consider it her duty to escort Trent safely back to his motor home.

He squinted at her as if he was having trouble focusing. "Huh?"

It was sneaky, arguably unworthy of her, but Kelly knew she had to take the opportunity presented by Trent being under the influence. If he was going to keep racing the way he did today, she'd never win their bet. The bet *he'd* devised and which was every bit as sneaky and unworthy as what she was about to do.

"I'm offering to help you get home," she coaxed him. "All you have to say is, 'Yes, please, Kelly, I need you.'"

He blinked, and she detected a barely discernible sway to his stance. She kept her voice soothing, her eyes filled with nothing more than warm concern. "What do you say?"

"You'll take me home?" he said, as if he'd finally understood.

"That's right," she assured him. "Just say, 'I need you, Kelly,' and we'll leave. You must be tired."

"Tired," he slurred.

She nodded and prompted him, "'I need you, Kelly.'"

"I need—"

Just when she thought he would say the words that would secure her job, he stopped. He laughed, his head thrown back, his eyes alight with humor. When he spoke, all trace of a slur had vanished. "I admire your gumption, sugar, but you're out of luck."

For the briefest moment, he smiled at her in a way he never had before. Kelly saw the admiration he'd mentioned, maybe even respect. Her insides might have turned to mush, if she hadn't also discerned something irritatingly like sympathy. Then the smile was gone, so fast she wondered if she'd imagined it. When he turned to the blondes and said, "Say, girls, is there room for one more in your car? Maybe we could party on at your place," she knew she had.

Their squeals of excitement—and the steadiness of Trent's gait as he left with them—told Kelly she'd lost. He hadn't been drunk at all. Just playing some stupid game with her. Again.

Trent Matheson had never needed her less.

TRENT WOKE UP on Monday morning with a thumping headache.

He couldn't blame excessive alcohol consumption. As always, he'd limited himself to two beers last night. Experience had taught him it paid to keep his wits about him when sponsors wanted intelligent conversation, and women wanted him in their beds—and they weren't too fussy about whether he was conscious or not. Thankfully he'd convinced the girls to take him straight home after the party, pleading exhaustion after his big race.

The exhaustion was real. He'd had something to prove yesterday, then he'd stayed on a high through the party, capping it off with that trick he'd played on Kelly. This headache was a natural result of coming down from that euphoric state. He reminded himself a sore head was a small price to pay for a victory that had been all the sweeter because he'd ignored Kelly's advice and raced his own race.

She was one devious woman, trying to make him say he needed her when she thought he was less than sober. He tried to summon outrage, but found instead that a smile twitched on his lips. Okay, so it was the kind of thing he'd have done himself. But he expected more from a professional like her.

The grinding in his head intensified. Trent shoved aside the unpalatable thought that his desire to prove Kelly wrong had fueled his brilliant performance. From there, it would be only a small step to saying he needed her.

IN PENNSYLVANIA, Kelly watched in awe as Trent wowed the crowds with his mastery of the track's famously difficult "tunnel turn." He finished fourth in Sunday's race, which lifted him one position, to fifteenth on the leaderboard for series points.

Monday was spent in intensive debriefings with the crew, trying to pinpoint where things had gone right, and how they could make it happen again next week. Kelly's heels were dragging with exhaustion as she let herself into her condo after work. She had an hour to change before Trent picked her up for tonight's "family" dinner at his father's house, to which sponsors and crew had also been invited.

Turned out when Chad Matheson had said she'd be minding Trent 24/7, he meant it. Kelly was earning every penny of the fee she'd considered generous. Mornings weren't so bad—Trent tended to roll up at the workshop around nine-thirty, and after three days with him she knew why and adjusted her schedule accordingly.

The man partied every night. *All* night. Okay, he got home in the small hours of the morning—but by then Kelly was wiped. Just making sure Trent went home alone was a full-time job in itself. The first night they'd been out, she'd waded into the crowd of girls at midnight and said, "Trent, you need your sleep, let's go."

But that had produced a chorus of offers of beds for the night from the girls, and annoyance from Trent at being bossed around. Since then, she'd exercised her creativity to the fullest, devising reasons why he had to say goodbye to Melinda and Lacey and Mary-Anne *right now*.

"You have a 2:00 a.m. workout scheduled at the gym."

"According to this magazine, men who get to bed before 1:00 a.m. have twice the sexual stamina of other men." The girls had been happy to let Trent go at that one.

"That laxative you took is about to kick in." One of her less successful efforts from Trent's perspective, but unarguably effective.

Most nights, he would untangle himself from the fans with a show of regret at her intrusion, and head home.

When Trent had offered her his stupid bet eleven days ago, she'd assumed getting him to admit he needed her would be, if not easy, at least doable.

Today, their bet would expire, and she was no closer to her goal.

Last Monday, the day after the race at Dover, he'd had a headache—served him right for pulling that stunt pretending to be drunk—and had not been inclined toward serious conversation. Tuesday, he'd worked with the crew on the Number 186 race car, as well as the backup car. While Kelly had been able to make several suggestions about his performance, she doubted he listened. Then he'd gone AWOL for all of Wednesday and half of Thursday. When he finally arrived at Thursday lunchtime, just in time to board the plane to Pennsylvania, he refused to say where he'd been.

Friday through Sunday had been frantic with qualifying and practicing, then the race itself.

Today, Kelly had managed to pin him down between meetings for an hour of real discussion. He'd listened to everything she said about next weekend's race in Michigan with apparent interest. Just when she thought she was getting somewhere, he'd said, "So, which uniform do you think I should wear? The red looks powerful, but the blue matches my eyes."

"Jerk." Too tired now even to curse the man's idiocy with the vehemence it deserved, Kelly grumbled under her breath as she poured boiling water over the peppermint tea bag she hoped would revive her.

Tonight was her last chance to get Trent to say those magic words: *I need you.* Tomorrow, she was out of a job.

Despondent, she sat on the couch and sipped her tea. How could she be her persuasive best when fatigue left her as flat as a burst tire? Maybe she should give in now, forget all about persuading Trent he needed her. She had no chance of changing his mind in the next few hours.

Kelly squeezed her eyes shut against the pricking of a defeat made no less depressing by its inevitability. It hardly seemed worth the effort to get ready for tonight's dinner. Maybe she should take a short nap, get this exhaustion out of her system.

HE'D DONE IT! Trent had won the NASCAR NEXTEL Cup Series. With one hand, he brandished the trophy, and with the other, he lifted Kelly's arm in triumphant salute to the crowds.

He moved to the microphone and a hush, punctuated by the occasional cheer, fell over the speedway at Homestead, near Miami. "I owe everything to Kelly Greenwood," he said.

The fans went wild, but it was as if Trent didn't hear them. He looked deep into Kelly's eyes, all mockery gone, and said loud enough for the world to hear, "I need you, Kelly."

The chime of the doorbell woke Kelly just as he was about to give her a victory kiss. She unglued her palm from her cheek and looked at her watch. Six o'clock! She half rolled off the sofa, found her feet and stumbled to the door, patting her hair down as she went.

She pulled the door open a sliver. Trent—right on time. He stuck his foot in the door, forcing it open a few more inches.

"I'm not—" The words came out raspy with sleep and she tried again. "I'm not ready yet."

He pushed his sunglasses up onto his head. "That's a relief. Because I have to tell you, that's not a good look."

"What's not?" She glanced down at her rumpled clothes, began to retuck the shirt that had come out of her skirt. Trent took advantage of her inattention to barge his way into her condo.

"Why don't you come in?" She closed the door behind him.

He sauntered to the sofa she'd just vacated and sat down.

"Have a seat," she said.

He stretched out so he was lying the length of the sofa, right where she'd been sleeping.

"Why don't you put your feet up?" Kelly snapped.

"Thanks, sugar." He grinned. "All I need now is a drink to keep me going while you get dressed." He reached for the cup of peppermint tea on the coffee table and sniffed it. "This stuff stinks. Got any beer?"

Kelly snatched the cup from him and took a gulp of the tea. Ugh, stone cold. She forced the liquid down and said, "Beer's in the fridge."

He sighed. "Service is terrible here, I don't know how you tolerate it."

Kelly meant to go and change while he found a beer. But he looked so darned good—or rather, so darned *bad*—in his dark pants and long-sleeved black polo, she couldn't take her eyes off him. Trent was tall for a NASCAR driver, she guessed just shy of six feet, but it was his sheer presence, not his height, that dwarfed her kitchen. Like a magnet, that presence drew her until she was standing at the high counter that separated the kitchen from the living room.

He twisted the top off his beer, then turned and caught her gawking. He raised an eyebrow as he stepped over to the counter, where he pulled out a bar stool and sat. "How do I look?"

Despicably weak at the knees, Kelly took the stool next to him. She sighed. "Good enough that every girl there will throw herself at you as if tonight's her last night on Earth before she gets beamed back to Planet Belly Button." His fan club would make Kelly's job even more difficult. Or it would have, if it hadn't already been impossible.

Trent roared with laughter, and his face looked less world-weary, the sparkle in his eyes genuine and warm.

"And you know they're from Planet Belly Button... how?" he asked.

"It's the uniform that gives it away," Kelly confided. "Those tight skirts or pants and low-cut, clingy tops. And between the skirt and the top..." She shrugged.

"The belly button revealed in all its glory," he said.

"Usually pierced," she confirmed.

He chuckled.

"Don't you get sick of them?" Simple curiosity prompted the question. "Those bevies of beauties flashing their navels at you?"

"When you put it like that it sounds really sickening," he deadpanned.

Kelly took another sip of her cold tea. "You're always so nice to them." Indeed, he greeted each woman with a smile brewed specially for her, followed by a compliment on how great she looked and then the teasing banter that ramped up the giggle decibels. The beauties lapped it up. "Some of those girls are in love with you at hello."

He frowned. "I don't encourage that. Or at least, I don't encourage any one girl more than the others."

It was true. If Trent got serious with any of those girls, he was very discreet. As far as Kelly could see, he handed his favors around indiscriminately. If he slung an arm around one girl in greeting, he gave the next one a shoulder squeeze. If one was reckless enough to grab him and kiss him, he'd gently detach her and tease her with, "Hey, my girlfriends will get jealous."

Kelly sighed once more. "True, you're an equal opportunity flirt."

"That's a compliment, right?" His hopeful smile weakened her knees all over again.

She rolled her eyes and he laughed. Then his teasing gaze skimmed over her curves—Kelly realized the top two buttons of her shirt had come undone while she slept, and tugged the lapels together—and down to her waist.

"You said every woman there tonight will throw herself at me," he said. "Does that include you?"

"I'm not from Planet Belly Button."

"So—" his gaze sharpened as if he could see right through her shirt "—no piercing?"

She didn't need to answer. One look at the hands she'd inadvertently folded across her navel and Trent laughed out loud again.

"Come to think of it, you don't even have pierced ears." Now his scrutiny was on her face, and Kelly felt herself color.

"I used to," she admitted. "But they interfered with my…sport."

"The sport you don't like to talk about."

She pressed her lips together.

He thought for a moment. "Shooting."

"Excuse me?"

"Your sport," he said. "Earrings might get in the way of your earmuffs."

She shook her head. "It wasn't shooting."

He reached out and touched a finger to her left earlobe, to the faint scar which was all that remained of that teenage piercing.

Pleasure darted in all directions from that sensitive spot, tingling down her veins. Kelly drew in a shuddery breath. She should pull away, she really should. But a toe-curling awareness of his touch paralyzed her. In the sudden, utter silence that filled the kitchen, she saw Trent swallow, met the dark intensity of his gaze. His finger trailed the soft curve of her ear, then he reached to tuck a strand of hair behind it.

He pulled his hand back and stuffed it into the pocket of his pants. "Your hair—" He cleared his throat. "It's, uh, kind of messy. And we have to leave soon."

She snapped out of her trance. "Of course it's messy when you've got your hands all over it." She forced a laugh, hoped it didn't sound hysterical. "Cut it out, Trent. I appreciate expert attention as much as the next woman, but I'm not one of the millions who find you irresistible."

He was oddly silent, and mortifying heat flooded Kelly. She pushed herself off the stool and swigged the rest of the cold tea with the crazy idea it might cool her down. "I'll get changed—and brush my hair—and then we can go."

Still overheated, she searched her closet for something to wear. Nothing too short or too tight—she didn't want to look as if she was applying for citizenship of Planet Belly Button. But it had to be cool, or her fair skin would be flushing like a beet every time she remembered the way she'd reacted just now.

She rejected a sleeveless red satin shift in favor of a halter-necked sundress. The sundress had the disadvantage of requiring her to go braless, but its lilac color could never be construed as a come-on.

She slipped the dress over her head, then brushed out her sleep-tangled hair. Next, her makeup. She looked in the mirror and sighed. There wasn't enough concealer in Nordstrom's to hide the dark circles under her eyes.

"Maybe the panda look is in this year," she muttered.

When she got back out to the living room, Trent was watching sports on TV. Golf.

Without looking around he said, "Your sister's playing."

"I know, I'm taping it."

"She doesn't look much like you."

Kelly had always thought Stacey was prettier than she was. "Are you ready to leave?" she said, trying not to snap.

Trent hit the remote and the picture died. He stood up.

"Sorry about…the ear thing," he said. "It wasn't very professional of me."

Kelly waved a hand. "I don't expect you to be professional."

"There is that." He grinned and the lingering awkwardness in the atmosphere eased. He ran his gaze over her, taking in her bare shoulders, the fullness of her curves emphasized by the halter top and the flare of the skirt over her hips. "You look…better than usual."

How come he smooth-talked every other woman in the world, but with her it was one wiseass comment after another? She should have laughed it off; instead, an unreasonable hurt needled her. "Appearances don't matter, it's what's underneath that counts." Darn, she'd meant to say inside, not underneath.

She might have known Trent wasn't about to pass up an opportunity like that. He slipped his sunglasses down from his head. "Let me check that out with my X-ray glasses."

Kelly rolled her eyes.

"Just as I thought," he said happily. "No bra."

She gasped and wrapped her arms across her chest. Trent laughed so hard he dropped the car keys he'd pulled from his pocket. He swooped to snag them in one graceful movement, then escorted her to the door. "Let's go, sugar."

TRENT MIGHT HAVE KNOWN the sight of his car would have Kelly rolling her eyes again. The things that impressed other women seemed to either annoy her or make her laugh. Either way, he found himself enjoying her reactions.

"Is there a problem?" he asked.

"What is this thing?" She wrinkled her nose at his bright orange Lamborghini Gallardo.

"Uh…a car?"

She projected eloquent silence until he said, "Okay it's a babe-mobile."

She tsked. "That's what I thought."

"Don't tell me," he said as he opened her door, "you think it's an airhead car."

She tucked that flirty skirt around her knees and looked up at him, all wide-eyed innocence. "I wouldn't tell you that."

He pulled out into the traffic and headed for his father's house.

For all her ennui, Kelly appeared to be enjoying the Lamborghini. She checked her appearance in the mirror, fiddled with the sound system and pressed every button she could reach, including one tucked down the side of her seat.

"Yikes!" she squawked as her seatback reclined, taking her with it so she ended up almost lying down, that sexy dress riding up her thighs.

Trent eyed her legs and tightened his grip on the steering wheel. "That's one of the car's more convenient features."

She tutted and got the seat upright again. He watched her hands as they smoothed her skirt.

"Tell me about your father," she demanded.

"Quit analyzing me," he said good-naturedly.

She rolled her eyes again. "He's the host tonight, and I'd like to know something about him."

After a moment he said, "Dad's been in NASCAR forever."

She nodded. Anyone who knew anything about NASCAR had heard of Matheson Performance Industries, the company Brady Matheson had founded after he quit his career as stock car driver. MPI had a stellar track record in building winning engines, not just in NASCAR, but also in Indy racing.

"Are you close to him?"

Now that definitely counted as analyzing. But Trent didn't see the harm in answering.

"Dad doesn't suffer fools and he can be a hard man. But he always loved us kids, we never doubted that."

"What about your mother?"

"Mom died when I was sixteen. She was Dad's second wife."

Her curious eyes tried to bore a hole in his head. What the heck, he might as well tell her all of it. Since she'd be quitting tomorrow.

"Chad is thirty-five, and I have another half brother, Zack, who used to race but now lives in Atlanta. He's thirty-three. Dad married my mom the day after his divorce came through, and I was born a month later. I'm thirty-one."

Even an airhead could do the math on that one and figure things hadn't been plain sailing in the Matheson family for a while back then. And Kelly was no airhead.

"Is your father one of the distractions you want me to deal with? You looked pretty riled when Chad mentioned him last week."

He knew he shouldn't have talked about his family. "Very good, Sherlock. But I don't need you to deal with Dad." The thought of his fiery little shrink "dealing with" Brady Matheson lit a funny glow inside him.

Trent found himself whistling as he drove. This was shaping up to be a great night. He had an idea that would impress the heck out of Dad, and he was about to unload Kelly permanently.

Which was just as well, given the way he'd manhandled her ear earlier. He couldn't explain why he'd made that physical contact. Nor why that slightest of touches should have arrested all reason and left him thinking about things such as whether or not she was wearing a bra.

It was the sort of juvenile mentality he'd grown out of back in high school.

But there was something different about Kelly tonight. He'd gotten used to his uptight shrink constantly probing for any sign of weakness, of need. He knew exactly where he stood with her. The just-woken-up Kelly who'd talked about belly buttons and piercings had thrown him off balance.

She'd been just as disturbed by his touch, he knew that for sure. If she hadn't been about to quit, that might have worried him. As it was, he could chalk up tonight to the growing list of enjoyable memories of his brief association with Kelly Greenwood.

CHAPTER FIVE

As THEY LEFT CONCORD, Kelly's cell phone rang.

"Hi, Mom." Darn, she didn't need to hear from Mom right now, not when she was feeling such a failure.

"Stacey just birdied the eighteenth, did you see?" Merle Greenwood's voice rose to a squeak of excitement.

"I'm taping it, I'm on my way out. But that's great."

"I have news—your brother's getting married."

Dave was already married, so that left… "*Josh* is getting married?" Josh was twenty-five, a year younger than Kelly.

"Her name's Nikki, they've been dating three months."

Kelly sensed this information was new to her mother, too.

"The wedding will be here in Richmond in September," her mom continued.

"He can't get married in the middle of the series," Kelly protested. Trent glanced at her.

"They'll take their honeymoon at Christmas." Her mother added meaningfully, "They have a *reason* to get married, and they want to do it before that *reason* starts to show."

"Mom, why don't you just say she's pregnant?" Kelly caught Trent's grin from the corner of her eye.

"It'll be a midweek wedding, the week of the race at Richmond." Mom told her the date. "We'll expect you here, sweetheart."

"Of course I'll be there." After tonight she wouldn't have any other demands on her time.

"I can't wait to see you again, Kelly. We were so disappointed when you only stayed a weekend after you got back from New Zealand."

Tears smarted behind Kelly's eyes. "I know, Mom. I wanted to stay longer, but I was—" *too ashamed* "—busy trying to make this NASCAR thing work."

"And now you've done it."

Kelly heard the smile in her voice. What would Mom think when she heard Kelly had quit?

"We're so proud of you, sweetheart."

"You are?" Okay, this was new. Even though she'd always told herself it didn't matter that her parents weren't proud of her the way they were of the others, Kelly's heart expanded in her chest, and she felt a lump in her throat.

"It can't have been easy getting into Matheson Racing. Working with Trent Matheson will make you a household name."

And if you're not a household name in this family, you're no one. Kelly cursed the excited impulse that had prompted her to phone Mom the day she got the job with Trent.

Her mother said, "When you come for the wedding, we all want to hear every detail."

After the usual protracted goodbyes, Kelly put her phone back in her purse. She massaged her temples.

"Trouble?" Trent asked.

Thanks to your stupid bet my family is about to think I'm a loser yet again. She should tell him now that she quit, spare herself the humiliation of being fired later. Instead, she said, "Nothing I can't handle."

Maybe she could leave the country again, be on the other side of the world by the time her family found out she'd failed.

TRENT'S FATHER lived on the south side of Charlotte, almost in the country. They traveled down a long driveway, the

Lamborghini's tires spitting gravel into the beds of wild-flowers that edged it. Around a bend in the end of the drive-way, Kelly saw a huge house of timber and stone set among rolling lawns.

About a dozen cars were already parked out front, but there was room on the square of pavement for ten more. Trent pulled in next to a black BMW that Kelly recognized as Chad's.

Trent shrugged into a black linen jacket and came around to open Kelly's door.

She clambered out of the low-slung car, then scraped the sharp corner of the door across her ankle as she pushed it shut. "Ouch." She hopped away from the car.

"Are you okay?"

Kelly looked down at her foot, saw beads of red where her skin had torn. "I'm bleeding." The stinging sensation wasn't painful enough to draw tears. Yet, idiotically, she felt the buildup of pressure behind her eyes. She bit down hard on her lip.

"Hey, you're really hurt." Trent sounded worried.

Oh, great. He'd picked this moment to get sensitive. He pulled a handkerchief from his pocket, then hunkered down and reached for her foot. He lifted it off the ground, forcing Kelly to put a hand on his shoulder to maintain her balance. Holding aside the strap of her sandal, he dabbed at the abrasion with unexpected gentleness.

She held herself completely rigid. "Really, it's just a scrape. You don't need to—"

"You can't walk in there with blood on your foot." Finished with his wiping, he folded the handkerchief into a pad and used it to blot the wound. He looked up at her. Awkward, Kelly let her gaze slide away. "You realize this is just an excuse to grope your legs, right?" he teased.

Against her will, she smiled. He stood up, and she in-spected her ankle. No sign of any blood. "Thanks," she said.

He tossed the dirty handkerchief into the car and pressed

the remote lock. "That's the third time I've seen you collide with something."

"I'm a klutz," she said. "So shoot me."

"It surprises me, given you went to college on a sports scholarship and all. What sport did you say you played?"

"I didn't." Kelly straightened her dress unnecessarily.

"Must be tough," he mused, "being a klutz in a family of super-athletes."

"I'm the shrink here," she said crossly.

He chuckled, then took her elbow and steered her toward the house. "Whatever you say, sugar."

Just like that, the man who'd tended her graze was gone, and playboy Trent was back. Frustration welled up. "Don't call me *sugar.* Not ever, but especially not tonight."

"Okay, honey."

"Or honey, or sweetcakes, or any other edible endearment," she said, exasperated.

"Okay…Kelly." He'd said her name so seldom, it still shocked her on his lips. This time he said it lingeringly, tenderly, and her ankle tingled at the memory of his touch.

"No flirting, either."

"You mean I'll have to flirt with someone else?"

Kelly searched his face, tried to see beneath that lightly mocking smile. If she could somehow figure out how to get him to be serious, maybe she had a chance of resurrecting her job at Matheson Racing. Then she wouldn't have to give Mom and Dad the bad news. "Can't you just…not flirt?"

"Not flirt?" He sounded horrified. "But what about my ego that's in need of constant pandering?"

"For Pete's sake, I'll pander to you if that's what it'll take to keep you away from those women."

He snorted. "You wouldn't know how to pander to me."

"I would." She took a deep breath. "You're gorgeous."

He scowled. "You don't think that."

"This isn't about what I think, it's about pandering to you."

"It has to sound convincing," he said, "or it won't work."

Kelly said in a slow, breathy voice, "Trent, you…are… goooorgeous."

His lips quirked. "Better."

She fluttered her eyelids. "You're the best driver in NASCAR. You're incredible out on the track."

"I'm incredible other places, too," he said modestly. When she didn't say anything else he said, "Keep going, this is good. I can feel the desire to flirt ebbing away."

She thought hard. "Just looking at you makes my pulse race." To her shock, her pulse did actually skip a beat and start thudding with renewed vigor.

He stared. "What kind of books do you read? I like that."

She flushed. "You're my hero."

"Too corny. Not to mention unbelievable."

"You're the sexiest guy alive," she snapped.

He chuckled. "How do I know you're not making that up?"

Kelly tired of the game. "I guess you'll never know." She turned away, ready to head inside.

Trent grabbed her arm, spun her back to face him. He'd stepped so close she could see the tiny lines at the corner of his mouth. He wasn't smiling, but his tone was light when he said, "I think I can figure it out."

Just the slightest movement on his part joined his lips to hers. The contact sent a spark arcing between them. Kelly's eyes widened. She pulled away, touched a finger to her mouth.

"Let's try that again." Trent sounded perplexed, so far from his usual cocky certainty, that she didn't resist when he cupped her face in his hands and drew her back to him. His mouth pressed against hers and Kelly was unable to do anything except kiss him back. Immediately, his tongue parted her lips.

Her eager response told him to make himself right at home, and he deepened the kiss. His hands swept the bare expanse of her back and settled just above her waist, where her dress began. Kelly wound her arms around his neck, her fingers burrowing into his dark hair. He pressed her hard against him, and without a bra she felt almost naked against his chest.

His hands found and molded the curves of her bottom. Kelly squirmed against him, heard his grunt of need, felt his response to her movement.

Voices drifted from the house, reminding her just how public this embrace was. Somehow she got her hands between them and pushed against Trent's chest. He released her right away, and she stepped back, her breath embarrassingly close to panting.

Trent's mouth tightened. He jammed his hands into his pockets. "That was goodbye."

Her mind reeled. "Goodbye?"

The eyes that had glowed cobalt with passion were now opaque, unreadable. "You're quitting tomorrow. Have you written your letter of resignation?"

"No, I—"

"That's what I thought. So I took the liberty of preparing one for you." He pulled a folded piece of paper from his jacket pocket and held it out.

Kelly recoiled. Had that kiss been his idea of having the last word? Anger welled up from the pit of her stomach, burning its way through her system. Anger at herself—how stupid could she be, letting him toy with her just now? Anger at Trent for his arrogant assumption that she couldn't win this stupid bet. Anger that he was forcing her to once again disappoint her family. Fury forged into a new resolve and she said, "I won't need that."

His laugh both mocked and pitied her. "Sugar, your time is up."

She jabbed a finger at his chest. "You might be done with me, but I am *not* done with you, Mr. Hotshot NASCAR

Driver. It's still Monday, and our bet's still on. Now get inside and get ready to tell me you need me, because that's what's going to happen."

She stalked up the path, not caring if he followed.

"You have until midnight," he called after her.

Their arrival at the dinner caused a minor sensation. Or rather, Trent's did. Girls came unglued from their boyfriends, grown men grinned like boys who'd been given their first train set, and older women planted less-than-motherly kisses full on Trent's mouth.

Kelly was invisible.

Or she would have been, but she had to give Trent credit for introducing her, furious and standing stiffly beside him, to every one of the people who fawned over him. It wasn't his fault if they glanced her way for a nanosecond then returned their attention to him.

She soon realized there was method in the way he greeted, charmed and moved swiftly on. They were making slow but inexorable progress toward the tall, broad-shouldered man at the end of the enormous living room.

He watched their approach, a resigned grin creasing his rugged face. "I thought you were never going to get past Elspeth Tanner," he said. "Since she walked in that door she's been asking when you were going to get here."

"Dad." Trent shook his father's hand, allowed himself to be clapped on the back in a half hug. "This is Kelly Greenwood. Kelly, Brady Matheson, my father."

Brady was a spooky incarnation of Chad in twenty years' time. The hair was more gray than dark, the blue eyes had a lot more laugh lines about them, but this was the origin of Chad's steely charm.

"Mr. Matheson." Kelly didn't even try to match his grip for firmness.

"Brady," he corrected her. "I saw you on TV during the race

at Charlotte." She'd already decided she was no longer apologizing for that particular incident, but still his chuckle surprised her. "I nearly spilled my beer, I laughed so hard."

Trent didn't look thrilled, so Kelly beamed.

"I'm glad you're on board, Kelly," Brady continued. "What's happening to Trent out on the track is just a glitch. Chad tells me you can help us through it."

Since, despite her fighting words to Trent, she had only five hours left in the job, Kelly doubted that.

"Trent can win the Cup, no doubt about that," Brady said. "He's a better driver than I ever was, and that's saying something. In fact, he's the best damned driver in NASCAR." That he had so much pride in his son, despite Trent's erratic performance, warmed Kelly.

"He certainly has the potential to be," she said.

Trent scowled at her. "How's the business, Dad?"

Brady grimaced. "Margie quit today—her daughter was taken suddenly ill, so Margie's going to live with her and the grandkids in Miami."

Trent told Kelly, "Margie is Dad's assistant, she's been with him for ten years."

"She's gold," Brady said. "The most important person in the organization, after me. I'll never find anyone like her. I don't have the time right now to run interviews, but if I let an agency choose they'll get it wrong."

"So how're things working out with Energy Oil?" Trent asked.

"The new oil is testing great," Brady said. "But renegotiating the joint venture is taking a lot of my time. Margie's had to keep the place running, I've been so tied up." He shook his head. "I don't know what I'm going to do without her."

Chad approached and the conversation began to delve into technicalities beyond Kelly's understanding. She kept looking for a way to steer it back to Trent's need for her, but after half an hour she gave up and moved away to talk to some of the women who wanted to know what it was like to work with Trent Matheson.

She encountered Trent again at the dinner buffet, but he spurned every attempt she made at serious conversation. She sat outside with Chad to eat her meal of baked ham and potato salad. Brady and Trent joined them for the dessert of blueberry pie, and soon a crowd surrounded them.

After coffee, the conversation turned technical again, punctuated by Brady's complaints about the departure of his assistant. People drifted away, leaving Kelly with the three Matheson men.

Chad said, "Dad, what do you think about getting into building Formula One engines? We have the capacity, and it would complement our NASCAR and Indy Racing League business. If you like, I'll do an analysis of the opportunity and write up a report."

Brady's face lit up. "Great idea." The two men began to talk out Chad's proposal. Though Trent nodded and made the occasional suggestion, he'd tensed up. It wasn't the first time Kelly had noticed rivalry between the brothers. Quick as Chad was to give Trent the glory for his racing abilities, he liked to make digs about his brother's charm being even greater than his driving skills.

As Brady waxed increasingly enthusiastic about Chad's idea, Trent grew more silent and watchful. This was a big deal to him, Kelly could tell. In fact, it was the first time she'd seen him care about anything other than winning a race. This might be her chance to cut through his arrogant self-regard.

"Mr. Matheson—Brady," she said when the conversation lulled, "why not let Trent hire your new assistant?"

Trent and Chad stared at her as if she'd lost her mind. But Brady rubbed his chin, and his brow furrowed as he considered her suggestion.

"Trent's good at reading people," she said. He certainly seemed to know how to press all Kelly's buttons. "You don't have time for interviews. He could do them for you."

Chad looked as if he wished he'd thought of it himself. But Trent shifted uncomfortably.

"Not a bad idea," Brady said, turning toward his son. "I've got a hell of a week coming up, and Trent, if you could take that off my hands…"

"Dad, what I'd rather do is—"

"Do this." Brady's tone was incisive. "I'd appreciate it."

Trent nodded with obvious reluctance. What was wrong with the man?

"I have a bunch of candidates lined up for interviews on Wednesday," Brady said. "I was going to cancel because of the Energy Oil negotiations, but you can do them."

"Wednesday's not good for me," Trent said. "In fact, the whole week is a problem."

Brady's eyebrows drew together. "That's a real shame. If I could get it sorted this week, it'd make a big difference."

"Wednesday's great," Kelly said.

TRENT DRAGGED Kelly through the kitchen where the catering staff was cleaning up and out to the utility room. He congratulated himself on not having throttled her en route—this way he could savor that pleasure fully later.

"Why the hell did you say that?" he demanded.

She stumbled over a broom that protruded from an open cupboard, but shook off the hand he extended to steady her. "I was helping you. I could see you wanted to do something for your father."

"So I get to choose his *secretary?*"

"You'll do great," she assured him. "You're a people person. Look how well you get on with women."

"Dad doesn't respect people people," he snapped. "He

likes numbers people, machine people. That's why Chad was talking engines." That was why Trent was convinced Dad would love his ideas for the business, if he'd just give him an hour of serious listening.

She planted her hands on her hips. "It's obvious your father respects you both. So why are you and Chad acting like two kids fighting over a piece of candy?"

"That's none of your business. Anyway, I can't do those interviews on Wednesday." He almost regretted missing out, because maybe if he did this secretary thing, he'd have Dad's ear long enough to tell him his ideas.

"Why not?"

"I have to be elsewhere."

"Another blonde?" she said cuttingly.

Trent leaned against the counter. He narrowed his gaze to tell her it was none of her business. "As a matter of fact, she is."

Kelly made a disgusted sound. "So," she said, and now her brown eyes held a curious satisfaction, "you need to choose the perfect secretary for your father, and you don't have the time."

"Exactly," he said. "And for reasons I don't intend to share with you, the last thing I need right now is for Dad to think I'm unreliable. Thanks to you, I'm screwed."

She dazzled him with a smile that drew his eyes to her mouth and his brain back to that kiss that had rocked his senses so violently he'd been tempted to jump in his car and hightail it out of here.

"How about I do the initial interviews for you?" she said. "I'm great at assessing people, and since you plan on sneaking off to see a blonde, I'm free on Wednesday. You can make the final choice on Thursday."

He should tell her to butt out. He didn't want her hanging around through this week. But she'd got him into this mess, and she was bound to do a better job of the interviews than he would. "Fine," he said.

"Not quite." She folded her arms, the movement pushing her breasts up in that halter dress.

Trent remembered she wasn't wearing a bra—actually, the thought had crossed his mind about a hundred times—and kept his eyes on her face.

Kelly said, "You need to say the magic words."

"Please?" he said, and when she shook her head, "Pretty please?"

She grabbed his wrist and Trent found the sight of her pale fingers on his tanned forearm incredibly alluring. She looked at his watch. "It's ten to twelve. You have ten minutes."

Those magic words? Not a chance.

Trent heard his father's laugh booming all the way from the living room. Dad wouldn't be laughing if he messed this up. He jerked his arm out of Kelly's grip and paced the small utility room. For a full minute he tossed his options around. But he couldn't think of a way out of it. There was little chance another nine minutes would prove any more fruitful.

He stopped right in front of Kelly, so close his chest almost grazed hers. She didn't step back, just lifted her chin and met his eyes. Her brown gaze held all the determination he'd assumed she lacked.

Trent parted his lips the minimum necessary to get the words out. "I need you, Kelly."

CHAPTER SIX

THE FINAL INTERVIEWS for Brady's secretary took place on Thursday morning at the offices of Matheson Performance Industries, located just a few hundred yards from the racing team in the same business park. Kelly took it as a good sign that, after two days of not speaking to her, Trent asked her to sit in.

Not that he said *please*. And it wasn't so much a request as a command.

But they were a team now. Of course, teammates didn't normally kiss each other—unless they were European soccer players—so there would be no repeat of that kiss she and Trent had shared the other night. Kelly put that moment's aberration down to stress, hers and Trent's, and the irregular nature of their bet. Now they'd set their relationship on a professional footing, she was confident they could both forget all about the kiss and start building the trust they needed to work together.

Deliberately, she sidelined the niggling thought that trust couldn't be complete when she hadn't been totally honest with Trent about her past. She would tell him about New Zealand when the time was right.

First, they had to find Brady a secretary. While Trent had been entertaining a blonde yesterday, Kelly had interviewed eight women. She'd shortlisted the two who most closely matched the briefing Brady had given Trent, along with another woman who didn't have secretarial experience but knew a lot about NASCAR.

Trent would make a decision before he flew out to Michigan this afternoon for the weekend's racing.

He sprawled back in his father's leather office chair, hands clasped behind his head, his boot-shod feet up on the desk, as if he owned the world. "Who are we meeting first?"

"Edith Sloan." Kelly passed him the woman's résumé. "Her former boss retired, and the new guy wanted someone younger. She's quiet, no-fuss, she has years of secretarial experience. I'd say she's in her fifties."

"Dad likes 'em old," Trent approved.

"We're assessing her on the basis of her abilities," Kelly said sternly, and he flashed her a grin that did something to her insides. *Don't think about that kiss.* She cleared her throat. "Mrs. Sloan is very competent, I think she and your father will be a perfect match."

When Edith Sloan tapped on the door and came in, Trent swung his feet down from the desk. He got up and shook her hand. "Mrs. Sloan, nice to meet you. I'm Trent Matheson."

The woman greeted him coolly, sending a pointed look to the spot where Trent's feet had rested. *Uh-oh,* Kelly thought.

Unfazed, Trent worked his way down the list of questions Kelly had given him. He kept his feet on the floor and didn't once call Mrs. Sloan "sugar," but the woman didn't warm up. Kelly would have bet money that Trent didn't like her, no matter that she was eminently capable of doing the job.

After he'd finished Kelly's questions, Trent added one of his own. "Do you like NASCAR, Mrs. Sloan?"

Kelly should have thought of the question herself. She awaited the response with interest.

The woman pursed her lips, tilted her head to one side so that her short, iron-gray curls brushed the starched collar of her blouse. "I find it noisy."

"So it is," Trent said thoughtfully. "So it is."

When the interview ended Kelly showed the woman out.

"We're not hiring her," Trent said.

Kelly humphed. "Because she didn't succumb to your charm?"

"Because she's scary," he corrected her.

"Trent, that woman could do this job blindfolded. She's exactly what your father wants."

"You might hire on ability," he said, "but I hire on personality."

"Which sheds a whole new light on why you didn't want to hire me," she said drily.

He laughed. "Where do I start, sugar, where do I start?"

"*Don't* start." She handed him another résumé. "Next up is Marjorie Foster, who recently moved to Charlotte from Salt Lake City to be near her son and his family. She's not at all scary."

"So you think she's the one for the job?"

Kelly wished she could answer an authoritative yes. "She's well qualified, pleasant, cooperative. But something about her is a little off."

"What sort of something?"

"I don't know. Just…something."

"You're probably overanalyzing," he told her. "You do that."

When Mrs. Foster walked in, Trent directed an approving nod at Kelly. The secretary's wavy white hair framed her round, bespectacled face and her two chins creased as she smiled warmly. She squeaked with excitement at the sight of Trent. "Look at you," she cooed. "You're even more handsome than you are on television."

Trent took the adulation with his usual look of charmed, "Who, me?" surprise and waved her into a seat.

The interview went well, and Kelly started to relax. The way Trent was leaning across the desk toward the candidate suggested he liked her. There was no sign of whatever had seemed off yesterday. Maybe he was right, and Kelly had been worrying unnecessarily.

After he'd worked his way through the list of questions,

and Kelly had mentally applied ticks to every one of Marjorie Foster's answers, Trent said, "I have to say, Marjorie, I'm very impressed."

Kelly sent him a warning look. They'd agreed he wouldn't offer anyone the position before discussing it with Kelly. And they still had one more interview. He raised his eyebrows as if to say he had no idea what she meant by that look, then turned back to Marjorie. "In fact, you're perfect for the job. Can you start Monday?"

"Why, yes, I can." She clasped her hands together. "This is so exciting."

This is so annoying, Kelly amended, fuming. They'd agreed to a procedure for these interviews, and it didn't involve Trent making unilateral decisions. So much for teamwork.

"Is there anything else you need to know?" he asked, avoiding eye contact with Kelly.

"Well, this may sound silly...." Marjorie's apple cheeks pinkened.

"Go ahead," Trent told her.

"My youngest daughter, she's twenty-three, she's a big fan of yours."

Kelly smirked. Older women often said that sort of thing to Trent. But after he autographed whatever they handed over, they scuttled away with it clutched to their chest in a way that suggested if the daughter existed, she'd have to fight Mom for her piece of Trent Matheson memorabilia.

"You want me to sign something?" His smile tolerant, Trent picked up a pen.

"Oh, no," Marjorie twittered, and her face went even pinker. "I wondered if you'd like to marry her."

"Well, sure I—" Trent came to a sudden stop as the words sank in.

Marjorie sat there, her hands fluttering in front of her like butterflies.

Deranged butterflies.

Her voice high with the effort not to laugh, Kelly said, "Er, Marjorie, did you just ask if Trent would like to marry your daughter?" *Get yourself out of this one, Trent. And next time, don't hire someone without my say-so.*

Marjorie nodded. She reached for her handbag, scrabbled in its depths. "She's very pretty, I have a photo…."

"I'm sure she's lovely." Trent cast a longing glance at the window. If it had been the kind that opened, Kelly suspected he'd have jumped out. "But the fact is, Marjorie, I'm not good husband material. I can't see myself being tied to one woman." He spread his hands in apology for his own shallowness.

Kelly had to admire the way the legendary Trent Matheson charm had smoothed an awkward moment. In his own way, Trent was quite the professional. Maybe this didn't have to be the end of the road for Marjorie Foster. Maybe she could still work for Brady, if she promised to drop the subject of marriage to her daughter.

Marjorie continued to rummage in her purse. With a cry of triumph she pulled out…not a photo. A booklet. She slid it across the desk, face up. The title stood out in bold red letters: *Polygamy and the Virile Young Man*.

Kelly whimpered. She thought Trent did, too.

"A man like you shouldn't be expected to tie himself to one woman—it's not natural." Marjorie's blue eyes took on an earnest gleam. "Why should you conform to a society that says you can only have one wife?" She tapped the leaflet meaningfully. "I wrote this especially for men like you, men who have…needs. Back where I come from near Salt Lake City, there are plenty of men with three, even four—"

Kelly jumped to her feet and snatched up the booklet. "Mrs. Foster, it's been a pleasure to meet you. You've given Trent a lot to think about."

"I'll see you Monday," Marjorie called over her shoulder as Kelly bundled her out the door.

Kelly dusted her hands together as she sat back down. "Good job," she told Trent brightly. "I'll go ahead and cancel our last interview."

"Fire her," he said.

She widened her eyes. "But you only just hired her." She pressed a fist to her mouth to keep from laughing.

"I mean it, Kelly," he said darkly. "You put that woman on the shortlist, you have to get rid of her."

"Don't you think you should at least meet her daughter first?" At his look of horror, she crumpled into laughter. She laughed so hard that she cried, for the first time since she got back from New Zealand.

"It's not funny," Trent said irritably. "People like her can be a danger to—" His lips twitched. "Okay, it's a little bit funny, but you still shouldn't—"

"When she gave you—" Kelly gasped for air, then tried again. "When she gave you that booklet, the look on your face…" She collapsed into mirth again, knuckling her eyes.

Oh, what the hell. Trent gave in to the laugh that had been building inside him ever since that crackpot woman had mentioned her daughter. His chuckle became a guffaw, and soon his laughter was as uncontrollable as Kelly's.

It was a good couple of minutes before just thinking about Marjorie Foster didn't trigger another bout of hilarity.

At last Trent pulled himself together. He got up and poured two glasses of water from the dispenser. He took a sip from one, placed the other on the desktop in front of Kelly and perched on the edge of the desk.

He hadn't wanted to believe her when she said she had an instinct about Marjorie Foster. Was that because he might have to admit her instincts about his racing could be valid?

A tiny part of him almost wanted to work with Kelly,

almost believed she could help him. But a larger chunk of him clung to his sense of self-preservation, warned him that revealing too much to her would backfire. Not that, right now, Kelly looked remotely like a threat to his ambitions. With her cheeks flushed and her eyes still bright with dampness, she looked cute and soft and warm. Huggable. *Make that kissable.* Trent tried to steer his mind away from the way her lips had felt beneath his. But it was darned difficult when those same lips were right in front of him, slightly parted so he got a glimpse of white teeth and the soft pink of her tongue.

He took another sip of the ice-cold water and reminded himself this was a business meeting.

Yeah, but who said a meeting couldn't sometimes take a detour? Right now, his gut told him he should kiss her. And a good driver always went with his gut. He leaned toward Kelly, saw something leap in her eyes. He read it as the surefire knowledge that this kiss would be very enjoyable.

But the second his lips grazed hers, she jerked away.

"Stop it." That was unmistakably annoyance, not desire, in her voice. The shared laughter had evaporated, and Trent was surprised to find he missed it. She said, "I'm part of your team now, Trent. So unless you make a habit of kissing Rod Sutton and the mechanics, don't try it on me."

"But you kiss way better than Rod," he joked in an attempt to recapture that intriguing, unfamiliar intimacy. She didn't smile, not even a flicker. So much for his instincts. Not content with messing with his mind, her brown eyes and soft lips were screwing with his gut. Trent sighed. "Sorry."

She nodded abrupt acceptance of his apology.

He couldn't resist adding, "Though I think the no-kissing rule is a little harsh. One thing about Mrs. Foster, she understands men like me."

Now Kelly did smile. Trent liked the way her lips seemed to curve against her will, a little at a time until her eyes lit up.

"Understanding you isn't difficult, Trent," she said. "You're an open book—and a junior reader at that."

"Ouch." He feigned a hurt expression. "I want Mrs. Foster, go call her back."

A knock on the office door startled them both.

"Be careful what you wish for," Kelly warned. She called out, "Come in."

To Trent's relief, the woman who entered Brady's office bore no resemblance to Mrs. Foster.

Petite, with dark hair and dark eyes, she seemed to bounce forward, hand outstretched. "I'm Julie-Anne Blake."

"Ms. Blake is our last candidate," Kelly said.

This one didn't look like a psycho. But neither had Mrs. Foster. Trent gave her a restrained version of his smile. She looked to be in her forties, so she might consider herself dating material—he didn't want to encourage any marital aspirations. "Nice to meet you, Ms. Blake."

"Julie-Anne," she insisted as she took the seat Mrs. Foster had vacated. "And you're Trent Matheson, I'd know you anywhere."

Kelly said sweetly, "Julie-Anne, do you have any leaflets you'd like to pass over to Trent?"

Trent gave Kelly a black look. "Don't listen to her," he told Julie-Anne. He picked up his list of questions. "Tell me a little about your work experience."

"I've worked in NASCAR a long time," Julie-Anne said. She outlined what sounded like a hundred jobs involving everything from driving a hauler through to catering and handling fan requests for photographs. The nearest she'd come to secretarial work was a receptionist position for one of the smaller teams.

But Trent liked her relaxed warmth. She was completely different from his father's former secretary, but she knew a heck of a lot about NASCAR. That knowledge might help ease the load on Brady.

"Julie-Anne," Trent said, "can you use a computer?"

The question elicited a dazzling smile. "Absolutely. My daughter spends her time traveling the world. To keep in touch I have to read her blog or send her an e-mail. Actually, I was in one of your fan chat rooms the other day and folk were describing your race at Dover a couple of weeks back as your finest moment."

"Yeah?"

Kelly had to hand it to Julie-Anne. Buttering Trent up was a smart job interview tactic. He wore that pleased smile he got whenever people said nice things to him. The one Kelly never saw when it was just her and him.

"I didn't agree," Julie-Anne said. The statement wiped the smile off Trent's face and put it on Kelly's. Julie-Anne continued, "You seemed tense, and in the early laps I thought you might not pull it off. If I had to pick your finest moment, I'd go for—" she thought a moment "—the first race at Daytona last year."

Trent weighed that up, then smiled, a genuine smile this time. "You're right."

Julie-Anne *was* right, Kelly agreed silently. Trent had lucked out with that win at Dover—he couldn't afford to get overconfident.

But overconfidence seemed to be hardwired into him and she wasn't surprised when, undaunted by the disaster of the previous interview, Trent offered Julie-Anne the job, starting Monday. Having apparently conveniently forgotten Marjorie Foster was also starting Monday.

Trent ushered Julie-Anne to the door and closed it behind her. "That's what I call a result," he said to Kelly.

Kelly packed her papers into her briefcase. "Julie-Anne's very attractive and she paid you some nice compliments. But I think your father would prefer Mrs. Sloan."

He gave her a superior look. "I know my own father better

than you do, Ms. Smarty Pants. Julie-Anne will lighten the atmosphere around here. Dad sometimes looks like he's about to blow a gasket, he gets so stressed."

She clucked disapprovingly. "You can't decide what's best for someone else. You have to listen to what they really want and work with that."

"Then how come," Trent said, "you seem to think you know what's best for my racing?"

Kelly snapped her briefcase shut. "Trent, all I've been doing is throwing out some ideas. Until you start talking to me, nothing I come up with will really resonate with you." She gave him a hard look. "Now that I'm officially part of the team, I expect you to keep your promise to cooperate."

They headed out into the parking lot, where the sun beat down on the pavement, making shimmering waves of heat. They skirted the side of the building, then walked across the grass in the direction of the Matheson Racing headquarters.

Trent was an enigma, Kelly decided. A brilliant driver, professional when it suited him, but more often than not a playboy charmer. Somewhere in all that was the cause of his distraction from his racing.

Maybe if he had more consistency in his personal life, it would spill over into his driving.

"Perhaps you should find a serious girlfriend," she mused aloud.

"Yeah," he said. "One with a lucky belly button ring."

"Excuse me?"

"Danny Cruise's girlfriend has a lucky belly button ring. He rubs it right before he gets in his car on race day."

"Ugh." Someone else who'd feel right at home on Planet Belly Button. Kelly revised her opinion of Danny Cruise downward. "I meant a steadying influence might help you."

"Like I told Marjorie, I don't see myself settling down with one woman."

"Don't you want to get married, have kids?"

"In theory? Sure I do." He grabbed her elbow briefly as her heel sank into the soft ground. The moment she freed her shoe, he released her. "But marriage is a partnership, right? Two people supporting each other."

"Very good." She slid a glance at him; he appeared to mean what he said. "You're quite the New Age guy." They reached the start of the Matheson Racing parking lot. Kelly felt steadier back on pavement.

"Wrong," he said. "I can't do that two-way thing. To win races, I need to focus on me. Having to be there for someone else would be a distraction."

Kelly stopped, and he did, too. "Other drivers manage."

He lifted one shoulder. "Not me. The women I date…it's enough for them that I want to be with them, they don't expect any more."

"So it's all about you," Kelly said.

He grinned with a blatant satisfaction no New Age guy would dare display. "Exactly."

At least he was honest. Any woman dumb enough to fall in love with him would have only herself to blame.

Again, Kelly felt a twinge of guilt that she hadn't been entirely honest with him in return.

"Maybe your self-absorption is a good thing," she told him as they climbed the steps of the building.

"How do you mean?"

She lifted her shirt where the heat had stuck it to her skin and flapped it to admit some air. Trent eyed her movements with interest. "Now that you're cooperating with me, your self-awareness will make it very easy for you to answer my questions." With relish, she added, "It won't take me long to have your soul laid bare."

His eyebrows rose on the word *bare,* but he didn't flinch. "Sugar, I'm all yours."

THEY FLEW TO MICHIGAN that afternoon on Trent's jet. The royal-blue leather seats were deep and comfortable, and the spacious cabin felt more like a living room than an aircraft, with its plush maroon carpet, oak-fronted bar and full-scale entertainment system. It sure beat traveling coach, Kelly thought.

Somewhere in the sky behind them, the crew was flying on the Matheson Racing team aircraft. Below them, a hauler transported two Number 186 cars, and a driver was delivering Trent's motor home to the track. Matheson's NASCAR Craftsman Truck Series team was also out there somewhere, but Kelly had no involvement with Brad Thorne, that team's driver, whose consistent performance suggested he didn't have any kind of focus problem.

Kelly flicked through a motor sports magazine as she watched Trent out of the corner of her eye. To judge by the intensity with which he was reviewing a tape of his last race in Michigan, you wouldn't guess he suffered from distraction. Unless you knew that his nineteenth-place finish back then had been his worst result in a glorious year. And that, just shy of this season's midpoint, he'd finished worse than that five times.

The past couple of weeks had given her some insight into Trent's personality and his racing, but to make a real difference they had to get down to the nitty-gritty. That soul-baring stuff.

For a half second, the Trent on the video screen scowled as he got out of the car. Then he caught sight of the camera and flashed a don't-care grin.

"The next three days I'll be hanging around you a lot," she told the real Trent. "I'll be logging your routines up to and including race day."

He hit the stop button, unclipped his seat belt, stood and stretched. The movement drew Kelly's gaze to his lean strength. "How about I just tell you my routines, and you stay away from me?"

She ignored him. "How you drive can be affected by a whole lot of things, right down to what you eat, how much sleep you get, who you listen to ahead of a race. My job is to discern behavior patterns, then figure out which ones help you win, and which ones contribute to bad results."

"Sounds a lot like the superstition you accused me of relying on."

"Not really. Later on, we can reduce your reliance on the ones that are just plain lucky, and focus on those that work for a logical reason."

Trent walked over to the bar fridge and pulled out a soda. He waved the can at Kelly, and she nodded. He popped the top and handed it to her.

"If we work hard, I'm sure we can identify the problems," she said.

Trent took a swig from his own can. "I already identified one."

"Really? What's that?" She waited, pen poised over her notebook.

"You're no fun."

Kelly had to bite her lip, lest she prove him wrong by grinning. "You're a faster learner than I thought."

His rich, warm laugh washed over her. She smiled back, and it occurred to her that although Trent was the most infuriating and annoying man she'd ever met, she'd smiled more in the last few weeks than she had in years.

I like him. The thought rose unbidden, and her first instinct was to deny it. Then reason asserted herself. He was her client, it was okay to like him. It was easier to work with someone you like.

I like his kisses. Now that was not okay. That was bad. *I like them a lot,* her mind added. *Stop that,* she admonished

herself. Using a relaxation technique she sometimes recom-
mended to anxious clients, she discarded every thought from
her mind, one by one.

The memory of Trent's kiss was the last to go.

TRENT'S QUALIFYING LAP at the Michigan track was a non-
event. Halfway around, the Number 186 car's transmission
went south and Trent limped onto the infield. NASCAR allo-
cated him a provisional entry for the race, but it meant Trent
was starting on the back row, forty-second out of the forty-
three cars that would race on Sunday.

Rod and the team put their usual one hundred percent into
setting up the car, but the mood in the Matheson garage was grim.

Trent, however, seemed invigorated by the challenge.
When the green flag fell, he proceeded to turn his back-row
start into a sizzling run around the wide track. He stuck to the
low groove when he could, made the most of Michigan's
generous passing room, and set the fastest lap time ever
recorded at the track on lap ninety-eight. On lap 140, he broke
his own record.

Kelly wore a microphone headset, but she didn't talk to
Trent during the race. Instead, she hung around Rod Sutton,
sitting in the war wagon hunched over the television screen.
She listened to the instructions Trent gave the team ahead of
his pit stops, and to the crew chief's comments about his performance.

"He's going a hell of a lot better than he did last time he
was here." Rod stated the obvious to no one in particular.

"Why do you think that is?"

He shot her an impatient look, but he answered the
question. "We pitted earlier this time. Seems to take some of
the worry out of him."

"Does he know that?" Kelly asked.

Rod frowned. "I guess."

When Trent flew past the checkered flag in ninth place, the crowd cheered him harder than they had the winner. In the pits, Kelly yelled herself hoarse. She didn't doubt Trent had what it took to win the series. All he had to do was focus that incredible determination.

When he got out of the car, everyone wanted to clap him on the back, shake his hand, high-five him. He took it all in stride, laughed and joked with the guys, relived the crucial moments of the race, thanked the team for their good work.

At last he got to Kelly. She wanted to throw her arms around him, tell him he was the best thing she'd ever seen. For one long moment, he looked at her. Then he slapped her on the back, not painfully, but solidly enough for her to lurch forward. "Great race, huh?"

"Great," Kelly said between coughs induced by that thump on the back.

"I'm treating you like one of the guys, sugar." He grinned. "Just like you said."

The reporters obviously viewed Trent's ride as the high point of the day's race. After they were done in Victory Lane, they descended on the Matheson team. Trent posed for the cameras, flanked by two gorgeous blondes, whose tight T-shirts bore the Energy Oil logo.

When one of the girls pulled Trent into an embrace, he kissed her hard on the lips, much to the delight of the whooping media. He ended the kiss when he was good and ready—about ten seconds later, Kelly estimated. His eyes met hers over the girl's head. He raised his eyebrows and shrugged slightly, as if to say, "See, one woman isn't enough."

Kelly told herself she didn't care how many women he needed, as long as, when it came to his racing, he only needed her.

WHEN TRENT TURNED UP at work at ten o'clock Monday morning, Kelly informed him in her most businesslike manner that she still had several questions about his race weekend routines. She didn't actually use the words *bare your soul,* but from the way he groaned, she figured he knew what lay ahead.

They sat at the meeting table in his office, and she showed him what she'd logged over the past four days. Although Trent cracked a few jokes about the level of detail she'd gone into, he paid close attention. He leaned over to peruse her notes.

"There are still some gaps in this." She shifted away from him, from the bent head she could touch if she reached out the tiniest bit. "Like, where did you have dinner on Saturday night?"

"I went to a Japanese restaurant with Chad and Rod." He leaned back in his chair. "Since you seem to want every detail, I guess I should tell you a couple of girls joined us."

Kelly swallowed a mouthful of coffee while she waited for the flare of irritation to pass. "What did you eat?"

"Sushi. Plus a couple of beers." He added helpfully, "The girls drank wine."

She ignored that last irrelevance, wrote the rest down. "What time did you go to bed?"

"Two a.m."

She steeled herself. "Were you...alone?"

CHAPTER SEVEN

TRENT REARED BACK. "That's none of your business."

Kelly looked flustered, as she damn well should. Her gaze fell to the page in front of her, and she applied intense concentration to scratching out something she'd written. But her voice was cool when she said, "If intimate relations are part of your pre-race routine, I need to know."

"Are you saying I can't have sex before a race?"

"I'm saying I need to know whether you did or not, so we can assess the impact it had on your racing, good or bad." With exaggerated patience, she said, "Trent, you had no qualms about making out with that girl in front of millions of TV viewers after the race. Telling me whether or not you slept with someone can't be that big a deal."

Trent was so busy trying to figure out a way around her original question, it took a moment for Kelly's comment to sink in.

"Making out—?" Realization dawned. "*She* kissed *me*. In a moment of excitement."

"For you, too, it seemed."

He snorted. "The media wanted the shot. I gave it to them."

"That's a good reason to kiss someone." Her tone said, *Not*.

He wasn't about to tell her the real reason. That he'd seized the chance to overlay the plaguing memory of that Kelly kiss with something more ordinary. Nor would he tell her that it hadn't worked.

"You still haven't answered my question," she said. "Did you have sex the night before the race?"

Damn, she was back on that. To his chagrin, he couldn't hold her gaze. "No," he mumbled. He watched as she put a little *X* next to the word *Sex* on the page in front of her.

"How about before the race at Dover?"

"No," he said tightly.

"Before Charlotte?"

Trent stirred in his seat. "Are you going to ask this about every race?"

"I'm trying to compare your performance—on the track," she added hastily, "in different races. If you spent the night with a woman then had a bad race. Or had a good race after you…you know."

He managed no more than a strangled sound. And sensed the balance of power in this conversation slipping from his grasp.

"We agreed we were going to lay your soul bare." Sure enough, Kelly looked as if she'd started to enjoy this discussion.

"There's bare, and there's indecent exposure," he retorted.

"Think of me as your accountant, or your lawyer," she said, and he detected teasing beneath the soothing tone.

"I never discuss my sex life with my lawyer. Or my accountant."

"A doctor, then," she said. "You need to be able to tell me anything and everything."

Trent eyed her as she sat there in her knee-length blue skirt and her short-sleeved white blouse done up all the way to her neck. That he was even tempted to indulge in a stethoscope-and-skimpy-white-coat fantasy told him he could never have a doctor-patient relationship with Kelly. He shook his head. He had to stop thinking about kissing her.

She tsked. "Would it be easier if I ask when was the last time you had sex?"

"I'll tell you if you'll tell me," he said. He stopped short, his next smart comment forgotten. The thought of Kelly sleeping with someone burned like battery acid.

"I'm not leaving until you answer the question," she said with that mule-like stubbornness that was a match for anything Trent could throw at her.

He gave up. It wasn't as if he wanted to impress her. If such a thing was even possible. His voice level, he said, "There's no link between my love life and my race results. I haven't been with anyone all season."

Her mouth dropped open, and she quickly clamped it shut.

"To be sure we're on the same page here," she said carefully, "I should tell you it's not only the night before a race that could be relevant. I need to know if you've—"

"I have not had sex this season," he enunciated slowly, for complete clarity. What the heck, he might as well totally destroy his reputation. "Not the night before a race, not after a race, not midweek, not on Monday, not on Tuesday, not on—"

"Hell, no wonder you've been cranky," Chad said from the open doorway.

Oh, great.

Kelly choked on her coffee, coughing until tears streamed from her eyes. Trent sprang forward and grabbed her mug before she emptied it all over the floor. He thumped her on the back—until he realized her coughing had turned to laughter, silent at first, then giggles that she tried to suppress but which soon erupted into peals of mirth.

He gave Chad a scowl fierce enough to send his brother on his way, albeit with a jaunty grin. Chad hadn't dated in way longer than Trent—he was probably thrilled to find he wasn't the only loser on the block. "Could you pull yourself together?" Trent demanded of Kelly.

"I'm s-sorry," she sputtered. "I'm really not laughing at you." Then merriment overtook her again.

Trent shouldn't be feeling inclined to laugh himself. Not

when his ego had just been decimated, first by Kelly, then by Chad. But her irrepressible laughter tugged at the corners of his mouth. With difficulty, he got it back into line. "Can we move on to the next question? You don't need to know about my…intimate relations preseason, do you?"

She shook her head as she swiped tears from her eyes. "I've heard all I ever want to about your sex life."

Her statement wasn't strictly true, Kelly could admit to herself. Why would a man she'd pigeonholed as a shallow womanizer be living like a monk? She believed what he'd told her. There was no reason for him to lie, and plenty of embarrassment in his admission. He'd said he didn't want to settle with one woman, yet he wasn't interested in playing the field. If women weren't the distraction to his racing that she'd suspected, then what was?

"I meant what I said before," he prompted her. "I told you mine, now you have to tell me about your love life."

"I don't have to tell you anything."

"Trust goes both ways, don't you agree?"

"Not to that extent," she said shortly. But he was right. She should tell him what happened in New Zealand.

"At least tell me if you have a boyfriend," he wheedled.

Kelly grabbed at the reprieve. "No boyfriend." She'd learned to be so self-sufficient, she sometimes wondered if men found her aloof. She had plenty of male friends and sufficient dates that she didn't feel unattractive. But it had been a long time since she'd wanted to share enough of herself with someone that they might have a future together. This conversation with Trent felt more intimate than any date in recent memory.

"But surely you want to get married, have kids?" He parroted the question she'd asked him last week.

"I do," she said, then realized she sounded as if she was making a marriage vow. "Of course I want children," she hurried on. "But first I have to find a man I love. One who'll be there for me," she said, in pointed reference to his insistence that he wasn't that kind of guy. Just in case he thought she'd taken his kisses seriously.

Trent sat back, arms folded, his blue eyes gleaming with speculation. "So you want to get married, you want to have a family, but you don't have a boyfriend."

It struck Kelly that she'd never consciously articulated, before today, her desire to really *matter* to a man who loved her, and to create a loving family of her own. Nor had it struck her just how many million miles away she was from achieving it.

Something of her shock must have shown in her eyes, for Trent said with unexpected sympathy, "Tough luck."

No way would she let him feel sorry for her. She said brightly, "I guess it's no worse than wanting to win the NASCAR NEXTEL Cup Series but being unable to get into the top ten on points."

He laughed, her attempt at retaliation bouncing off him like a stone off a windshield.

Damn Trent Matheson. She'd come here to lay his soul bare. Instead, she found herself staring back at him, as raw as if someone had taken a scalpel and sliced open her vulnerable heart.

BRADY MATHESON looked at his watch. Again.

His new secretary was late.

He might have known Trent would hire someone unreliable—the only time the clock mattered to his youngest son was during a race.

Impatient, Brady tapped the face of his chunky stainless steel watch. The amount of work he had lined up the next couple of months, the last thing he needed was a secretary who couldn't be punctual. For just a second, the pressure set Brady's heart thumping like an engine on a dyno. Maybe he was being too ambitious, thinking he could grow the business at the rate he'd targeted. Maybe he should ease off into retirement....

Like hell he would. Brady wasn't going to hand the business over to Chad until its future was secure.

Of course, it would be a damned sight easier to secure it if he had a little help around here. He picked up the phone to call Trent and tell him to fix this mess.

A knock sounded on the door of his office. *About time.* Brady dropped the phone back onto its cradle. "Come in."

One look at the woman—a quick glance at her résumé reminded him her name was Julie-Anne Blake—told Brady which part of his anatomy Trent had been thinking with when he gave her the job.

Trent had suggested she was in her late forties, but that couldn't be right. Not with that thick, dark hair that fell unrestrained in waves below her shoulders. She looked like a gypsy—full-mouthed, dark-eyed, exotic. Brady put her at no more than five foot three, with enough curves packed into her small frame to attract any man's attention. Her green scoop-necked T-shirt molded a generous bust above her still-trim waist, emphasized by the wide belt on her full skirt.

She stepped lightly in her high-heeled sandals, with a rhythm that suggested she might at any minute break into a dance.

What was Trent thinking?

"Mr. Matheson?" She stopped in front of his desk. Her voice was light, musical, just as he might have guessed. "I'm Julie-Anne Blake. I'm sorry I'm late, I ran into Rod Sutton in the parking lot, and we got talking...." She stopped, maybe aware that gossiping with Trent's crew chief wasn't a satisfactory explanation for her tardiness. "It won't happen again."

Brady grunted. He judged people by what they did, not what they said. Nor, he reminded himself, what they looked like.

He shoved his chair back, stood, shook her hand. "Take a

seat, uh—" he darted a lightning glance at the fingers of her left hand "—Ms. Blake."

It didn't surprise him she was unmarried. She looked about as hard to hold as quicksilver.

He scanned her résumé again. The typed words swam in front of his eyes—he'd worked late last night, but even so he shouldn't feel this tired. Must be that stress Trent kept warning him about, which was easy for Trent to say. He lived his life as if he didn't have a care in the world. Trent didn't have a company to run, aggressive growth targets to meet and three squabbling sons to hold together in some kind of family. Brady could never tell how well he was doing with that last one.

He ran a hand over his face.

"Are you okay?" Julie-Anne asked.

With his scowl he told her his state of mind was none of her business. He shuffled her résumé, forced himself to concentrate. Trent had hired this gypsy-woman; she must have something going for her. Apart from the obvious.

"Have you worked as a secretary before, Ms. Blake?" Brady remembered that nowadays you were supposed to call secretaries personal assistants—presumably it sounded more important. Personally, Brady thought it sounded like he needed help going to the john. He sighed, and with what might have been his first ever nod to political correctness, said, "I mean, as a PA?"

"Secretary's fine," she said. That was something. "No, I haven't. But I'm good with computers, I can use a phone, I like dealing with people and I know NASCAR. Is there anything else I need?"

"I guess not," he said truculently. He could hardly expect her to have the experience of this specific job that had made Margie invaluable. And invisible.

He took another look at Julie-Anne. Not only did she look...*sexier* than any woman her age should, she projected a kind of energy a man would be hard put to ignore.

And there was something else about her....

"Have we met before?" Brady asked. "You seem familiar."

Julie-Anne crossed her arms. Her gaze centered somewhere on his forehead. "Possibly. I've had a lot of jobs in NASCAR."

He ran a finger down the page in front of him. "Sold souvenirs for Roush, catering for SouthMax, drove the show-car hauler for Cruise." He looked up. "Nope, I don't know you from any of these."

Julie-Anne smiled, a tight pressing of her lips. Brady looked down at the pages again. "How old are you?" He probably wasn't allowed to ask her that.

"Forty-eight."

"You don't look it," he said, aware he'd made that sound like a bad thing.

"I have help with my hair," she admitted, not appearing to take offence. She touched a hand to her dark locks. "In its natural state it has some gray."

Why the heck was he talking about his new secretary's hair? She could probably sue him for sexual harassment.

Focus, Brady told himself. *Think about what you're trying to do for the boys.* At their ages they didn't need anything else from him. The least he could do was keep their inheritance in decent shape.

"This job involves long hours," he warned her, "especially over the next couple of months. We're concluding the current phase of our testing program with Energy Oil, and then I'll be preparing a proposal for potential investors to fund the expansion of Matheson Performance Industries. I don't have a lot of time to show you the ropes. I expect you to be self-sufficient."

She looked faintly amused at his sternness. "Of course."

A female voice trilled from the doorway, "Brady, how are you?"

Brady looked up. "Come in, Patty."

Patty Selman sashayed into the room, holding a casserole

dish out in front of her. The blond divorcée was around
Brady's age, her figure still pretty good, as far as he could tell
through her jeans and sweater. He'd never seen her wearing
less—and he never wanted to.

"My beef Stroganoff," she announced with a pride that suggested she'd just given birth to the stuff.

"That's great, Patty." He cleared some papers from the
corner of the desk so she could put down the casserole.

"Forty-five minutes at three-fifty and it'll be piping hot."
She cocked her head to one side, batted her eyelashes. "Or
would you like me to come over and put it in the oven for you?"

"I can do it," he said, like he always did.

"My son is spit-roasting a pig this weekend."

Brady shook his head before she could invite him along.
"I'll be in Sonoma for the race." Truth was, he'd probably be
stuck here in the office.

"Come over Wednesday then," Patty said. "I'll do my
chicken pasta." Her chin jutted forward, daring him to find
another excuse.

Sometimes, it was easier not to argue. "Sure, Patty." He half
stood. "Thanks for the Stroganoff."

As Patty left, Brady caught Julie-Anne's quizzical glance.
He didn't owe her an explanation, but he found himself saying,
"Since my wife died, a bunch of ladies have taken it upon
themselves to bring me my dinner two or three times a week."

"I'm sorry," Julie-Anne said. "I didn't realize your wife's
death was so recent."

Brady shifted in his chair, scratched the back of his neck.
He muttered, "It was, uh, fifteen years ago."

"Oh." She paused. "So the self-sufficiency thing only
applies to me? Not to you?"

He felt himself flush. "A guy's gotta eat."

"Of course." But her eyes gleamed with what he suspected
was laughter. Then she asked, "Are you lonely?" as if that

might explain why he was still accepting dinners from desperate divorcées.

He recoiled. "I don't get lonely. I'm very busy. And I have my boys."

She smiled, no mockery in it. "The Brady Bunch."

He shook his head at the title the press often bestowed on Brady Matheson and his three sons. "They're good boys—men—all of them."

"I have a daughter," she said. "She's overseas, she travels a lot."

Unlike him, Julie-Anne did sound lonely. Brady didn't want to know. "We should get started."

"Before we do," she said, "maybe we should talk about how we're going to do things, how our relationship will work."

Our relationship? Brady almost groaned aloud. He shouldn't have mentioned his wife, his sons. A proper secretary would never take that as an invitation to get personal. Heck, until Margie had told him she was quitting because her daughter was ill Brady had forgotten she *had* a daughter.

Julie-Anne might like to get personal with her employers, but that didn't work for him. He'd better make it clear right now. He said, "How about I tell you what to do and you do it?"

She looked as if she might argue, so he added, "It's too busy around here for it to work any other way. I've put everything into this business. I'm fifty-eight years old, I have two years to build this place up before I retire, and I'm not going to waste a second."

"I see," she said, her dark eyes intent, knowing, as if she really did see into him.

Something flitted through Brady, a sucking, punching sensation that left him feeling empty, then full, then…hungry.

It was the feeling he'd had the day Chad was born, when he'd held his son in his arms for the first time. The same one he'd felt when he met Rosie, Trent's mother. Sixteen years of marriage to Rosie had passed in the blink of an eye.

Brady cursed Julie-Anne for making him think about loneliness. Cursed the fact that the familiarity he'd sensed about her suddenly seemed nothing to do with NASCAR. It felt soul-deep.

THIS SNEAKING AROUND is undignified. Kelly acknowledged the thought, then discarded it. After seven weeks trying to get to the bottom of Trent's focus problem, she was beyond worrying about dignity. If she had to resort to spying on him, then so be it.

She flattened herself against the bulk of a Jeep, hiding in its shadow so that if Trent turned around he wouldn't see her following him across the parking lot.

Every Wednesday, he disappeared for the day. Every week, she asked him who the blonde was he sneaked out to meet and where he met her. Every time, he said, "None of your business."

Since Michigan, he'd had a string of mediocre results—admittedly with a flash of brilliance at Daytona, where he came second. Kelly sensed the Wednesday Blonde, as she thought of her, was the key to his erratic performances. The woman had a strong enough claim on Trent's time that he wouldn't break their weekly commitment, not even for the sake of his career.

What if he was in love with her? The thought had prodded Kelly into action.

Trent got into the Lamborghini. Six cars away, Kelly slid into the aging Corvette she'd borrowed from one of the crew, just in case he recognized her Toyota. It wasn't as inconspicuous as she'd have liked, but guys who worked in NASCAR didn't own inconspicuous cars.

Trent pulled out of the parking lot. Kelly gave him a half minute to get ahead of her, then followed. He was headed south, which meant he wasn't meeting the blonde at the condo he owned at the race track, nor at his house. As they drove past a retail strip, Trent's turn signal flashed. He pulled into a parking space. Darn! Kelly couldn't stop without being too obvious. She cruised past, just in time to see Trent walk into a florist.

Buying flowers for the blonde. This was serious. To a guy like Trent, who was all take and no give where women were concerned, buying flowers probably counted as a commitment. Kelly circled back, found a space and parked, keeping an eye on the store through her rearview mirror. A couple of minutes later he emerged empty-handed.

Maybe the roses weren't red enough today, Kelly speculated as she pulled out into the traffic behind him. He drove another few blocks, then drew in again. This time, Kelly was able to park a couple of cars behind him, where she got a good view of him entering a fancy store called Chocolatier.

Her mouth watered. She loved chocolate. But yet again, Trent came out with no visible sign of any purchase. Unless he'd bought one very small, very expensive chocolate and stuck it in his pocket. Where it would melt, and the Wednesday Blonde would be so unimpressed she'd give Trent his marching orders and he'd get his driving back on track. Kelly entertained the fantasy briefly, then snapped to attention as Trent pulled back out into the traffic. He turned onto I-85, still headed south. A few exits later, he quit the interstate and turned into a shopping mall. Kelly parked within sight of the Lamborghini and waited.

And waited.

Two hours later, she conceded Trent must have seen her following him. He'd probably abandoned his car and taken a taxi to his rendezvous. Or maybe he was meeting the girl at the mall. Kelly turned the key in the Corvette's ignition and started back toward the office. Wherever Trent was, Kelly wasn't about to solve the mystery.

Stalemate.

CHAPTER EIGHT

WHEN KELLY ARRIVED home that evening, two dozen white roses and a deluxe assortment of Belgian chocolates greeted her on her doorstep.

If the flowers hadn't been so beautiful, she'd have kicked them in frustration. Instead, she buried her nose in their fragrance, relished the velvet stroke of their petals against her skin.

She set the roses down on her dining table, then went back to collect the chocolate. It, too, smelled divine.

When she put the roses into a vase, she found a card tucked among them. *Hope these revive you after your long day.* A scrawl that counted for Trent's signature. Then a PS: *I'm guessing your sport wasn't orienteering.*

Kelly fought the curving of her lips, tried to summon irritation. She'd wasted hours today. It would take more than a couple of gifts to make up for that.

She wondered, would Trent give her flowers and chocolates if he was serious about the Wednesday Blonde? Probably. Knowing him, he'd placed a bulk order at both stores today, had them delivering to women all over the county.

She tore the cellophane wrapper off the chocolate box, and started in on the praline creams.

WITH A TWO-WEEK BREAK between races, this week wasn't as busy as most others. Kelly planned to use the relative quiet to snag Trent's attention. When she found him in his office on

Thursday morning she didn't mention yesterday's abortive stalking episode, just launched right into what she had to say.

"Trent, we need to think harder about the way you're preparing for your races."

His face got that shuttered look it did every time she tried to make suggestions about his driving. Then he flashed her the charming smile he employed whenever he tried to fob her off. "Did you like the flowers?"

"Were they from you?" She feigned wide-eyed surprise. "I couldn't read the signature."

He chuckled. His gaze ran over her, touching on her waist, her legs, heating her skin before it returned to her face. "Doesn't look like you ate too many of those chocolates."

"I'm allergic to chocolate," she lied.

His grin widened. "That's a real shame. How about I come by tonight and take them off your hands?"

"I gave them to the poor," she said virtuously.

He chucked her under the chin. "That's my Saint Kelly."

She'd indulged him long enough. She said, "I've noticed when you start on the second or third row, like you did last week at Chicago, you tend to drop back pretty quickly."

"The car was too tight last week," he said. "The front was losing traction on the corners."

"What about at Sonoma? You finished thirtieth."

He scowled. "I know where I finished. That flat tire didn't help."

"Any driver can blame his car," she said. "It takes a great driver to admit something in his head is hurting his racing." She paused to let him absorb that. "Why don't you tell me what part you think *you* played in those bad results?"

He paced the office, until he stood as far away from her as possible. "It's complicated."

Kelly caught her breath. This was the closest he'd come to revealing anything personal. "Try me."

"You wouldn't understand."

She itched to shake him. "You'd be surprised what I understand," she said. "Josh had a similar problem last year." Despite her irritation with Trent, the thought of her kid brother made her smile.

Trent actually looked interested. "Josh is doing a heck of a lot better in the NASCAR Busch Series this season. Did he get some advice from you?"

"Well…no. He's a lot like you."

He grinned. "A great driver?"

She sent him a quelling look. "Egotistical. He always thinks he knows best."

"Are you as rude to him as you are to me?"

"I *love* him."

Her words sparked a strange, charged silence. Kelly felt as if someone had hit the pause button to her heart. The silence grew louder, heavier. Trent opened his mouth to say something. Then his gaze flicked past her to the doorway and he said, "Speaking of brothers…"

Chad walked in, followed by Brady. Kelly's heart resumed normal service.

Trent said mildly to his brother, "This looks like a deputation."

"Call it a progress review," Chad said.

"I didn't know we had one scheduled." Trent glanced at Kelly. She shook her head. He sat back, folded his arms. "Do you guys want to pull up a seat, or can you light a rocket under me from there?"

"No need for that kind of talk." Brady grabbed a chair. Chad did likewise. Brady nodded to Kelly. "You've been here nearly a couple of months—I'm interested to know how Trent's getting on."

Before she could speak, Trent said, "Dad, this isn't grade school, you can't come in for a parent-teacher meeting."

Brady looked perplexed. "I'm taking an interest."

Kelly sensed he meant it, however heavy-handed his approach.

"I'm taking a *vested* interest," Chad said. "I want to know what we're getting for our money." His smile toward Kelly was friendly, telling her any doubts he had related to Trent, not to her.

She'd expected something like this to happen, and it meant she was ready to account for herself and Trent.

"Let me run through what we've done so far." She walked over to the whiteboard on the back wall of the office and picked up a marker. "I spent the first few weeks observing Trent's racing and his routines, as well as studying his past form. I was trying to identify the combination of circumstances that allows him to race at his best." She scribbled some points on the board. "For example, you know he does well when he starts on the pole, but not so well if he's a row or two behind. I'm trying to understand why things happen the way they do."

"So why do they?" Brady asked bluntly.

"I've figured out some of the what, but not so much of the why," she admitted. "I expect to progress that, now that Trent and I have built a rapport."

"Have you?" Chad said, surprised.

Kelly swallowed. She glanced at Trent, still sitting with his arms folded, his expression giving nothing away. "Maybe you should ask Trent."

The two men turned to Trent. If he wanted to get rid of her, he could probably say something now that would set his brother against Kelly irrevocably. Trent's gaze measured her, and at last he spoke.

"Kelly can be challenging to work with," he said. "But that's good for me." She let out a breath. Trent added, "She's also very generous." At his brother's querying look, he added, "She gives to the poor."

Chad's eyebrows drew together in puzzlement. Kelly

choked back a wholly inappropriate giggle. "Now that Trent and I have this affinity," she said hastily, "we can dig deeper."

"I struck a glitch like this once, back when I was racing," Brady said thoughtfully. "I was leading the Busch Series, and then it all went south. Turned out I was too busy with other things. I'd already started the engine business, but I had to pull out of that for a few months while I got my racing under control."

"Dad," Trent said, "you and I are different."

Brady stiffened. "The difference is, I knuckled down and solved the problem." Contrition flashed across his weathered face, and Kelly could tell he regretted the harsh words. But he sat there, unyielding, patriarchal.

She said, "Trent's right, Brady. What's going on with him is particular to his situation. You'll see the progress we've made reflected in his racing very soon." Brady looked only slightly mollified, so she added, "I'm convinced Trent has it in him to win the Cup."

Her confidence pleased Brady and at the very least placated Chad. The two men left soon after that.

"Did you mean what you told Dad?" Trent said. "That I can win the Cup?"

She nodded.

Not looking at her, he drummed his fingers on the table. "When I said before that the reason I have a problem with a row two or three start is complicated…"

Kelly waited, not daring to speak.

"I'm close enough to the front to see the open space ahead," he said. "Somehow, that makes the gap between those front row cars look tiny. Coming up to the green flag, I find myself thinking there's no way I can get through. Next thing I know, I've lost four or five places, as all the other drivers who don't see it that way get past me." Frustration burned in his blue eyes.

Kelly clutched the edge of the table, light-headed with relief. "I can do something about that."

JULIE-ANNE DIALED through to Brady's office. "Zack's on the line from Atlanta."

"Put him through." Pleasure made Brady sound ten years younger.

She transferred the call, then turned back to her computer screen. Through the open door of Brady's office she heard his voice, booming with good cheer. No hint that he'd been fretting all week that his middle son hadn't called. Fretting enough to ask Julie-Anne if maybe she'd forgotten to pass on a message.

She heard Brady ask with studied casualness why Zack hadn't been in touch.

She tsked. Why didn't he just tell Zack he wanted to hear from him more often? Or better yet, pick up the phone and make the call himself? In the nearly two months she'd worked here, it had become clear the Matheson men were pretty screwed up in their relationships. Chad and Trent came in every Monday for a debrief of the weekend's race, and each time Julie-Anne was amused—and bemused—by the way the two brothers angled for their father's attention. Brady seemed oblivious to their posturing. Toward Chad, he was serious, businesslike, seeming not to notice that Chad was occasionally looking for a little warmth. Trent, Brady treated with indulgence, when anyone could see Trent had long tired of being the petted baby of the family.

None of them talked much about Zack, who three years ago had come within a whisker of winning the NASCAR NEXTEL Cup Series. The following year, the NASCAR world had been shocked when Zack left Matheson Racing for another team. At the end of that season, after he was knocked out of contention—in an accident caused by Trent—Zack had quit racing altogether. All of them had refused to discuss Zack's departure—from racing and the family.

Now, it was obvious Brady missed his son. But to admit

that would be to reveal neediness. Heaven forbid that any Matheson male should be needy.

Julie-Anne spent on average ten hours a day in Brady's company, five days a week and sometimes six. She'd grown to admire his strength of character, even if it made him too darned unbending. If he would just soften up a little, let someone behind that tough facade... Like the sons he loved so deeply and who she could tell loved him back. Or maybe a woman...

"Let's face it," she murmured, confident Brady wouldn't hear her over his phone conversation, "I like the guy."

She'd never expected to feel this way. She'd been so hurt by her marriage she hadn't wanted to risk another serious relationship. But Brady's self-control, integrity and loyalty couldn't be more of a contrast with her late husband.

"Blast." Somehow, in the middle of a letter to one of the other teams that used MPI's engine shop, she'd typed, *It's not a crime to need someone.* She held down the backspace key.

She heard Brady say, "I'm kinda busy, buddy. Getting down to Atlanta right now wouldn't be easy."

She groaned aloud. How could a man so intelligent in his work be so dumb when it came to his sons? The light on her own phone indicated Brady's call was over. No doubt Zack hadn't taken his father's refusal to visit well.

Exasperation propelled Julie-Anne into his office. "I think you're foolish to reject Zack's attempts at reconciliation," she said.

Brady stared at her. A dull red seeped beneath his tan. "Did I ask your opinion?"

Uninvited, she sat in the chair in front of the desk. "It's obvious Zack has ended up the odd one out in your family. That's tough on a kid, even when he's grown up. You need to accept his overtures."

"I did," he growled. "I said I'd like to see him, but now's not a good time for me to go to Atlanta. He can come up here."

"It doesn't work like that." The bitterness of her experience with her daughter colored her words. "All he heard is that you don't want to visit him."

Brady shot her a disgusted look. "He's a grown man, for Pete's sake. We're not kids sulking in our corners."

"Aren't you?" She ignored the angry working of his jaw. "It looks to me like you won't call him unless he calls you first. That's the sort of thing kids do."

In a movement unexpectedly fluid for such a bulky man, he rose and rounded the desk. Julie-Anne scrambled out of her chair—and found herself chest-to-chest with him. Something snapped between them, like static electricity. Or maybe it was the blast of heat in his blue eyes. She took a hasty step backward and bumped against the chair she'd vacated. Brady stepped toward her, and her awareness of him was so palpable, the desire to draw close to him and comfort him so seductive, that she shrank away.

"Hey." He stopped, shocked. "I wasn't going to—I wouldn't hurt you."

"I know that." Julie-Anne sidestepped him and headed toward the outer office. He stayed her with a hand on her arm, firm but not ungentle.

"Then what was that about?"

She looked down at his hand, embarrassed that his touch made her stomach flip like a nervous sixteen-year-old's. She really had to get out more, stop sitting at home in her little cottage weaving romantic fantasies about turning gruff, tough Brady Matheson into a warm, tender lover.

"I'll make us some coffee." She didn't answer his question.

He released her, but he didn't move away. "My sons and I get along just fine."

Brady found himself following her, watching as she poured coffee from the pot on the warmer next to her desk. As so often happened when he was with Julie-Anne, a sense of familiarity nagged him.

More like *over*familiarity, given the way she liked to venture her opinion on most aspects of his life. Brady frequently told her to butt out, often in those exact words, but he found himself opening up to her more and more, and he liked her too much to get really annoyed. And she knew it.

At least, he assumed she knew why he got so jumpy around her. She'd proven as difficult to ignore as he'd predicted the day he met her. Each week that passed he got more pleased to see her in the mornings, more reluctant to say goodbye to her in the evenings. More inclined to ignore that she never did things exactly the way he told her, and now when he looked for something in his office, he could never find it.

"Maybe you're right about Zack," he said abruptly.

Her smile lit her face, made him glad he'd said it. "Zack's not like the others. He doesn't have Chad's interest in the business. He was a great driver, but he never had the charisma that makes Trent so much fun to have around." Brady chuckled at the thought of his youngest son. "Zack's the serious one."

Julie-Anne handed him the coffee. Deliberately, his fingers brushed hers. Pathetic behavior for a man his age. Still, he enjoyed it.

"Maybe you need to tell Zack you love him."

Why did he let her suck him into these sentimental conversations? "We're *guys*," he said. "We don't hug and kiss—" mentally he measured the span of her lips, and he wished he hadn't said the K word "—and we don't spout declarations of love." When she eyed him steadily he protested, "Zack knows I love him."

Brady had a job to do for his sons, and he would do it. That's how you showed love.

"Did you sort out the purchasing agreement for the new rod supplier?" he asked, a change of subject so clumsy that she laughed.

"I started, but then I saw you only locked in the price for a year. I thought you might want to go back and ask for a longer term."

"I tried that, but they wouldn't do it."

"But what if you—"

"Just do as I ask," he said, suddenly convinced that if he kept letting her think she knew best she'd get the wrong idea. He swigged his coffee, then cursed when he burnt his mouth. "Energy Oil has a new VP of sponsorship starting in September. Word is he's not easy to deal with. I need you to set up a series of meetings with his staff between now and then, to make sure they're all on our side. Then I'll need a meeting with the new guy in his first week on the job. Make it breakfast."

"Wouldn't it be better to—?"

He massaged his right temple where a headache had started to kick. *Too much caffeine.* "Just arrange the meeting." She looked hurt so, not entirely sure what he was asking of her, he added softly, "Please, Julie-Anne."

THE ANXIETY Trent had confessed he felt about those early row starts was almost laughably easy to fix. Kelly had given him a half-hour "harden-up" chat that strengthened Trent's resolve. When he'd started on row three at Indianapolis on Sunday, he'd passed two cars on the first lap. Later in the race he slipped back, but not as much as usual. His tenth-place finish put him at twelfth in the series point standings.

But Kelly was every bit as conscious as Trent that there were no guarantees he'd make the cut for the Chase next month.

She had to deal with his primary distraction. The Wednesday Blonde.

Last Wednesday he hadn't even come into the office before he disappeared on his mystery excursion. If he did the same today, Kelly would be ready for him.

She took a taxi to Trent's house, which was about a mile from her condo geographically and about a million miles away in luxury. On this dazzling summer morning, the sun warmed the two-story French-style mansion's pale plaster to a creamy color and the shadow of the wrought-iron gates striped the crushed limestone driveway.

There was no sign of life in the house, but then, 8:00 a.m. was the crack of dawn by Trent's standards. Kelly slunk low in her seat so he wouldn't see her if he looked out a window, and prepared to wait. She'd told the cab driver to set the whole morning aside, brushing off his dire predictions as to how much it would cost. She would submit an expense claim to Matheson Racing—Chad was as concerned as she was about Trent's absences.

It was just gone nine o'clock when the garage door opened, and the orange Lamborghini emerged. The gates opened automatically, and the car exited the driveway in front of the taxi, its engine no more than a throaty purr at low speed.

Kelly gave Trent a few seconds, then sat upright. "Follow that car," she said with a pleasing sense of drama.

Her plan almost came unstuck right there. The driver twisted around to face her. "You want me to follow Trent Matheson?"

She might have known Trent's babe-mobile would be widely recognized. "That's right." She squirmed on her seat, seeing Trent getting away from her. "Could you hurry, please?"

"Are you some kind of a stalker?" the driver demanded. "You can't just follow a guy like Trent Matheson around."

"It's a free country," she snapped. The driver's eyebrows knitted. She drew a breath. "I work with Trent. We have a…a meeting, and I didn't bring the address with me."

"So why didn't you go with him?"

Kelly thought fast. And came up blank. "I'll double your money." It was, after all, a tactic after Chad's own heart.

The driver humphed disapprovingly, but the lure proved too great. When he pulled out into the traffic she almost kissed him. At the next intersection, there was no sign of Trent in either direction. "Do you know where he was going?" the driver asked.

"If I knew that," Kelly said, "I wouldn't have to follow him." How much of Trent's journey the last time she'd tailed him had been bogus? Lacking any better ideas, she said, "Head for I-85."

Mercifully, they caught up with Trent at the interstate's southern on-ramp. This time he drove farther south, past Charlotte's airport. He exited the interstate and drove into a leafy campus.

Kelly read the signboard. Belmont Abby College. Ugh! She shuddered at the thought of Trent dating a coed.

The taxi tailed him to a parking lot. Kelly handed over her life's savings to pay the driver, then scrambled out to follow Trent at a discreet distance.

He headed into a building labeled Business Management. She followed him down hallways deserted for the summer vacation. Trent was so focused on the Wednesday Blonde, he didn't look behind him once.

At the end of a short, narrow corridor, he tapped on a door, then entered, closing it behind him.

Kelly read the brass nameplate: Prof. Elizabeth Biggs.

Trent was dating a professor? Kelly tried to imagine what they had in common, and came up with only one answer.

"Okay, lover boy," she muttered, "you've had your fun. No more distractions."

Prepared to avert her eyes, she pushed open the door and stepped inside.

And found Trent sitting in front of a desk. The woman on

the other side, facing the door, was in her late fifties, Kelly estimated. Her beige sweater set cloaked a bosom that was ample but undeniably matronly. She wore no makeup to hide the lines of age. Her blond hair was cropped short against her head. She looked like…a professor.

Nothing like Trent Matheson's crush.

At Kelly's entrance, Professor Biggs looked up from the document she was reading. Trent turned in his seat. His jaw dropped. Then his eyes narrowed.

"May I help you?" the professor asked.

"I—uh…" Kelly made a helpless gesture toward Trent. "I'm here for him."

The professor sighed. "Oh, dear, another one," she said to Trent. "Shall I call security?"

Trent shifted his chair around, a tight smile on his face. "Maybe you should."

The woman picked up her phone.

"I'm not one of Trent's fans," Kelly said.

"Sure you are, sugar. You said it yourself, I'm brilliant."

"I said you're unreliable," she retorted.

"And you're spying on me. That's not exactly professional."

The professor put down the phone, realizing there was more going on here than a star-crazed fan episode.

Kelly refused to feel guilty for sneaking around. Staking her claim to the moral high ground, she planted her hands on hips. "You're supposed to be focusing on next Sunday's race. What are you doing here?"

"I'm focusing," he said, "on the rest of my life."

His words stopped Kelly in her tracks.

"Perhaps you and Trent could continue your discussion later," the professor suggested. "He and I have work to do."

"He and *I* have work to do, too," Kelly said, with less conviction than she'd have liked.

"Kelly, I'll be done here in fifteen minutes. I'll meet you in the student cafeteria. Please?" He was so serious, so un-Trent-like, that she shivered.

"You'll really be there?" she said. "You won't disappear on me?"

"I'll be there."

IT WAS TWENTY minutes before Trent bought a coffee and doughnut and sat down opposite Kelly at a plastic table in the cafeteria. The sunlight that streamed from behind him into the glass-fronted space threw his face into shadow. Kelly darted a tentative smile at him. She couldn't tell if he returned it.

Without preamble, he said, "I'm telling you this in confidence. Chad might pay your wages, but I'm your client and I don't want you repeating this to him."

"Fine," she said, because she'd give anything to know what was going on.

"I want to take over as head of Matheson Performance Industries when Dad retires."

She hadn't expected that. "But I thought Chad—"

"Right now, Chad has the job sewn up," he interrupted her. "He's better educated than I am, and he's used to running a business."

"So why not let him take over?" Kelly said, and he scowled.

"With Chad in charge, the business will carry on like it is now—building engines, maybe branching out into Formula One and other areas of motor sport, but it'll still be an engine business."

"Is that a problem?"

He raked a hand through his hair. "It could be so much more. With a little vision, MPI could dominate the entire performance enhancement industry. Shock engineering—a lot of the teams buy in consultancy services for their shock absorber strategy. Maybe we'd do telemetry-based driver performance analysis. Heck, I don't know, maybe we'd even provide driver fitness trainers. Anything that impacts performance."

"And sport psychology," Kelly said. "You could offer that, too."

He frowned. "Yeah, maybe."

"Have you told your father your ideas?"

Trent's hands fisted on the table. "Every time I suggest an improvement to the business, Dad more or less tells me not to worry my tiny mind. I enrolled part-time for a degree in motor sports management so he'll see I'm serious."

Kelly grappled to reconcile this new side of Trent with the playboy charmer she knew. "So every Wednesday…"

"During the semester I had lectures," he said. "The day you were interviewing for Dad's secretary was the day of my first tutorial with Elizabeth—Professor Biggs. She came back off her vacation especially, so I didn't want to miss it. Accountancy doesn't come naturally to me, I need all the extra tutoring I can get."

Trent found Kelly's bemusement almost comical. Twice, she started to say something, then stopped. He was surprised how relieved he felt to have told someone his ambitions, and how relieved he was it was Kelly he'd told. At that meeting with his father and Chad last week, he'd realized she was on his side. It felt good.

"Trent," she said at last, "you're incredible." She'd told him that once before, jokingly, the night she'd won that bet at his father's house. Now, she said it as if she meant it, and Trent *felt* incredible in a way the cheering of a hundred thousand fans had never done for him.

Then she added, "But you're deluded."

Dammit, couldn't she ever pay him a compliment that didn't have a sting in the tail?

"Tell me this." She leaned forward. "Who will take over from you in the Number 186 car?"

He sat back, relieved. If that was all that was worrying her… "They'll be lining up."

"Ah," Kelly said, "but are any of them as good as you?"

Why did Trent feel as if this was a trick question? He gave an honest answer. "Probably not."

She pushed her empty coffee cup away and folded her arms. "Then you have a problem."

He sighed. "Don't you ever look on the bright side?"

"Think about it," she said. "If you win the Cup, your father won't want to pull you out of that race car to run the business."

The thought had crossed his mind. "Dad won't expect me to race forever."

"Nor will he want you to quit when you're at your peak." She paused. "Are you prepared to lose the series to get that job?"

"The hell I am." No way would he ever throw a race. Even if his brain entertained the thought—which it wouldn't—his racing instinct wouldn't allow it.

"What do you want more, the job or the Cup?" Her brown gaze didn't waver.

Her acuity pierced Trent's confidence. Bereft of an answer—a glib answer, a charming answer, any answer at all—he scowled.

When he was out on the track, he wanted that silver trophy so badly, it just about ate him up. But other times, he hungered to have a say in the future of the business his father had built. He wanted to take it to the top.

Kelly read his lack of response. "That," she said, "is why you won't win the series."

Was that supposed to be in any way logical? "That's garbage."

"There's no easy answer. If you don't win, Brady will ask himself, if you can't even be relied on to do what you're best at, how can he rely on you in the business? If you do win, he'll think you should stick with the driving. Because if you quit the team, and they can't replace you with someone as good, won't that hurt his relationship with Energy Oil?"

Trent swallowed on a bitter taste. Kelly wasn't saying anything he hadn't already thought of, but he'd hoped he was wrong. "You're overanalyzing," he said. "We Matheson men are simple creatures. One plus one equals two. If Dad sees me as a credible candidate to run the business, he'll give me a fair shot at the job. You're dividing and multiplying where a simple addition will do."

"In your heart," Kelly said, "you know you're damned if you do, damned if you don't." She crumpled the paper coffee cup in her hand. "Trent, if you're torn in two directions, there's no way you can win the Cup."

"CAN'T WIN, HUH?" Trent yelled the words in a burst of exhilaration as he spun a doughnut on the track at Pennsylvania. He'd just won the round and that had escalated him to number nine in the NASCAR NEXTEL Cup Series standings. If he kept this up, he would qualify for the Chase without a problem.

"You did great, Trent." Kelly's voice came through the radio, warm with genuine pleasure. Trent waited for the rider in the tail of her praise. It didn't come.

"She's right," Rod Sutton said. "Great job, buddy."

"Hear, hear." Chad. Normally, that would have been the voice that mattered. But now he had Kelly's seal of approval, Trent found he couldn't care less about the rest.

IN THE MONTH that followed, Trent's results were more consistent, but far from brilliant.

While the team set up at the Richmond track on the Wednesday afternoon ahead of Saturday's race, Kelly sat in the small office in the front of the hauler, reviewing their progress to date and planning her next move.

A familiar voice called her name from outside.

"Josh!" She scooted through the hauler and into the sunshine outside, where her brother caught her up in a bear hug.

"Hey, sis, I thought I'd give you a ride home."

"Thanks, I'll just grab my stuff."

When she got back outside, Trent was waiting. He must have overheard her and Josh, because he'd interrupted his conversation with Rod Sutton to stroll over. "Going somewhere?"

Aware her brother was shifting closer to Trent as if he could soak up Trent's aura, Kelly had no choice but to perform the introductions. She kept them brief, her tone discouraging. Trent was perceptive enough to read the dynamic between Kelly and her family; if he saw how little they respected her, it would affect his opinion of her work.

"You'll have to excuse us," she told him. "We're going to my parents' house for dinner."

"But what about our meeting?"

"I'll meet with you first thing tomorrow."

"I don't do first thing," he reminded her. "And our prequalifying meeting is part of the routine you're so fond of."

Darn, he was right. She'd been so caught up in the wedding details her mother had been e-mailing and calling her about, she'd overlooked the meeting.

"You'd better tell Mom I'll come by later," she told Josh.

He blanched. "You can't do that. She'll kill you—and she'll kill me, too, if I arrive home without you."

Mom *had* sounded somewhat fraught the last time they'd spoken. But Kelly knew where her duty lay. "I'm sorry."

Josh turned to Trent. "Why don't you come with us, Trent? Come for dinner, then Mom can do her wedding thing, and after that you and Kelly can have your meeting."

"He can't," Kelly said, and there was enough alarm in her

voice to draw curious glances from the others. "It would break his routine."

"Dinner is part of my routine," Trent said.

"You wouldn't enjoy it," she told him. "My family can be a little overwhelming."

"What do you mean?" Josh said, mystified.

"Now you've got me interested," Trent said.

"Mom's cooking is very plain." Kelly edged away, but Josh didn't move. "You said you wanted to try that Italian place where Chad has a reservation. You'll eat much better there."

Josh said, "I'll tell Mom you said that."

"I'd love to come for dinner." Trent might have directed his response to Josh, but Kelly would have bet a large chunk of her inflated pay packet that he accepted the invitation mainly to annoy her.

CHAPTER NINE

TRENT DIDN'T for one moment believe what Kelly said about her family being overwhelming. When he entered the Greenwoods' Victorian-style family home, located in a leafy suburb of Richmond, he knew he was right.

The whole family was in the living room watching the sports news. The atmosphere was relaxed, warm. Kelly's father turned off the TV when they walked into the room, and Kelly introduced everyone.

"Great drive at Pennsylvania," Dave Greenwood said.

"Great touchdown at Texas Stadium," Trent returned.

Kelly's sister Stacey shook his hand then turned to Kelly, eyebrows raised. "He's hot," she whispered, so loudly that everyone caught her words.

"He's not, he just thinks he is," Kelly said.

"Honey!" Merle sounded shocked. "Trent's a client."

"She talks like that all the time, I'm used to it," Trent said.

When her family rounded on Kelly with advice and recriminations, he wished he hadn't. She took their interference much better than he would have, but he noticed the tautness of her smile.

They sat down to a meal of roast beef, plenty of crispy roast potatoes and broiled vegetables, with an assortment of breads on the side. Plain food? Trent would have called it hearty, athlete's fare.

He already knew Kelly's father Rob had been an NFL coach

in his younger days. But he hadn't realized Merle, her mother, was a long jumper who'd once been selected for the U.S. Olympic squad, though she hadn't actually competed. Both her parents still looked fit and strong, and they carried themselves with the confidence of people used to being watched.

Trent normally only saw this many sports stars at one table on awards nights. On those occasions everyone was on their best behavior, mindful of the cameras panning the room. He imagined tonight was what one of those dinners might be like without the cameras.

Six enormous egos—he counted his own in that tally— vied for their share of the food, the conversation, the adulation. Even the table space was up for contention. People planted elbows well outside the span of their place mats, and stretched legs far and wide beneath the table, moving them only grudgingly when someone else protested.

Trent held his own, of course. He entertained the Greenwoods with a couple of behind-the-scenes NASCAR stories, but he also made sure to listen up when Josh or Dave had an anecdote to share. He must have done okay, because partway through the meal, Mrs. Greenwood said, "Trent, we'd love you to come to the wedding on Tuesday."

"Trent will be back in Charlotte by then." It was more than Kelly had said all evening. The woman who ordinarily had no trouble putting Trent in his place, and who would argue a green light was red and almost convince him she was right, became a different person among her family. She said little, seemed to make herself smaller with her economical movements and few words. The one time her mother had tried to bring her into the conversation, by asking about her work in New Zealand, Kelly had muttered something inaudible then clammed up. Her eyes and her voice were warm when she spoke to her family, and that warmth was reciprocated. But she wasn't the Kelly Greenwood Trent had come to know and…like.

Interested to see if she would stand up for what she wanted—and clearly what she wanted was for him not to come to the wedding—he said, "The wedding sounds great, count me in."

He heard her sharp breath, saw the pursing of her lips. But Kelly didn't say a word.

"WHY ARE YOU such a wimp with your family?" he demanded after they'd adjourned to her father's den for their meeting while the rest of the family cleared away before dessert.

"That's off-topic," she said. "And I'm not a wimp."

"You're more klutzy than normal, too." He paused. "If that's possible."

She frowned. "I wouldn't have dropped those plates if I hadn't tripped over your big feet."

"You've been around my big feet for months but this is the first time you've fallen over them."

"Mom didn't mind about the plates."

"She looked as if she half expected it," Trent agreed. He remembered the way Dave had handed Josh a five-dollar bill when Kelly stumbled—apparently the two brothers had a bet on as to how long it would be before their sister did something clumsy. Brothers did that kind of thing, of course, but still… "Your family isn't very nice to you."

Her eyes clouded. "I'm different from them," she said tightly.

"You're more polite," he agreed. "And that's something I never thought I'd say about you."

Her tentative smile told him he'd done the right thing by lightening up the conversation. He added, "You're the best-looking."

"That's not true." But now her smile turned shy in a way he found incredibly cute.

"You're the only one I—" Trent bit down on the rest of his sentence. *The only one I want to make love to.* No way! He didn't want to, so why was he even thinking it? He looked at

Kelly. Her tailored pants and pin-striped blouse formed the sort of outfit a schoolteacher wary of shocking the PTA might wear. He definitely didn't want to make love with her.

"Let's talk about Sunday's race," he said abruptly.

A HALF HOUR LATER, Mrs. Greenwood summoned Kelly to the living room for the meeting about the wedding. Kelly urged Trent to stay where he was, but he'd caught a glimpse of the enormous, freshly baked apple pie Merle planned to serve for dessert. No way was he going to miss that.

Kelly sat down on the brown corduroy couch at the far end of the room, so Trent plunked himself next to her. With Stacey on the other side of him, the couch was cramped. His thigh rested against the soft firmness of Kelly's leg.

As everyone dug into their dessert, Merle began to run through her list of who was doing what on the big day. Trent gathered that because the wedding was in Richmond, rather than the bride's hometown, the groom's family had a few more responsibilities than they might otherwise.

"Dave, I picked up your groomsman tuxedo from the hire shop today, along with the ones for Nikki's brothers." Merle looked up from her list. "Stacey, I gave the dressmaker your measurements for your bridesmaid dress, but you need to go over there tomorrow for a fitting."

Stacey pulled a face. "I hate wearing long dresses."

"Is Kelly a bridesmaid, too?" Trent asked.

Kelly said quickly, "Josh's fiancée has two sisters, as well as a best friend who are in the wedding party. There's only room for one Greenwood bridesmaid."

Trent remembered how Kelly had once told him she loved Josh. On the other occasions she'd mentioned her younger brother, she always had a tender, indulgent smile on her face. The two were obviously close. "If Stacey doesn't like long dresses, maybe you should be the bridesmaid," he told her. Kelly glared.

Merle said apologetically, *"Today's Woman* magazine is doing a profile of Stacey. Bridesmaid photos are just the kind of thing they want." She smiled sympathetically at Kelly. "I'm sorry, sweetie."

Darn Trent Matheson! Kelly had gotten over her disappointment at not being a bridesmaid weeks ago, and she was certain she hadn't betrayed her feelings to her family. Why was Trent doing this? She pasted on a don't-care smile. "I'm sure there's something else I can do. Usher, maybe?"

"A couple of my teammates are ushering," Josh said.

Her mother ran a finger down her list. She flipped over one page, then another.

"I have one job here—it isn't very glamorous, sweetie," she said at last.

Kelly waved a hand. "I don't need glamorous, just give me something to do." Had anyone else picked up on her desperation?

"We need someone to set up the display of wedding gifts, and to record who gave what. I don't trust the staff at the reception venue. If you could take that on, sweetie…"

"No problems." Kelly heard her own voice go high, and hated herself for it. What did it matter if she was a bridesmaid or a gift arranger? She'd never wanted the limelight the way her siblings did, so it was no surprise that no one offered it to her.

Trent took her hand in his and pulled it into his lap. Kelly sensed a sudden stilling around the room. She looked down at Trent's long fingers, which he was now lacing between hers, and noted the contrast of the thick strength of his hand against her fair skin.

She made to pull away, but he pressed down on her hand with an iron grip.

"Sugar." He lowered his voice so it took on a gravelly texture that raised a cloud of butterflies in her stomach. "If you're busy arranging gifts, how will you entertain me?" He lifted her hand to his lips and dusted a kiss across her knuckles.

She should tell him to cut it out, should wrench her hand away. But she was mesmerized, just like those inhabitants of Planet Belly Button. Mesmerized by the deep blue of his eyes, by the crinkle of smile lines at their corners, by the strong white teeth revealed when his mouth curved in that lopsided smile.

He was looking at her as if she was the most important woman in the world.

What the heck was he playing at?

Then Josh said, "Kelly needs a better job than that, Mom," at the same moment as their mother said, "Trent's right, sweetie, we can't have you away from all the action. You're a major player, for goodness sake." She spoke with a genuine brightness and outrage that told Kelly that sidelining her had never been the family's intention. It had just…happened.

"There really is no room for another bridesmaid," her Mom continued. "But how about we have you do the Bible reading?"

Mortified that Trent was trying to force them to treat her as if she was someone special, Kelly said, "Isn't someone else doing the reading?"

"No one that matters," she said airily.

"Mom, that's my crew chief," Josh protested. "Maybe Kelly could—" He quailed under his mother's gimlet eye. "You do the reading, Kel," he mumbled. "Please."

If she protested, she'd make this even more of a debacle than it already was. Kelly forced a smile and said, "Whatever you all want."

Trent's grip relaxed a fraction, and Kelly tugged her hand away. He winked at her—as if they were coconspirators in his stupid behavior—then stood up. "Sugar, it's time I got some shut-eye. Maybe you could call a cab to take me back to the track."

She doubted he planned to go back to his motor home. Trent "Night-Owl" Matheson was probably bored with a family-style evening. Now that he'd done his good deed for the night, he wanted out.

Kelly stood, too. She'd show him out, all right. She'd show him the door and tell him he wasn't welcome at this wedding and he wasn't welcome to interfere in her life.

Trent farewelled her family while she phoned for a taxi. Then he followed her out onto the porch. She pulled the front door shut behind them.

"That was totally uncalled-for," she said.

"What was?" he said innocently.

"The hand-holding, the sappy looks, the...the *sugar*." She clamped her hands on her hips. "Every stupid thing you did in there."

"Hey," he said. "I got you a promotion. If it wasn't for me you'd miss most of your brother's wedding. A simple thank-you would do."

"It's none of your business," she said. "It just so happens I don't want to be in the public eye."

Trent leaned against the porch railing. "You don't deserve the disrespect your family dishes out."

"They respect me."

He snorted. "They don't."

Why was she arguing, when she knew he was right? Kelly dropped her hands to her sides, let her shoulders sag. "They love me," she said, "and that's what matters."

For one awful moment she thought he would say they didn't love her, and she'd lose even that precious assurance. But after a long, hard look at her, he gave a brief nod of his head. "They do love you. But you deserve more."

"If I'd insisted on being a bridesmaid, Mom would have found a way to make it happen," she said, almost certain she was right.

"Then why didn't you insist? I could see you wanted the job."
He patted the space next to him on the railing, and Kelly found
herself going over there to sit shoulder to shoulder with him.

"Every person in my family is a star. They expect star
treatment and they get it." She shrugged. "I learned a long
time ago my folks measure success in newspaper column
inches. I'm never going to be famous. This job with you is
the nearest I've ever been to it." She looked momentarily
appalled at the thought. "I don't feel I can ask for special treatment when I haven't earned it." When his mouth tightened,
she added, "My family isn't perfect, but it works okay."

He must have heard the pleading note in her voice that
begged him to drop the subject. He joked, "Maybe they'd be
nicer if you'd made it to the top in your chosen sport. In
swimming." When she blinked, confused, he added, "Swim
caps are hell on earrings."

She rolled her eyes. "I can't swim to save myself."

"No wonder you quit," he said.

She swatted him. With lightning-quick reflexes, he caught
her hand, held it in place on his forearm. Kelly was dismayed
to feel a tremor in her fingers.

"No one's watching," she said. "You don't need to play
games now."

His eyes darkened. "Who says I'm playing games?"

Out on the street, Trent's taxi pulled up. Kelly should let
him go, but she needed to have this out with him. "I'm not a
charity case, Trent."

"There are some things I'll never do for charity," he said.
"Like this."

He pushed away from the railing, then tugged her to him,
just with that powerful hand over hers. Kelly bumped against
his chest, and he let out a soft laugh that shivered over her.

"My little klutz." The teasing tenderness in his voice
tempted her to lean into him. "You're standing on my foot."

"If you'd just let me go—" Kelly was horrified to find her voice had gone all breathy "—I'll get out of your way."

His head dipped and he kissed her hard. Kelly was still trying to decide if she should open her mouth and welcome him in, or if she should lift her shoe off his foot and stamp her heel back down onto it, when he ended the kiss. He touched a finger to her lips.

"Good night, sugar." He waved to someone over her shoulder, then headed down the walk with a jaunty step.

Kelly turned around too fast for her brothers to drop the curtain they were peering around. Josh gave her a thumbs-up.

Darn it! Trent had kissed her to impress her goon-head brothers. Somehow she was wishing he'd done it just because he wanted to.

ON FRIDAY, much to the excitement of the hometown crowd, Josh Greenwood won the NASCAR Busch Series race, his first win of the season.

But it was Saturday's race that had everyone on tenterhooks. This race would determine which ten cars qualified for the Chase for the Cup. The other drivers would continue to race, but only the top ten in the series standings would have the chance of the ultimate glory, winning the NASCAR NEXTEL Cup Series.

Trent was sitting eleventh in series points. At twelfth, Davey Hayes was just three points behind Trent, which made him a real threat today. The drivers immediately below Hayes were far enough away not to pose a challenge, unless something completely unexpected happened. The drivers above Trent were all exceedingly tough competitors. The ones nearer the top held a points lead that was unassailable, and of the more vulnerable—those sitting eighth, ninth and tenth in the rankings—none would give up their slot in the Chase without a hell of a fight.

Consequently, the whole Matheson team was extra tense. Even though Trent loved the short, three-quarters-of-a-mile Richmond track, he, too, was more anxious than normal.

It was a nighttime race, so the day dragged for everyone.

Trent was relieved to hop into his car the moment the flyby finished. Thanks to the night racing, he felt much cooler than usual. But every other driver had the same advantage.

He buckled himself in, inserted his earpieces, fitted his helmet and gloves. Next, he attached the steering wheel, then confirmed with Rod that the radio was working. He was in third place on the starting grid, which a few weeks ago might have fazed him. Tonight, he was confident he could get out front early on. Whether he could stay out there was another matter. On a track this short, and wide enough to make a pass just about anywhere, four hundred miles was a lot of laps to try and hold the lead.

As he moved into formation to circle the track ahead of the start, Trent ran through a relaxation breathing exercise Kelly had taught him. It helped. Actually, pretty much everything she'd done with him had helped.

These days, he had a clearer head at the start of each race. They still had some work to do to make it consistent, but Trent owed Kelly. Even if she'd been so on edge about this race that she'd been nagging him all week.

He pushed her out of his mind, concentrated on memorizing the bumps and dips of the track. It was easier to see them with the floodlighting than it was in the daytime, but once the race started, he wouldn't have a lot of time to look.

Up ahead, Danny Cruise led the cars that circled the track. As they moved into the final circuit prerace, the atmosphere changed—in the car and in the stands. That expectant hush— or as much of a hush as you could get with a sellout crowd— fell, and the muscles in Trent's forearms tensed. He breathed out, willed himself to relax, visualized his muscles uncording. *Better.*

Ahead of him, the green flag dropped, and Trent floored it.

The familiar markers—the pit road entry, the scoreboard, the NEXTEL logo on the trackside hoardings, flashed around much faster on a short track, increasing the sense of urgency.

Trent passed the rookie in the Number 63 car, who'd had a lucky break in qualifying, on lap two. He had Cruise in his sights, but the other driver was too experienced to let Trent pass him easily.

He might not pass Cruise at all, the way the car was feeling. Way too tight—Trent couldn't get through the corners as sharply as he'd like. And corners came up a lot more often on a short track. Trent cursed under his breath.

"Number 53 low," his spotter said. Sure enough, Tony Stevens had come up alongside Trent, racing at the bottom of the track.

They raced into Turn One neck-and-neck. Coming off Turn Two into the straightaway, Stevens moved higher. Trent felt the bump of the black car against his. He didn't look, just concentrated on keeping his hands on the wheel and the car in its line. But he saw the shower of sparks the contact generated arcing through the night air, and heard the delighted roar of the crowd. Nothing like a bit of contact to get everyone excited.

Everyone except Trent. Stevens had pulled in front.

Trent took advantage of a caution to pit early, on lap thirty. It was a four-tire change, and the track bar needed lowering to loosen the car up. That all took 15.9 seconds. *Too long*.

A bunch of the other front-runners pitted at the same time, and Trent had dropped back to sixth by the time he got back out on track. A dozen laps later, he was twelfth.

"Relax." Kelly's voice came over the radio.

Trent barked a laugh, surprising himself.

"Look ahead," she told him. "There's plenty of room for you up there."

She was right, of course.

"I'm not afraid to pass," he grumbled.

"Then what are you waiting for?"

It took a long time, but by lap three hundred he was in sixth place. He couldn't get any higher, but he held it right through the checkered flag.

Sixth gave him a hundred and fifty points. Whether that was enough to get him into the Chase depended on how everyone else had done.

Trent got out of the car. Rod was yelling something, but the words wouldn't penetrate. Trent found himself praying as he checked the scoreboard, tried to figure out who'd come in ahead, where the points would fall. The car numbers in the first several places were the same ones that topped the standings. But—yes!—the driver who'd been ninth in the standings had finished near the back of the field, which meant Trent could— His heart stopped. *Damn.* Davey Hayes, who'd been twelfth in the standings, three points behind Trent, had come in fifth, so he now had two points on Trent.

Hayes had taken that last precious top-ten slot.

Trent's eyes hazed over, and he couldn't swallow the bitterness that filled his mouth. He turned away from the scoreboard, seeking Kelly. And found her right beside him, tears streaming down her face.

Smiling from ear to ear.

"You did it," she yelled, above the chaos.

"But—" Trent waved vaguely in the direction of the scoreboard. "Hayes…"

Now she was squeezing him in a hug of surprising strength. "You led three laps, you idiot," she half sobbed, half laughed. "Hayes didn't lead any."

For the first time, Trent wondered if she was right about the airhead thing. In his panic, he'd forgotten he'd earned five bonus points for being a lap leader, which put him three points ahead of Hayes.

He'd made the Chase for the NASCAR NEXTEL Cup.

Josh Greenwood turned up in the Matheson Racing garage after Trent's race, while the crew was packing up.

Like everyone, Kelly was moving around in a state of euphoria.

"The Harveys had their baby early," Josh told her. His fellow NASCAR Busch Series driver Bob Harvey was best man for Tuesday's wedding. "Bob's wife needed a cesarean section, so Bob flew home to help look after the kid until she's back on her feet. Seems he won't make the wedding."

Kelly murmured sympathetically, but her mind wasn't on her brother's words. A few feet away from them, Trent faced a barrage of media cameras and microphones with his usual blend of easy charm and slow-witted responses.

Josh eyed Trent with envy. "I didn't get that many reporters taking an interest in me after I won yesterday," he grumbled. "I've got my sponsor telling me I'm not getting enough media coverage, and Trent's fighting them off over *sixth* place."

"Don't take it personally. Trent is a lot of people's favorite."

To her horror, Josh called out to Trent, "Hey, Trent, buddy, how about being my best man?"

Kelly hissed and grabbed her brother's arm with the idea of dragging him away. But the cameras had already swung in their direction. "I'm getting married Tuesday," he told the journalists. "Bob Harvey was my best man."

Murmurs of understanding rose from the media, who'd obviously heard about Bob's new baby.

Kelly cringed as Josh elaborated on how Bob's departure might ruin the best day of Josh's life. How could he make such a blatant play for attention? She looked at Trent. He wore a dazed-and-confused airhead look that didn't fool her for one second. His eyes met hers and turned assessing, enigmatic.

She tried to transmit a mute apology.

The cameras were about to swing back to Trent. Kelly stepped forward, pulling the attention her way.

"Trent won't be able to take you up on that kind invitation, Josh," she said, directing a smile at her brother that threatened unspeakable violence later. "We're working on a new weekly routine and we can't afford to—"

"Kelly, sugar." Trent's sweet-coated words stopped her. "You know I love a party." He turned to Josh. "I'd be pleased to be your best man, Josh, thanks for asking."

Josh showed what a seasoned professional he was by not betraying even a hint of surprise. He stepped forward and clapped Trent on the back as he shook his hand, all the while keeping the two of them pointed toward the cameras.

In his answers to the barrage of questions that followed, Josh managed to name his sponsor at least five times.

At last the journalists ebbed away, which meant Kelly was free to strangle her brother without any pesky witnesses. When she took a step in his direction, Josh backed off.

"Now, Kel," he said. "This is between me and Trent, nothing to do with you."

"How could you do that?" she demanded.

"Trent was okay with it," Josh said. "So he should be, given he's your boyfriend."

"Trent is not my boyfriend." She turned to Trent. "Tell him." So what if it meant she got demoted to gift arranger again.

Trent shrugged. "Whatever you say, sugar."

Josh's smirk told her which of them he believed. But he made a politic decision to get out of there. "Kelly can bring you to the rehearsal on Monday night," he told Trent as he left.

"Why did you go along with him?" Kelly asked Trent. "He only wants you for the publicity."

"You mean he thinks as little of my charming personality as you do?"

"Probably less," she said bluntly. "So if you want to pull out…"

"I thought me being best man might help you with your folks," Trent said. "It seemed the right thing to do. We're friends, right?"

Friends? Her and Trent? A ball of warmth expanded in the pit of her stomach and spread right through her. "I don't… need your help," she said uncertainly.

Annoyance flickered across his face. "I'm in a good mood," he said. "Don't spoil it. You know I never do anything that doesn't suit me."

For some reason, that eased her discomfort. "You don't need the publicity," she felt obliged to point out.

"I need you off my case." He picked up a wrench one of the crew members had dropped as he hurried past, and handed it back to the guy. "You haven't stopped telling me what to do for one minute this week. I figured I'll do you a deal. I'll be Josh's best man if you quit nagging."

She swallowed. "You should have checked with me before you made your generous offer to Josh. I'll never quit nagging."

Trent sighed. "I was afraid of that."

ON MONDAY NIGHT, Brady paced the outer office as he waited for Julie-Anne to appear. Dammit, how had he ended up going on a date with her?

He'd told her to organize breakfast for him with Rick Johnstone, the new investment manager at Energy Oil. Instead, he and Julie-Anne were about to join Rick and his wife in a cozy foursome for dinner. Julie-Anne had invited the wife, then invited herself along, too, on the basis that Amy Johnstone was an old friend of hers. She'd all but ignored Brady's complaints about the switch from breakfast to dinner.

As if Brady didn't have enough to worry about, without being hyperconscious of Julie-Anne's presence next to him all evening. He still hadn't met Rick, but everything he'd heard suggested the guy was moody and capricious. Brady looked at his watch. She'd gone to the bathroom to change; if she didn't get out here right now, they'd be late. Either way, she shouldn't expect a warm reception from him. The simplest way to deal with her unwanted presence at dinner was to ignore her.

Julie-Anne stepped into the office.

"I hope I didn't keep you waiting," she said in that musical voice.

Brady couldn't answer. His mouth was as dry as a leaky radiator in the desert, and keeping his eyeballs in his head required every scrap of effort he could muster. Somehow he grunted, a sound that might have been yes or no.

She looked incredible. The greeny-blue of her dress caught the light and shimmered where it hugged her figure. Her shoulders were bare, apart from two thin straps that flattered the light olive of her skin.

Gold hoops in her ears reminded him of that gypsy streak that so unsettled him. She wore more makeup than she did during the day, and it suited her, made her lips look fuller and her eyes darker.

So much for ignoring her.

"Are you ready?" she said, her gaze quizzical.

"Let's go." Brady hadn't intended to, but he took her arm as they headed out to the parking lot.

CHAPTER TEN

KELLY'S MOTHER had organized the seating plan for the rehearsal dinner roughly in order of each person's importance in tomorrow's proceedings. Josh and Nikki, who turned out to be a gorgeous, all-American blonde, had the center seats at the long table in downtown Richmond's Chez Nico restaurant. Their parents would sit either side of them. Then came Trent and the maid of honor, Nikki's friend Amanda. Then assorted bridesmaids and groomsmen, and at the far end of the table, Kelly. Seated next to Pastor Giles.

Trent grabbed Kelly's arm as she headed toward her seat. "You shouldn't be sitting down there."

She tugged away, looking anxiously at her parents to check they hadn't overheard. "Pastor Giles is blessed with the gift of abundant small talk. I'm looking forward to it."

"Tell your mom you want to sit with me."

Whatever point he was making, she wished he wouldn't. "I *don't* want to sit with you," she lied.

Something flashed in his eyes, something almost like hurt. Kelly hurried to her seat, where she invited the pastor to update her on the happenings in the church community.

But she listened to him with only half an ear. She would have given anything to be closer to Trent and Amanda. Amanda of the long blond hair, almond-shaped blue eyes and a smile that Kelly found too wide to be attractive. Trent seemed enthralled by those pearly white teeth and the frequent laughter of their owner.

Amanda leaned into him as she spoke, and Kelly was fairly sure he had a great view of the maid of honor's cleavage in her strappy top. Amanda's hand fluttered alluringly over Trent's, occasionally alighting on his just long enough to make him want more.

But while Amanda might be blatant, she wasn't stupid. She was a lawyer, and from the few snatches Kelly caught of their conversation, she was keeping Trent amused with anecdotes of cases she'd tried.

When Kelly bent down to pick up a fork she'd dropped, she used the opportunity to check under the table. She found the woman's leg pressed the length of Trent's. Kelly ignored the fact that he didn't have much room to move at the crowded table. If he wanted to, he'd find somewhere else to put his leg.

Thinking back to that look in his eyes when they'd sat down, Kelly half wondered if he was responding to Amanda just to annoy her. But why would he do that? More likely, given he hadn't made love to a woman all season, he was succumbing to Amanda's overt appeal.

The thought of him giving in to temptation caused a stabbing pain behind Kelly's ribs.

She told herself she was worried how such a dramatic change in his routine might affect his driving. He'd be distracted, he'd probably want a repeat performance every night this week, and who knew what that would do to his racing on Sunday?

She glared down the table at Amanda. Trent intercepted the look and raised his eyebrows. Kelly composed her face into a mask of serenity. But not fast enough, going by the quirk of his lips. And by the attentive way he inclined his head to whatever Amanda was saying now.

Someone asked the waiter to put on some music, and Josh and Nikki began to dance on the restaurant's tiny dance floor.

Amanda wasted no time dragging Trent out of his chair. Not that he put up much of a fight.

Why were this woman's antics bugging Kelly so much? It wasn't as if she didn't see the same behavior every weekend at the track. It wasn't as if love letters and photos of women in their underwear—even the underwear itself—didn't arrive in the mail at Matheson Racing every day.

Something, she acknowledged, had changed between her and Trent. He'd gotten involved in her family but it hadn't made him respect her any less. His admission that he hadn't made love with anyone recently had changed her view of him as a womanizer. Then there was his casual declaration that they were friends, which to Kelly was starting to feel like an understatement.

It was getting too easy to take Trent's ingrained flirtatiousness personally. Which was a dumb idea, given she knew him to be unashamedly selfish.

She watched him dancing with Amanda. The blond woman had both arms around his neck, her face so close to his that if he whistled along to the music he'd be kissing her. Trent's hands rested at her waist, though as far as Kelly could tell he wasn't holding tight.

She made a decision in her professional capacity to interrupt the dance. Just in case he was about to be…distracted.

She moved to the edge of the dance floor, and when Trent and Amanda came within reach, she tapped Amanda on the shoulder. "May I cut in?"

Amanda looked far from thrilled. But only for a moment. Then that wide, wide smile appeared and she stepped out of Trent's arms without any apparent reluctance. "Absolutely." She turned the smile on Trent, and it became lingering, suggestive. "See you later."

Kelly stepped into the position she'd vacated. But she kept a good two feet of space between her and Trent. With

"Unchained Melody" playing over the sound system, this had to be a slow dance, but she was darned if she was going to wrap herself around him the way Amanda had.

They didn't speak for a minute. Then Kelly couldn't help herself. "You look like you were having a good time."

"Amanda's a nice girl." He added, "In an obvious kind of way."

"You like obvious," she reminded him.

He chuckled. "That's true." He tugged her closer, until she brushed against the firm expanse of his chest.

She stiffened. "Amanda is smart, too. Interesting. And she likes you."

"All true," Trent agreed.

A little worm of jealousy burrowed deep, undermining Kelly's intention to keep this strictly business. "If you were thinking of…" No, she couldn't say that.

She felt the tension in his chin where it rested on her head.

"Breaking the drought?" he suggested coolly.

She squirmed. "Er, yes."

"What if I am?"

The words hit her harder than she could have imagined. She blurted, "You can't."

He pulled away from her, and she saw his eyebrows raised in spuriously polite inquiry. *"Can't?"*

"We don't know what effect it will have on your driving," she said. "It's not worth the risk."

He laughed, his face suddenly boyish. "You're the boss."

"Really? In that case—"

He tugged her close again. "Don't push your luck."

They swayed together a little longer. Then Kelly said, "So how come you haven't…been with a woman in so long?"

"Are you asking as my shrink?"

"I'm not sure," she admitted.

He shook his head, almost imperceptibly. "I haven't met anyone I liked that much."

"Out of all the women you meet?" she said, disbelieving.

"Out of all those women." Then he added, "Though Amanda's nice."

Kelly glowered. He was saying that just to annoy her, surely he was.

"Like you said, she's smart," Trent mused. "I think I'm developing a taste for smart women."

Kelly bit down hard on her cheek so she wouldn't blurt out that she had an IQ of 132.

THE JOHNSTONES hadn't arrived at the restaurant by the time Brady and Julie-Anne got there in their separate cars, so Brady was able to regroup his scattered thoughts as they perused the menu.

"Here they are." Julie-Anne got to her feet, as a man, dressed like Brady in a suit and tie, and a plump woman in a long black dress joined them.

"Amy!" Julie-Anne hugged Rick's wife, then accepted a smacking kiss on the cheek from Rick.

She introduced Brady, and they all sat. When the waiter had brought a round of beers, Brady said, "Rick, I appreciate you giving up your evening so we could meet. I'd planned on us having breakfast—"

Amy Johnstone put a hand over her husband's on the table. "You don't want to meet this guy in the mornings—he's a total grouch. Rick doesn't start to warm up until around 4:00 p.m. I always say he should work the night shift."

"There isn't a night shift," her husband pointed out with fond exasperation.

Brady felt a sharp kick on his ankle. He didn't need to look at Julie-Anne to know she was telegraphing, "I told you so."

"Why don't you two boys talk business while Julie-Anne

and I do some catching up," Amy suggested. "Then we can all relax and enjoy our evening."

Brady's discussion with Rick went better than he'd hoped. The guy had strong views, but he wasn't unreasonable. Their meals arrived just as they reached an agreement on where they should go from here in their partnership.

Brady proposed a toast, and they clinked the glasses of red wine the waiter had poured.

The talk turned to reminiscences of previous championships. Rick was new to Energy Oil, but he'd been involved in NASCAR sponsorship back when Brady was racing.

"Remember that time you persuaded Billy to give you a ride around the track at Las Vegas?" Amy said to Julie-Anne. "It was your first time out in one of the cars. We could hear you hollering over the radio the whole way around."

Julie-Anne joined in the Johnstones' good-natured laughter, but Brady saw the shadow in her eyes. Who was Billy? The ex-husband she never said much about? He must have been a NASCAR driver to have given Julie-Anne a ride at the—

Realization hit Brady, and he jerked back in his seat. He stared at her, shocked, his breathing suddenly constricted.

Julie-Anne lifted her wineglass. "Let's drink to partnership," she said. "To Energy Oil, Matheson Racing and Matheson Performance Industries."

Rick and Amy knocked their glasses against hers. So did Brady, after she kicked him.

AFTER THE REHEARSAL DINNER, Kelly sat next to Trent in a cab headed for the Greenwood home. Amanda sat on the other side of him. Turned out she was staying with them tonight—something to do with an overflow at the motel where the bridal party was staying.

Kelly moved in with her sister for the night, so Amanda

could have her room. Trent was accorded the fold-out couch in her father's den.

Kelly didn't miss the calculating look in Amanda's eyes when she heard the sleeping arrangements. Telling her sister not to wait up, and ignoring Stacey's avid curiosity, she pulled a robe over her cotton pajamas, then went downstairs. She tapped on the door of the den.

"Come in," Trent called.

Kelly sighed. If he was going to invite in anyone who knocked, there was no hope. She slipped inside, shut the door behind her. She leaned against it, facing Trent, who stood next to the sofa bed, dressed only in his jeans. His bare, muscular chest looked golden in the dim light of the lamp next to the bed. Those workouts at the company gym had honed enviable abs. His torso was pure male perfection.

Trent quirked an eyebrow. "Hey, sugar, are you here to break the drought?"

Kelly tsked. "I'm here to protect you from Amanda."

"She's not here," he said.

"She will be," Kelly said, walking over to the couch. "I saw it in her eyes."

He laughed. "I'm not denying she was interested. But, sugar, she already made the offer and I told her no."

"She already offered?" Kelly summoned outrage to hide her relief at Trent's response. "The maid of honor isn't supposed to proposition the best man until after the wedding."

He laughed again, a lazy sound that made Kelly think of a bed with tangled sheets and the comfort of strong arms.

"I'll tell her no again tomorrow," he promised.

"She's pretty determined," Kelly warned him.

Annoyance crossed his face. "Are you saying I don't have any willpower?"

She dragged her eyes from his chest. "I'm saying you're only human."

"Gee, thanks." His eyes narrowed. "I don't suppose you ever give in to temptation?"

She swallowed. "Not that I can recall."

"Maybe we should test that." He took a step toward her.

Kelly perched on the edge of bed, bunching the duvet beneath her fingers, avoiding his scrutiny. "It's late, Trent, let's talk about something else until she gets here."

"And then what do we do?"

"Leave it to me."

Trent looked at the couch. "So I can go to bed?"

That seemed too intimate. "I thought you like to stay up until 2:00 a.m.?"

"Only the night before a race." He unsnapped his jeans. Hastily, Kelly turned away. She heard a rustle, then the dull thud of the jeans hitting the floor.

"It's safe," he said, a grin in his voice.

She turned around. And smiled when she saw the sheet pulled up to his chin in exaggerated modesty.

"What shall we do now?" He sat up, and the sheet fell away.

Kelly looked around wildly. She grabbed a book from her father's desk, then perched back on the bed. "You go to sleep. I'll read this."

He snickered. *"Football Rules Illustrated?"*

She pretended an interest in the pages. "It's riveting stuff."

"Would I be right in saying, sugar, that you're uncomfortable to be on my bed?"

"It's not your bed," she said shortly.

"Semantics," he chided her.

Kelly closed the book with a thump. "I thought you wanted to sleep."

Trent turned off the lamp, leaving the room dark save for the pale illumination of the stars and the crescent moon in the cloudless sky filtering through the sash window. Kelly could make him out only as a dark shape, but his presence was just as potent as if it had been broad daylight.

"Do I get a kiss good-night?" he said.

"What do you think?"

He sighed, and lay down.

"I'll wait until Amanda gets here," she said. "I'll leave just as soon as I've got rid of her."

"YOU'RE BILLY BLAKE'S WIFE!" The Johnstones had barely gotten into their car, leaving Brady and Julie-Anne alone in the restaurant's parking lot, when Brady threw out his outraged accusation.

"His widow," Julie-Anne corrected. "It's been ten years." Ten years since she'd been let out of hell.

"I knew I'd met you before. Why didn't you tell me?"

"What difference would it—" She saw by the gathering darkness in his face that she couldn't get away with that. "It was a long time ago, Brady. To be honest, I don't have a lot of happy memories of my marriage." She opened her car door and got in. "It's late, I have to go."

But he went around the other side of her car and climbed into the passenger seat.

"Billy was always angry," he said. "Unpredictable on the track, mean as hell if you got in his way. The rest of us used to say he wouldn't last in NASCAR."

"That pretty much sums him up," Julie-Anne agreed. She inserted the key into the ignition. "Thanks for dinner."

Brady stared intently at her, as if he could peel away the layers of the past. "I met you at the end-of-season awards night," he said. "The year I won the NASCAR Busch Series. Rosie and I were on the same table as you two."

"I remember your wife." She darted a look of apology at him. "I don't remember you from that night, though I met you a couple of other occasions. But your wife was so lovely, she was wearing this long cream-colored dress, off the shoulder, and she had a beautiful pendant, with a ruby."

"That's right." Brady smiled. "It was our wedding anniversary—I gave her the necklace before we came out that night."

Julie-Anne turned in her seat to face him. "Maybe that's why she looked so happy," she said gently. When he frowned she said, "Not because of the necklace. Because of your anniversary, because you had a good marriage."

"It was the best," he agreed. The creases in his face softened in a way Julie-Anne had never seen. "I loved that woman."

Julie-Anne stared out through the windshield, and Brady read her silence. "Was your marriage to Billy that awful?"

She turned the engine on. "It's late, Brady, and I'm tired. We can talk about this some other time."

He reached across her, and before she figured out what he was up to, he'd switched off the engine and taken the key.

"I said—" she began.

"You've worked for me for three months without mentioning Billy. What did he do to you?"

Why not say it all now, then never have to mention her husband to Brady again? "He drank a lot, you probably know that. He'd kept it under control while he was racing open wheel, but when he made it into NASCAR he couldn't handle the pressure. Those two seasons he raced NASCAR, he would quit drinking for race weekends, then on Monday he'd be back on the booze. Like you said, he was mean. Angry."

"Did he hit you?" Brady growled.

Julie-Anne shook her head. "He was abusive, verbally and emotionally, but he didn't hit me. If he had, it would have made the decision to leave much easier."

"I didn't know you left him," Brady said.

"I didn't," she said flatly. "NASCAR suspended him from racing right before the end of the Busch Series—he threw a punch at another driver. His team fired him for breaching the good behavior clause in his contract. I always knew it was only a matter of time before they found out what he was like, but Billy was spitting mad he couldn't finish the series—he was the favorite to win. He had nothing to sober up for, and he started seeing other women.

"Amber, our daughter, was twelve, and his behavior sickened her at best, scared her at worst. I arranged for both of us to live with my sister in California. But it took time to set up. I wasn't ready to leave until March."

Brady froze. "The accident."

She nodded. Even now, bitterness welled up in her throat, making speech impossible. She clenched her eyes shut, willed it away. Then she said, "Billy was drunk."

Brady nodded. Everyone knew that when Billy Blake had crashed spectacularly on the interstate, injuring himself and the driver of another car, blood tests had revealed his intoxication.

"So…you didn't leave?" Brady said.

"Billy couldn't walk. He was paralyzed from the waist down," she said. "But it got worse. They removed his spleen because of internal injuries, and one of the pre-op scans revealed he had stomach cancer. The doctors said Billy only had a few months to live."

"You didn't leave," Brady said again.

"When Billy got fired, his insurance ceased. NASCAR provided some assistance, which was more than he deserved, and there were benefit events that helped with the medical expenses. We sold our home to pay medical bills, bought a smaller house fitted with disabled access. I sent Amber to my sister—I couldn't ask her to stay with me, not the way things were."

"Then what?"

Julie-Anne looked him in the eye. "I waited for Billy to die."

Brady didn't blink.

"But it wasn't a few months. It was *seven* years," she said. "He was in pain, though thankfully the amount of drugs he was taking minimized that. But his temper didn't improve over that time."

"Did he sober up?"

"I refused to buy the stuff, but his buddies would come around bringing beers and whisky—Billy could be charm itself when a drink was at stake." She shrugged. "I always wondered which would kill him first, the cancer or his liver." She paused, then said quietly, "It was the cancer."

Then she'd gotten to see her daughter again, for more than the occasional visits they'd had over those years. A daughter who had become almost a stranger, who still loved her, but who didn't see how a few months could easily become another few months and then another. Who didn't understand why her mother had chosen her abusive husband over her child.

Julie-Anne's hands fisted with the remnants of the anger she sometimes thought might never die.

"I was eighteen when I married him," she told Brady. "Nineteen when I had Amber. I didn't know what to expect, it took me years to realize I was worth more than what he dished out."

"I'm sorry," Brady said.

She put her hands on the steering wheel. "Why should you be sorry?"

"I'm sorry you were going through so much and none of us knew. I'm sorry that jerk treated you so badly, and you lost your daughter."

"I didn't lose her," she lied. "She'll come back."

Brady touched a finger to her cheek. He said roughly, "You've got guts, Julie-Anne."

It was hardly the most tender of compliments, yet her eyes filled with tears.

"Don't cry," Brady begged, and she sensed the effort it cost him not to move away from her.

She forced a shaky smile.

"Ah, dammit," he said, and brought his mouth down on hers.

Julie-Anne put her hands to his upper arms and yielded to the demands of his firm lips. He tasted of red wine and the chocolate dessert he'd eaten. She molded herself against him—he felt as solid and as real as a rock.

Brady held off on burying his fingers in Julie-Anne's thick, dark hair as long as he could. Not very long. He'd ached to touch her for so long now, and top of his list was running his fingers through that hair while his mouth mated with hers.

She quivered against him, every bit as hungry for him as he was for her. If he didn't stop this now, he never would.

Painful though it was, he drew away. Then came back for one more kiss. Then away again.

He cleared his throat. "We shouldn't have done that."

Her chin tilted. "Shouldn't we?"

"We work together, Julie-Anne."

"We're also strongly attracted to each other."

"I like you a lot," he said, "but I don't want a relationship."

She wrapped her arms around herself, as if she was cold. "I see."

"It's not a good idea," he said. "I'm not good at relationships. I mean, I was with Rosie, but that was a once-in-a-lifetime thing. You know how I am with the boys. I'm hopeless at touchy-feely stuff."

Julie-Anne picked up the key from where he'd left it on the dash, put it back in the ignition. "You're the boss."

So why did he feel like a total loser?

"WAKE UP." Trent's whisper dragged Kelly from a deep sleep. It took her a moment to remember she was in her father's den, and to realize it was the middle of the night, not morning. Somehow she'd ended up lying across the end of Trent's bed.

"What's wrong?" She blinked when he switched on the lamp.

Trent pointed toward the door. As Kelly watched, the

handle jiggled as someone tried to open the door. Its alignment had slipped over the years, and family members knew you had to lift at the same time as you turned the handle. Whoever was outside wasn't a Greenwood. "I told you so," she said smugly.

Trent clambered out of bed, and hopped as he dragged his jeans on over his boxers.

The door opened. Amanda slipped in and closed it behind her. When she spoke, her voice was throaty, as if she'd just woken up. "I couldn't sleep and I thought you might like some—"

She broke off when she saw Kelly, sitting rumpled and sleepy-eyed on the end of the bed. Her lips quirked in resignation. Then she shrugged. "Or maybe not. I'll leave you guys to it."

She was gone, closing the door behind her, before Kelly could tell Amanda she was here on business.

"Okay," Trent said, bemused, "you were right." When she opened her mouth to gloat, he held up a hand. "Just this once."

As an admission, it was better than nothing. Kelly yawned, then stood. "It's time I was in bed."

His gaze swept her. Kelly's hand went to the belt of her robe, checking it was still knotted.

"You make cute noises when you sleep," he said.

"I do not— What sort of noises?"

"Snuffling sounds, and the occasional squeak. You sound like a hedgehog."

"I don't." She glared.

He took a step toward her, bringing that chest within tantalizing touching distance. "You know, you don't have to go back to your own room. If you think you could be comfortable sleeping here." He held a hand out to her. "With me."

Kelly backed away, stumbling in her shock. "That's not a good idea."

"Because you don't want to?"

"That's right." Her voice went high, betraying the lie.

He grinned, his teeth a white flash in the dim light of the lamp. "Sooner or later, this drought has to break. Wouldn't you like to be in charge of that?"

Should she be relieved or annoyed that his invitation had turned out to be about nothing more than relieving his frustration? She pursed her lips. "I suggest you pray for rain."

He guffawed, and Kelly looked up at the ceiling, expecting to hear movement from someone woken by the noise. His fingers circled her wrist, snapping her attention back to him. He pulled her up against him—encountering no resistance whatsoever—and touched his mouth to hers.

This wasn't the first time he'd gotten her all hot and bothered with his kisses. But tonight, in the half light of a room made cozier by the darkness outside, at this late hour, following immediately on the peculiar intimacy of sharing the same bed... This particular kiss seemed more intimate than any other. It seemed to be about more than drought relief.

His mouth was gentle, experimental in his tasting, his exploration of hers. His tongue caressed the softness of her lower lip, moistening it, coaxing her to admit him.

She strained closer, heard his moan of appreciation. He stroked her back, then moved to cup her derriere, fitting her against him in a way that suggested they were made for each other. Somehow he got a hand between them and untied her robe. Kelly shrugged out of it, as he stepped her toward the bed.

Trent broke the contact of their mouths to murmur, "I want to make love with you."

At some deep, irrational core Kelly felt she'd waited all her life to hear those words. But the sensible part of her finally woke up. She pressed both hands against his chest, tried not to notice the firm smoothness beneath her palms, nor the roughness of the hair. "Trent, this is crazy."

"I like crazy."

She forced herself to leave the haven of his arms, then paced the area between the bed and the door. "You're a very attractive man—so naturally, I'm attracted to you," she rationalized.

"Naturally." His tone was light, but his eyes narrowed.

"But we work together, we're professionals."

"*You're* professional," he said. "You always tell me I'm not."

She ignored him. "Sleeping together would change that. It would let in all kinds of emotions, we'd start to…feel things."

Start to?

The awareness that it was too late—that already she felt more for Trent than she had any right to—swamped Kelly.

Aghast, she dropped her gaze before he could see her confusion. She bent to pick up the robe bunched at her feet, the robe he'd untied. She pushed one arm into a sleeve, then the other. "I have to go. Now."

Trent watched Kelly's jerky movements as she retied the robe and covered up her crisp cotton shortie pajamas. He couldn't believe how close he'd come to taking her to bed.

The whole situation was crazy. Sure he liked her, she was smart and pretty. But to feel this yearning, this hunger he sensed might be insatiable…

If she hadn't stopped him, he hoped he would have had the sense to stop himself. Kelly wasn't the sort of woman a guy could love and leave. She would demand so much more of Trent than he had to give. She was right. Sex would screw up their working relationship. And the threat of losing that made him realize how much he valued her.

"You're right," he told her. "Sleeping with you is a dumb idea."

Her head snapped up. "Really?" She sounded insulted.

"Like you said, there's a drought that needs breaking. But not at the expense of our friendship."

She nodded. "Or our working relationship."

"So we're agreed," he said. "No more unprofessional behavior."

Did he really say that? When Kelly burst out laughing, Trent couldn't decide if he should be amused or offended.

KELLY WAS UP AHEAD of everyone else next morning. Despite her interrupted sleep, dawn had found her wide-awake.

She tiptoed downstairs into the silent kitchen. As she measured coffee into the machine, she assured herself it wasn't too late to get out of this mess. Okay, she'd somehow allowed Trent to get to her. Not with his surface charm. The man she…liked…was the one who set his heart on something then went all out to get it. The one whose strong loyalty to his family gave him all kinds of conflicts. The one who cared whether or not Kelly's family respected her.

Any woman would appreciate those things. That doesn't mean I'm going to do something stupid like fall in love.

As a psychologist, she knew better than most people how to acknowledge her feelings without letting them dominate her. Like a plant left unwatered, this whatever-it-was she felt could be made to wither and die.

She'd just finished making a pot of coffee for the family and poured herself a glass of juice when Josh came into the kitchen.

"Hey, Kel." Her brother didn't look any better than she felt—pale with dark circles under his eyes. When he reached for the coffee she handed him, his hand shook. She knew he hadn't drunk much at dinner last night, so he couldn't be hung over.

"What's up, Josh?"

He waved to tell her he didn't want to talk about it. Which meant, she knew of old, that he wanted her to press him harder. "Spill," she demanded. "Or I'll pour my OJ down your shorts."

He managed a worn smile at the childhood threat, which

she'd last made good on when he was nine years old. "Just nervous about today, I guess."

"A little, or a lot?"

"A lot." He sipped his coffee, then put the mug back on the counter. "This all happened so fast. Nikki and I were dating, the next minute she was pregnant and we were getting married."

"Do you love her?" Kelly asked.

"Yeah…I think so. It's hard to know, with the baby pushing us into this wedding. I've always looked out for myself. Now I feel like there's a whole lot of responsibility coming my way that I never wanted."

The similarities between his self-absorption and Trent's amused her once again. But this wasn't a joke. "These days people don't necessarily get married because they're having a kid," Kelly reminded him. "That you wanted to marry Nikki, and that she said yes, means something."

"It means we both come from families that expect nothing less," he said wryly.

"There is that," she agreed.

"Right now," he said, "I can't say for sure if I love her or not." He took a deep breath. "I'll always be there for my kid. But if I'm not certain I love Nikki, I shouldn't marry her."

Josh's eyes glinted with the same kind of determination that had won him a ride in the NASCAR Busch Series. If Kelly had to put money on whether or not today's wedding would go ahead, she'd bet no.

Josh continued, "But Mom and Dad have organized the wedding, and Nikki's parents have paid for it. There'll be newspapers and TV there. Trent Matheson is my best man." He shook his head. "How can I even think about not going through with it?"

"It would be stupid to get married just because the wedding is paid for and you have a celebrity best man," Kelly pointed out. At the same time she felt sorry for Nikki—at yesterday's rehearsal it had been obvious the girl was crazy about Josh. "You shouldn't rush into a decision."

"I have to rush. The wedding's in—" he glanced at his watch "—eight hours' time." He looked frantically around the kitchen, as if he could see the walls closing in on him. "I have to think."

Kelly heard sounds of movement upstairs, and predicted that soon the family would descend en masse. She grabbed Josh's hand. "Come with me, I know how you can figure this out."

She led him down the hall to the den.

Trent sat up in bed, groggily rubbing his eyes. Nice to see someone had managed to sleep last night.

"Get up," she snapped. "Josh needs this room." She grabbed the towel hanging on the back of the door and threw it at Trent. "Go shower or something."

Trent raised his eyebrows at Josh, and evidently received enough back by way of silent male communication to follow orders. He shoved the sheets aside. Kelly averted her eyes while he got out of bed. He ambled from the room, grumbling under his breath.

"Sit." Kelly pushed Josh toward the sofa bed. She clambered over it to the desk and found a notepad and a pen. "You need to decide—fast—what you really feel for Nikki. I agree that if you don't love her, you shouldn't marry her."

"Thanks, Kel," Josh said.

"But don't go by what you're feeling right this minute. Sometimes, our emotions get screwed up, and they can make us think things that deep in our heart we know aren't true." *Like, that I feel something for Trent.*

"You need to ask yourself some questions that will help you understand your true feelings." She began to scribble on the notepad. When she had eight questions, she passed the paper over to Josh.

He scanned them. "This is great," he said, surprised.

"It's important to work through all of them. Otherwise you'll skew the answers."

"Sure." He sounded distracted, already absorbed in the first question.

Kelly handed him the pen. "Lock the door behind me, and don't come back until you've figured this out."

He looked up long enough to blow her a kiss. "Thanks, Kel, you're a star."

Kelly felt a little glow of warmth as she left the room. Someone in her family had finally seen she was good at her job.

TRENT ARRIVED in the kitchen around the same time as everyone else. Kelly eyed him with reluctant enjoyment. Freshly showered, dark hair ruffled where he'd toweled it dry, jaw smoother than it would be the rest of the day, he exuded relaxed male potency.

What would it have been like to wake up next to him?

Images and sensations welled up to fill her head. His chest, hard where she was soft, those strong arms around her, his mouth, warm with remembered loving...

She licked her lips, caught Trent's blue gaze on her. His eyes flicked up to meet hers. One side of his mouth moved in a restrained version of his usual smile.

Was that regret she saw there? Regret that she'd said no?

Most likely regret that he got woken up so early this morning. She turned away from Trent, pulled out a stool from the counter and poured cereal into a bowl.

Her mom offered him a cooked breakfast, which he readily accepted. While she prepared it, he remained on the other side of the kitchen, propped casually against the wall.

Kelly didn't expect Josh to emerge from the den just an hour after she'd left him there. Those questions took some thought—she'd have struggled to get through them herself in under two hours.

"Good morning, honey." Mom beamed as she put a hand on either side of his face, then kissed him. "All ready for your big day?"

Josh looked no better than he had first thing this morning. He cleared his throat, looked at the floor. *Uh-oh,* Kelly thought. She stood up, intending to drag him out of the kitchen before he could—

"There isn't going to be a wedding," he said.

CHAPTER ELEVEN

THE SILENCE THAT FOLLOWED Josh's pronouncement was utter and profound. But brief. Then a clamor of questions and protests turned the kitchen to chaos.

Just when Kelly's ears were starting to hurt, her father boomed, "Shut up," which silenced everyone.

"What's going on, Josh?" Rob Greenwood demanded.

Josh looked shell-shocked, as if he hadn't realized the effect his words would have. Kelly could have slapped him. She loved her brother but, like Trent, he was totally self-absorbed.

"I realized I don't love Nikki," he said. "I can't marry her."

"But you're having a baby," her mom protested.

"Sure you don't just have case of nerves?" her father said.

Josh's mouth set in a stubborn line. "It's not nerves. Kelly told me the questions I needed to ask myself to decide whether or not I love Nikki. The answer is no."

All eyes swung to Kelly.

"D-did you answer all the questions?" she stammered, uncomfortable at being the focus of attention.

He frowned. "I didn't need to. It was obvious by question four which way it was going."

"I told you it's essential to do them all." The last question had been the most important: *What are your goals for your life, and do you see Nikki as vital to achieving them?* Kelly had asked herself that question about Trent as she ate breakfast, and was relieved to find there was no way he fit with her goal of having a family of her own and a husband who was willing to put her first.

Stacey joked, "Wow, Kelly, way to go."

Her sister's reaction was mild in comparison with the haranguing her parents launched into. They bombarded her, not with outright accusations, but with doubts and questions that made it clear her family blamed her for Josh's change of heart.

Trent wondered if he was the only one who noticed Josh slinking out the back door.

So far, Trent had kept right out of this family fracas. But if Josh wasn't going to take some of the blame for his decision, someone had to help Kelly. Trent couldn't believe the way her family had rounded on her. Sure, his own father and Chad had high expectations of him, but even when he disappointed them, they never treated him with this lack of respect. "Hey!"

His call brought everyone to attention. Trent ranged himself alongside Kelly. His arm brushed against hers, and he felt the chill of goose bumps on her flesh, detected the faintest of quivers. He suspected she was only just holding herself together in the face of all this hostility.

"How about you all do Kelly the courtesy of hearing her side?" He sensed her startled look, but pinned his gaze on her parents as he said, "Whatever she did for Josh, you can bet it was based on her skills as a psychologist, which I happen to know are pretty impressive." He hadn't told her that before, but now was as good a time as any. He slid her a glance. "Go ahead, sugar, tell them what happened."

Kelly drew a shuddery breath. "Josh said this morning he had doubts about the wedding. I told him those were probably prewedding jitters." She went on to explain how she'd given Josh a series of questions to answer.

Trent frowned. Could you really figure out if you should marry someone just by answering a few questions?

"He didn't finish the exercise," Kelly said. "If he had, he might have come to a different conclusion."

Silence while they processed this information.

"I guess…you did your best," Merle said uncertainly. "You couldn't know Josh would be so stupid."

"You *should* have known he'd be so stupid," her father reproved her. "Josh never had two bits of sense upstairs."

When Dave and Stacey started relating examples of Josh's previous moments of idiocy, the tension in the kitchen eased. No one was commending Kelly for her actions, but nor were they laying the entire blame at her door.

Trent could see that Kelly didn't know whether to laugh or cry. Trent had done it again—used his clout in her defense. She met his eyes across the room. He winked.

He'd told her family she was good at her job. And he'd meant it.

JOSH DIDN'T BACK DOWN on his refusal to marry Nikki, which meant that while Kelly's parents consoled the bride's family and tried to figure out how to get the young couple back together, the Greenwood offspring bore the brunt of unraveling all the wedding arrangements.

Kelly and Trent didn't fly back to Charlotte until Wednesday, which gave them only twenty-four hours to prepare for the next race.

Maybe it was all that rushing, but Trent had a bad feeling about the race in Loudon. It started during his practice for qualifying, when the car they'd set up perfectly for the mile track developed a vibration. Trent called the problem in to Rod and headed for the pits. As he slowed to enter pit road, the right front tire burst. The car spun into a tire barrier. It was a write-off, and the crew worked through the night to set up the backup Number 186 car.

Trent's sensation of impending doom intensified during

qualifying itself. Matheson Racing drew the second slot, which meant he had to qualify when the track was at its hottest—and slowest—on an unseasonably warm September day.

His qualifying time wasn't bad, but it was bettered by a bunch of guys who qualified toward evening when the track was colder and faster, leaving Trent to start twelfth on the grid. Not what he needed for his first race in the Chase for the NASCAR NEXTEL Cup Championship.

He tried to listen to Kelly during their prerace briefing. But his mind kept flipping back to that kiss they'd shared in the middle of the night at her parents' house, to how he'd wanted to make love with her. He was relieved she'd said no—how the heck could he have faced her parents the next morning, knowing he didn't have it in him to commit to Kelly?—but he couldn't stop torturing himself with speculation as to what it would have been like to hold her in his arms all night.

Dammit, he needed to get his mind on the race. He didn't need to be wanting her. He especially didn't need to be worrying about her, noting the shadow in her eyes, the compression of her lips when one of her family hurt her feelings. He had enough worries of his own.

She'd warned him that if they slept together, they'd risk getting their emotions involved. He hadn't believed her. But he couldn't deny there was already something going on between them. Something not entirely physical. *Concentrate, dammit.*

SMALL WONDER that when the green flag fell on Sunday, Trent couldn't find his zone. By lap eighty, he'd passed no one and lost three places, which had his crew chief barking anxious questions over the radio.

"What's going on, Trent? Car too loose?" Rod demanded after Trent took one of the track's sharp turns so hard the car threatened to fishtail out behind him.

"Car's good," he said. *Can't say the same about the driver.* "Got any advice, Kelly?" Damn, he just wanted to hear her voice.

"She's not here," Rod said.

"Why the hell not? She's paid to be here, isn't she?" He cursed as another car—a guy who'd never once finished ahead of Trent—stole a pass on him.

"I don't know where *you* are, Trent, but you're sure as hell not in this race." Chad's angry accusation broke in.

Trent couldn't disagree.

"Trent, you were supposed to pit this lap." Rod's reminder was far more polite than Trent deserved.

Dammit, he'd missed his pit stop. They'd pushed the limits of their fuel cell already. Now, he risked running out of gas in the middle of the track. It didn't bear thinking about.

He made it into the pits on the next lap. The guys put their all into it and had him back out on track in an impressive 13.7 seconds, which served to emphasize that today's problems were all with the driver.

He finished an abysmal twenty-fourth. In the garage after the race, the crew was silent. Even Rod didn't meet Trent's eyes. Naturally, it was the two people he least wanted to talk to who had their gazes trained firmly on him. Kelly and Chad stood conferring to one side, obviously rehashing today's disaster. Trent strode over to them.

"So you decided to show up?" he snarled at Kelly. "Where were you when I needed you during the race?"

"You're blaming me for your poor performance?" she said coolly.

Hell, yes. Though he wasn't about to tell her it was because he couldn't stop thinking about her. "Your job is to get me into the zone, isn't it?"

Her lips tightened. "You're behaving like a spoiled brat."

Shame drained away his ire. She was right. Trent hated

drivers who blamed other people for their failures, and he was doing just that. He said to both her and Chad, "I'm sorry."

Kelly's mouth softened, but she didn't go as far as a smile. "Better."

Chad slung an arm around Kelly. "Where would we be without you to call Trent on his bad behavior? He never listens to me."

She grinned up at him.

What the—? Something fierce and sharp jabbed Trent. Chad hadn't looked at a woman with this much warmth in his eyes in over a year. Was he attracted to Kelly?

What's not to like? Kelly was smart, beautiful—just the kind of woman Chad went for. But Chad wasn't the guy she needed. He could be distant and cold when he chose. That would hurt her, and just the thought of Kelly getting hurt made Trent mad.

Not that Chad looked cold or distant right now. And going by the way Kelly's tawny brown eyes glowed warm as she looked at him, it was clear the two of them got along better than Trent had noticed.

"Depending how busy you are with Trent this week," Chad said to her, "I could use your help with Brad." Brad was Matheson Racing's driver in the NASCAR Craftsman Truck Series. "How about I clear my schedule so we can meet tomorrow morning?"

"Sure." Kelly smiled at him again.

"After that show I put on today, I'll need you full-time," Trent countered. The words were intended for Kelly, but he kept his eyes on Chad. "Every day. All day."

He didn't like the gleam of calculation in his brother's eyes. Let Chad think what he wanted. This wasn't about jealousy. If Kelly and Chad spent too much time together, she might blab Trent's secrets to his brother.

Chad shrugged. "Whatever you say."

"Let's start early tomorrow," Kelly said to Trent.

Great. He didn't want Kelly working with Chad, but suddenly he wasn't so sure he wanted to work with her himself. Today's race was proof he'd lost that essential self-focus that enabled him to win. Thinking about making love to Kelly, defending her against her family, had given him a warm, fuzzy feeling. The kind of warm, fuzzy feeling that killed a racing career.

ON MONDAY MORNING, Trent made a supreme effort and got to work before nine. It was part of his new resolution to be totally professional where Kelly was concerned. Much as it went against his laid-back nature, but he figured it was the only way to keep the kind of distance between them he needed if he was going to win races.

Kelly was already sitting in his office when he arrived; she handed him a notebook. He leafed through it. It was some kind of diary. A different day on each page, with notes in Kelly's messy handwriting that said things like, "Bkfst Froot Loops and coffee," and "Spk Brady 1pm."

"This is everything you've done ahead of every race since I started working with you," she said. "We've already homed in on some helpful things in your routine, but now we're taking it to a new level of detail."

"I only had Froot Loops for breakfast once, when I'd run out of Shreddies."

"Big mistake," she said. "That day you finished thirtieth at Sonoma."

"You think that's because I ate Froot Loops?"

"Not necessarily. It's more relevant that you ate Shreddies ahead of every top-five finish. You also spoke to your father in the two hours before the Sonoma race. You always do worse when you've talked to Brady."

"Go on," he said.

Kelly handed over a typed sheet of paper. "These are the elements that are common to the days you race well."

"Did you count the race at Watkins Glen?"

"Yes. I figured you couldn't have avoided Hayes hitting you and shunting you off the track on the second-last lap. Without that, you would have finished at least fourth."

Trent scanned the list. "You're suggesting I race best when I've had five hours sleep the night before the race?"

"You're pretty consistent about going to bed at two in the morning on a Saturday night," she said. "Normally, you set your alarm for eight. But twice, at Michigan and Daytona, you mentioned you'd woken early."

"Those were my two best runs this season."

"Uh-huh."

When a slow smile spread across Trent's face, Kelly knew she had him.

"Tell me what we need to do," he said.

She leaned forward, excited to share her ideas. "You need to be careful how many people you see the night before the race. Go to bed at 2:00 a.m., but cut down on the flirting and the women beforehand."

His eyes narrowed. "You just don't want me to have any fun."

She shook her head. "Your best races came after you spent the evening with Chad or a bunch of guys. Or with just one woman."

"I never see one woman at a time," he protested. "I'm a serial flirt."

"I hate to destroy your self-image," she said kindly, "but what about the night you and I grabbed a burger in Watkins Glen?"

"You don't count," he said.

"And the night you took Rod's niece on a date."

"Do you think I'm dumb enough to make a move on my crew chief's niece? That wasn't a date, I was doing Rod a favor—I don't even remember her name."

"Courtney, and she was twenty-one and gorgeous. It was a date." Still, Kelly couldn't help being pleased at his response.

Trent tapped the list. "What else?"

"Talking to Chad before a race seems to help you get in the zone." Kelly smiled. "Your brother can be very inspiring."

"You don't say," Trent growled.

"What happens in the early part of the race can make a big difference, too," she said. "I've noticed that when you pass several cars in the first few laps, you're on fire for the whole race. When you start on pole, you're often lagging by the midpoint. You pick up again later, but you're giving yourself unnecessary stress during the race."

"Fascinating," he said without a trace of sarcasm. "Now that I know that, what can I do about it?"

"We could try timing your midrace pit stops earlier," she said, "so we can counter the lethargy that kicks in at that stage. We can spread them out a bit in the early and late stages so we're not making more stops than we have to."

"Makes sense. As long as Rod's happy."

"But your best results," she said, "come when you get into the zone before you get into the car. If it takes you a couple of laps, you don't race as well."

"There's not a lot I can do about that. Except maybe try these." He indicated her list.

"These should help," she agreed. "Their familiarity can make it easier to get into the zone. But there's a risk if one of them goes wrong—say, you accidentally talk to your dad a half hour before the race starts—you'll get so psyched out you won't be able to find the zone."

"Why do I think you're about to tell me how to fix that?"

She grinned. "We're going to experiment with some key words you can say to yourself that will trigger your entry into the zone, and keep you there."

"Key words," he said doubtfully.

She passed over another piece of paper. Trent read aloud, "Smooth." He paused. "Faster."

Kelly felt herself blushing. When she'd devised those words she'd had no idea how they'd sound spoken in Trent's sensuous voice. She coughed, massaged her throat to ease the tension.

He read on. "Plenty of room. Stay in front."

Safer choices. Kelly blew out a relieved breath. "You'll use different words at different stages of the race," she said. "As you know, you feel better when you get away smoothly at the start. After your pit stops, you want to get back to speed as fast as possible. On a crowded track, you need to be confident in your passing. In the last quarter you want to take the lead and hold on to it. Your history shows you have a better chance of finishing in the top five if you lead at least twenty laps in the last quarter."

"Has this stuff worked for other clients?"

"The racer I worked with in New Zealand won his series." Once again, she longed to tell him about the fiasco with her rugby client. But now didn't seem the right time, not when he was so excited about her ideas.

"You know," he said, "it's hard for me to trust someone else with my racing. Like most things in my life, it's all about me." He grinned, and there was a wealth of self-knowledge in it. Then he sobered. "But, Kelly, I do trust you."

The words warmed her at least as much as any of his kisses had. She knew they'd make all the difference to their work. Yet a part of her wanted to urge him to take them back.

JULIE-ANNE hit the key to shut down her computer. The clock in the bottom corner of the display read 11:00 p.m. Another crazy day at Matheson Performance Industries.

Brady was still in his office, the door between his space and hers firmly closed, as it had been ever since that dinner with the Johnstones. As if it wasn't already perfectly clear he didn't want a relationship with her.

Over the past two weeks there had been none of what she now realized had been a special intimacy between them.

Those moments where they connected in a casual conversation or a shared opinion that morphed into something warmer. Now, it felt as if she was working with a stranger.

She tapped on Brady's door and went in. "I'm going home now."

He looked up from his screen, blinking with exhaustion. Julie-Anne longed to smooth the deep creases that ran from his nose down to his mouth. He pushed his chair back. "I'll see you to your car. It's late to be walking outside alone."

"My car's in the workshop," she said. "I'll call a cab."

For a charged moment, he looked at her. Then he grabbed the heavy cluster of keys from the corner of his desk and said, almost angrily, "I'll drive you home."

"There's no need."

He marched to the door, leaving her little option but to follow. Julie-Anne bit back further protest. Maybe he wanted to clear the air between them.

Or maybe not. He didn't say a word as they went out into the parking lot, where he held open the door of his classic Ford Mustang convertible.

"I live in NoDa," she said as she got in. "On North Mercer." He cast her a look of exasperation at the mention of the Bohemian area just north of uptown Charlotte.

Traffic was light this time of night, and Brady paid little regard to the speed limits. He didn't say anything the entire ten minutes or so it took to reach her place. So much for clearing the air.

Julie-Anne felt the familiar surge of comfort at the sight of her cottage, tucked back from the road in a quiet street. She hadn't lived there long, but already it felt like a home for her and Amber, if—when—Amber should decide to return. She unclipped her seat belt. "Thanks for the lift."

"I'll see you inside." He was out of the car before she could refuse.

The porch light came on automatically as they walked up the front path. When Julie-Anne turned to say good-night to Brady, the haggardness of his face in the harsh light shocked her.

"You look awful," she said.

His mouth tightened. "I'm hungry, that's all. I didn't eat tonight."

Neither had Julie-Anne. But she'd had a big lunch so skipping dinner wasn't a problem. She was pretty certain Brady hadn't eaten lunch, either. "I hope you have a meal from one of your lady friends waiting at home."

There was that angry light in his eyes again, momentarily stripping away the weariness. "I don't get those anymore."

"Since when?" she blurted. Just a couple of weeks ago she'd overheard him calling Gracie Manners to thank her for the mac-and-cheese she'd left.

"Since—" He scowled. "Since two weeks ago."

Since he'd kissed Julie-Anne? Her heart leapt.

"It's no big deal," he snapped. "I realized I couldn't keep taking food from those women when I would never be interested in them."

Certainty made her bold. "Does that mean you're interested in me?"

His chin jutted forward. "Can't say I want to be. But, yeah, it seems I am."

Puzzled, she said, "You've hardly spoken to me since that night."

"Like I told you, I don't want to be interested."

"So you like me enough to feel it's unfair to let other women cook you dinner, but not enough to date me."

He looked down at her, his face pensive. She couldn't read his hooded gaze. He jerked his head, as if to break some spell.

"You deserve a guy who's as generous with himself as you are," he said roughly. "I don't have that much to give."

That he'd thought it through to such an extent told Julie-Anne all she needed to know about what he was capable of giving. "You don't have to give it all at once," she said gently. "We could take it one step at a time."

He blinked, as if the thought had never occurred to him—silly man. Then hope lit his face, smoothed out some of those creases.

She said, "One *kiss* at a time."

His eyebrows shot up, and she nodded.

This kiss was more awkward than their first one, coming right after such a clinical conversation, rather than being born of a moment's heat. Brady stepped on Julie-Anne's foot as he moved closer to her, and then their teeth clashed.

He pulled away to rest his forehead against hers. His quiet chuckle sent warm breath fanning over her face. "Guess I'm rusty on the kissing front, too." He tilted her chin up with his finger. "Let's try that again."

This time, their lips melded perfectly in an embrace that was tender but demanding. Brady hauled her against him, and Julie-Anne guessed his little sound of triumph was pleasure in how well they fit together. She felt as if the connection stemmed right from her heart, and she gave all she could—without scaring him off—in her kisses.

At last, she eased back. "I'd better go in."

Brady grimaced his reluctance, but he took her key from her and unlocked the door.

She should invite him in, feed him something. Yesterday's leftover roast chicken would make a great sandwich…. Julie-Anne halted the thought. She wasn't about to become a one-woman Brady-feeding band to replace the divorcées. She'd probably still be doing it fifteen years later, still waiting for him to figure out what he had to give.

It pained her to send him out into the night unfed. But she did.

WHEN KELLY APPROACHED the car right before the start of the race at Dover, Trent unhooked his window net so he could see her better.

"You okay?" she asked.

"Great," he said, meaning it. "Thank you."

She smiled, but her voice was serious. "It's all you out there, Trent, and none of me."

He nodded. He'd earned a pole start in qualifying. He was ready to make the most of it.

Kelly stepped back and he rehooked the net, just in time to hear the command, "Gentlemen, start your engines."

He drove out of the pits. Man, he was tired—he'd hit the sack at 2:00 a.m. then been woken by his alarm clock at seven, just to be sure he didn't get more than five hours' sleep. He circled the track, waiting for the start, muttering, "Smooth," over and over again. It felt weird. But as he kept saying it, he felt the distractions seep away. Suddenly, he was in the zone.

The race was like no other Trent had experienced. He was relaxed yet energized, his performance automatically brilliant. From the moment the green flag fell, he didn't know and didn't care where anyone else was on the track—he was unbeatable.

Flying past the checkered flag in first place, he felt plenty of excitement but no surprise. When he got to Victory Lane he climbed out of the car to the adulation of the crowd.

He looked for Kelly.

And found her standing next to his brother, her grin matching Chad's in delight and excitement. Trent tried to quash the niggling jealousy, but he couldn't.

"Were you with Chad the whole race?" It was a dumb thing to say, but he had to ask.

She gave him a puzzled smile, and shook her head. "I just came to talk to Chad now. During the race I prefer to be next to Rod, so I can see the TV."

Chad pulled Trent into a rare and unexpected hug. "Stop bugging Kelly and just accept the glory that's coming your way, little brother."

TRENT MIGHT HAVE KNOWN winning the NASCAR NEXTEL Cup Series wasn't as easy as repeating a few magic words. The next week at Kansas City, a track relatively new to NASCAR and a favorite of many drivers—but not Trent—he managed to get into the zone ahead of the start, only to find that by lap 150 he was too tired to hold on to the race. He finished twelfth—could have been worse, but it was a far cry from last week's glory.

"Why didn't it work?" he demanded of Kelly on Tuesday, as they sat in his office at Matheson Racing watching a replay. "When I went so well at Dover?"

"It's not an instant fix," she said. "We know we're on the right track, but now we need to refine the routine. We'll get rid of the things that don't make much difference, focus on the ones that do. Plus, we need to look around at outside factors." She propped her chin on her hand and frowned at the television. "How about we spend tomorrow figuring out if there's anything we missed?"

"Tomorrow's my accountancy class." Trent had started another course this semester.

"Oh, yeah. Maybe on Thursday we could—" She stopped.

"We could what?"

"That's it," she said slowly. "That's the problem. Your college classes."

"I've had enough good results to know they don't affect my racing," he said irritably.

"The reason you're doing them affects your relationship with your father and your brother. And that affects your racing."

He groaned. "Not this again."

"You have all this stuff bottled up inside." She shook her head. "It's not good for you."

"I don't bottle it up, I share it with you."

"But I'm not emotionally important in your life."

She raised her eyebrows. The ready agreement Trent wanted to utter was nowhere to be found. Instead, he made a noncommittal sound.

"Our new routines have improved your focus, and the key words help get you in the zone. Right?"

"Right," he said suspiciously.

"Then trust me," she said. "Trust me that if you tell your father and your brother what you want, you'll clear some space in your head that will help your racing."

His instincts shrieked against it. But lately Kelly's instincts had proven more reliable than his. And if he talked to Dad, she'd stop badgering him about it. Trent swallowed. "I'll do it tomorrow after my class."

TRENT FELT JUST LIKE he had when he was ten years old and had to confess to his father that he'd buried the model race cars Zack and Chad had gotten for Christmas to punish them for breaking his slot-car set. He'd believed he had right on his side, but was certain his father wouldn't agree.

Back then, Dad hadn't agreed, and Trent had received a swat on the backside to prove it.

Trent dismissed the memory. This time, he really did have right on his side. He'd invited Chad to today's meeting with Dad—might as well handle all his conflicts in one hit. Kelly hadn't been certain this was the right way to go about it, but she'd left that judgment up to him.

Trent smiled at Julie-Anne, at her desk in the outer office. "Is he in?"

"Ready and waiting. And in a better mood than usual," she said with that lilt in her voice that Trent liked so much.

The news about Dad's state of mind encouraged him.

The door behind him opened and Chad came in. He nodded

at Julie-Anne. "What's so important, Trent? You know we have to get to the airport by six." The race at Talladega was on Saturday, which meant they moved the whole preparation schedule forward by a day, flying to the track on Wednesday instead of Thursday.

Julie-Anne tapped on the door and walked into Brady's office. "The boys are here."

Something about the warmth in her voice, the protectiveness, made Trent do a double take. She didn't sound like a secretary talking to her boss. He heard Dad's, "Send 'em in," spoken without his usual gruffness.

Trent would lay money there was something between Brady and Julie-Anne. *Go, Dad.* He grinned at Chad, but his brother seemed oblivious.

"You did okay on Sunday," Brady said when they were all sitting down.

"'Okay' about sums it up," Trent agreed. He knitted his fingers on the table in front of him. "I'm not here to talk about racing. There's something you both need to know." He looked his father in the eye. "I'm studying motor sports management at Belmont Abbey College. I took an accountancy course last semester, and I've just started another one. I hope to earn a degree out of it."

"Did you pass?" Brady's need to cut right to the chase overrode his obvious astonishment.

"I got a B plus." Trent enjoyed the surprise on his father's face.

"So that's why you've been disappearing. Why didn't you say?" Chad sounded suspicious, as he had every right to be.

"I wanted to prove I could do it before I discuss my goals with you guys."

"Your goal is to win the NASCAR NEXTEL Cup Series," Chad said. His father gave a grunt of agreement.

"That's this year's goal," Trent said. "Maybe even next

year's. But long-term, I'd like to run Matheson Performance Industries."

Chad jumped to his feet. "That's my job," he said, outraged. Brady's eyebrows shot up as he waved Chad back into his seat, but once again he grunted agreement. It was two immovable objects against one, and in that moment Trent knew he didn't stand a chance of winning.

"Dad, I don't expect you to hand me the job just because I want it," he persisted. He ignored Chad's snort. "All I ask is that you consider me as a candidate on an equal basis with Chad." He pulled out a slim file. "I have a lot of ideas for the business that I'll leave for you to read."

"What ideas?" Chad reached for the folder, but Brady put his palm down flat on top of it.

"You've never said before you want to work in the business," he said.

"I have," Trent said. "You haven't listened."

"I didn't know you meant it," Brady blustered. "Son, you're the best damned driver in the best damned sport in the world. Wouldn't you be better to race as long as you can, say another five or ten years, then take over running the team?"

"That's not what I want," he said.

"What exactly do you expect *me* to do?" Chad asked with a mildness that Trent recognized as deceptive.

"You do a great job running the team," Trent said. "I thought you enjoyed it."

Brady spread his hands. "We always said Chad would take over the company. He's the best qualified. Trent, I admire what you've done with these college classes, but I don't think you're the one to run MPI."

Trent recognized the finality in his father's words.

"Going to college is a great idea, but it's distracting you from your racing." Chad rubbed salt into the wound. "Maybe you should think about putting your studies on hold."

The discussion went downhill from there. It was obvious Brady and Chad wouldn't consider Trent had something to contribute to the business. He'd not only failed to pique his father's interest, he'd also alerted Chad to the fact he was after his job, and he'd revealed the source of his distraction.

As Trent left, Brady handed him back the file containing his ideas for the business. "I won't have time to read them the next couple of months," he said. "Maybe after that…"

Trent seethed at his father's intransigence as he walked back to the workshop.

He considered getting mad at Kelly, too, for forcing him to confront Dad and Brady. But she'd only been trying to help sort out his distraction, which was ironic, given she was proving more of a distraction than anything else.

Despite his irritation, the thought of Kelly put a smile on his face. She was so cute, the way she ordered him around, so certain she knew what was right. He liked the way she looked at him from beneath lowered lids when she thought he couldn't see her. They'd worked so closely the last few months, Trent felt as if he knew her better than he'd known any other woman.

Except, of course, there was one thing he didn't know about her.

Back in his office, he opened his laptop and loaded up Yahoo. He typed *Kelly Greenwood*.

The first few listings were a bunch of genealogical sites. Then a minor actress called Kelly Greenwood, a lawyer, a realtor. Trent clicked to the next page.

Item number seventeen jumped out at him. He clicked on the link and waited for the screen to load.

"Gotcha."

CHAPTER TWELVE

ON FRIDAY NIGHT, after a full day of practicing at the Talladega track, Trent invited Kelly to dinner with him and the crew at a steak restaurant in downtown Talladega. Kelly could tell he was on edge about tomorrow's race—he ate fast, then doodled on the paper place mat while he waited for everyone else to finish. Maybe he was still churned up about the meeting with Brady. When she'd asked him how it had gone, he'd said he would tell her later. But since then he'd avoided any opportunity for a private chat.

When they left the restaurant at nine, Kelly offered Trent a ride back to his motor home. They headed for her rental car, parked on the other side of Talladega's Memorial Park. Trent strode through the park so briskly he was almost jogging. Kelly slowed her own pace to a stroll, knowing his good manners would force him to do the same. He needed to relax.

"Just stick to your routines," she told him as they followed the Walk of Fame past the bronze plaques commemorating the achievements of some of NASCAR's greatest drivers. "You know what you have to do to win this race."

"Don't date, don't drink more than two beers, stay up until 2:00 a.m." He stopped under one of the old-fashioned streetlamps, and in its yellowish glow she saw his scowl. "I've had my two beers, what else is there to do?"

"You like watching TV," she reminded him. "There must be a game on."

"I guess." He took her arm and tugged her along at his pace. "Want to watch with me?"

"Not particularly."

He grinned. "That's my girl." They reached her car and he took her keys to open the door. "You'll watch with me, won't you?" he coaxed her. "Please?"

She rolled her eyes. "Fine."

KELLY HADN'T BEEN inside Trent's motor coach before. It was like stepping into a luxury apartment. Thick navy-blue carpet softened their tread. Leather couches in a lighter blue formed a cozy living area where a wide-screen TV was set into the wall. Polished wooden tables and shelves lent a rich warmth to the space. Beyond the kitchen area, through an open door, Kelly could see a king-size bed piled with pillows and a thick duvet.

Trent turned on the TV, then sat next to Kelly on the couch. They found a football replay and watched that, even though they both knew the final score.

When the game ended, Trent got up and put the kettle on.

Kelly looked at her watch. "It's eleven o'clock, I can't drink coffee now."

He spooned coffee out of a jar into two mugs. "You'll need it if you're going to stay up until two."

"I'm not staying up that late," she said, horrified.

"Sugar, I don't want to stay awake, either—just thinking about getting up at seven in the morning makes me tired. But we both know I'll race better if I do." He poured boiling water into the mugs.

Kelly couldn't argue with that. If he needed her help to stay awake, what else could she do?

"How are we supposed to pass the time?" she asked, then blushed at the direction her thoughts were headed.

He grinned. "I have just the idea." He leaned toward her, and she thought he was about to kiss her. Then he reached into the cupboard next to the couch and pulled out a folded board and a wooden box. A chess set.

Kelly's stomach flipped. She didn't believe in coincidence. Trent had been snooping. She moistened her lips. "You've figured out I went to college on a chess scholarship."

"With a little help from the Internet." He opened the box and began to set up the pieces. "Why didn't you tell me?"

"When we met, you wouldn't have had a lot of respect for that."

He nodded, confirming her view. "And how exactly did your earrings interfere with your chess? Or was that just to throw me off the trail?"

"Certainly not," she said indignantly. "Though it was more a matter of chess interfering with my earrings than the other way around." She touched a finger to her right ear, remembering. "I used to get pretty tense in competitions, and I'd sit there fiddling with an earring while I figured out my next move. In a really stressful match I'd end up with a bleeding earlobe."

Trent winced. "So, how far did you get in competition?"

"I was the American Under-Twenty-one Women's Chess Champion," she said. "I went to the World Under-Twenty-one Championship in London, but I lost to a Russian gal in the quarterfinals."

"Then what?"

"I stopped playing competitively."

The hand that held the white queen froze, poised over the board. "Because you lost one game?"

She knotted her fingers. "My family was so disappointed. They'd never really got the whole chess thing, but when it looked as if I might have a shot at a world title they were pretty excited. So when I lost…" She shrugged. "They were probably even more disappointed than I was. I realized I couldn't handle the pressure of competition at that level. The only reason I was trying to win was to impress my family. And if you don't really want to win, you can't get to the top."

"That's true." He placed the white queen in position.

Now that he'd discovered some of her past, Kelly decided it was time to tell him the whole truth. "Trent, there's something else I—"

"Dad said an outright no to me getting involved in the business," he announced. "Wanting to win that job isn't going to make it happen."

His tone was casual, but Kelly saw the disappointment in his eyes. She put her confession aside. "I'm sorry. Tell me what happened."

He recounted the meeting to her. "I know," he said, "you told me not to have Chad there. It might have gone better if I'd listened."

"A little better, maybe," she said. "But if your dad was that opposed… At least now you know where to focus—on your driving."

"Just because you don't need a college degree to drive a race car, doesn't mean you don't have a brain," he said. "Sometimes I think Dad thinks the same as you—that I'm an airhead."

"Now you're feeling sorry for yourself," she said.

He grinned. "No chance I'll overdose on self-pity with you around, sugar."

"If it's any consolation," she said, "I think you can do anything you set out to do, whether it's winning the NASCAR NEXTEL Cup Series or running MPI."

His eyes darkened. "That is…some consolation." He put the black king and queen, the last pieces, on their squares. "Ready?"

"Trent, I am not playing chess with you. You need to feel good about your race tomorrow."

He raised an eyebrow. "You think you'll beat me?"

"I know I will." Uh-oh. She saw the light of competition in his eyes, the smile that played at the corners of his mouth.

He indicated the board. "Black or white, you choose."

"Trent," she warned again, "this isn't wise."

"Sugar, if you won't play chess we'll have to find something else to fill the next three hours." His eyes traveled over her lips. "That might not be a bad idea."

Kelly pressed her lips together. "I'll be white." That way she would play first, and might discourage him from a foolish move that would lose him the game right away.

In fact, it might be a good idea to play along for a while then let him win, to bolster his confidence for tomorrow.

She made her move. Trent frowned in concentration as he eyed the board, then moved one of his center pawns. A classic rookie start. This game should be all over in fifteen minutes.

An hour later, they were still playing. Every time Kelly planned to put her king in mortal jeopardy and allow Trent to checkmate her, she couldn't bring herself to do it. He had a far better grasp on the game than she would have imagined. No wonder he was doing so well in his accountancy classes—he obviously had plenty of analytical skills.

"Who taught you to play?" she asked.

"Mom was her club champion, but Dad never learned the game. She got me up to speed so she'd have some competition."

"Did you join the club, too?"

He gave her a look that said he would eat his helmet before he joined a chess club.

Kelly made a deliberately stupid move with her knight, then faked disappointment when Trent captured it. Two turns later, she did the same with a pawn. She waited three turns before exposing her rook.

Trent didn't see the opportunity, and moved his bishop three diagonal spaces. It was a pointless move. She moved her rook so his bishop could take it. He didn't. Instead, he moved his queen to the center of the board, in a horizontal line with her rook.

Kelly's sensors went on alert. Nothing in Trent's play so far had indicated he was capable of such a basic mistake. "What are you doing?" she demanded. "Not even an airhead would have made that last move."

"So I'm running out of ideas." He yawned. "It's late."

"You're letting me win," she said, outraged.

He leaned back, arms clasped behind his head. "No, sugar, you're letting *me* win. And I'm not letting you do it."

"You replay that move right now," she ordered.

"Make me." His lazy smile taunted her.

She put his queen back where it came from and moved his bishop to a square that put pressure on her queen.

"I didn't want to do that," he protested.

She ignored him and made her own move. Trent put his hand on his knight.

"Don't you dare," she said.

"Now what?"

"You're doing it again." She slapped his hand away. Then she moved his bishop to put herself in check. "Say check."

"Check," he said.

She got herself out of check by moving her king one space to the left. Then she picked up Trent's knight and moved it forward.

"Kelly, what are you—?"

She squinted at the board and said through gritted teeth, "I'm not letting you throw the game." She slid her bishop four diagonal spaces, feinting a threat to Trent's knight. She moved his knight in an evasive action, then sneaked up behind it with her queen and captured it.

"Hey!" he protested.

"You would never have seen that coming."

Trent felt slightly better when she used his bishop to put herself in check again, which meant she had to move her king into the corner. He was about to pick up his rook and head for her queen when she did it for him. Trent struggled not to laugh as he watched Kelly play both sides of the game for a couple more minutes. He won.

She scowled at him. "You were right. You did beat me."

Trent couldn't hold back—he laughed out loud.

"It's no joke." Her voice quivered. "Chess is the one thing I'm good at, and now you've beaten me."

He almost fell for it. Then he saw the mischief that set her brown eyes alight.

"Suck it up, sugar," he said. "There's only room for one monster ego in this motor home."

She pulled a face, then laughed. As he helped her pack up the pieces, his hand brushed hers. Just the tiniest contact, but as always it left him wanting more. As if she'd felt the flare of his longing, she stilled, looked up at him.

"Damn but I like you, Kelly Greenwood," he said. He'd meant to state the obvious, that he wanted to kiss her, but somehow those words about liking had come out instead. They were true—just being with Kelly was more fun than a guy could have anywhere outside of a race car.

Maybe even more fun than a guy could have in a race car.

She flushed as if she'd heard his thoughts rather than his words.

"I like you, too." Her voice caught, and he could see she meant more than *like*.

Something shifted between them, and suddenly Trent saw possibilities that hadn't been there before, not even that night in Richmond when he'd invited her into his bed.

He took her hands in his, drew circles in her palms with his thumbs. She shivered, and just that simple touch made her pupils dilate.

"Maybe after the series finishes, when we're not working together," he said. "Maybe we could…date."

He heard her indrawn breath. "You mean, more than one

date?" she said lightly, but he saw she wanted to know exactly what he was offering.

He wasn't *exactly* certain. He'd spoken in the kind of nervous rush he hadn't felt since high school. "More than one date," he confirmed. "We could go steady." Man, now he sounded like he *was* in high school.

She giggled, and he liked it.

"So, how about it?" he said, and found himself holding his breath.

She pulled her hands from his, clasped them in her lap. "Trent, I can't."

The words hit him like a hammer blow, all the more powerful for their unexpectedness.

"What do you mean *can't?*"

She twisted her fingers. "Like I told you, I want a man who'll be there for me, who'll put my needs ahead of his when he has to. You're not that kind of guy."

He struggled to breathe over the tightness in his chest. "I was only talking about going steady for a few weeks. Or months."

She swallowed, but her gaze didn't waver. "I think I'd start to like you a lot more if we dated. I'd want more than weeks or months. I've lived my whole life with people who see me as a second-class citizen. I don't want to fall in love with a man like my family."

"I don't see you as a second-class citizen," he said, stung.

"You said there's only room for one monster ego in this motor home," she reminded him. "I've decided there's no room at all for a monster ego in my life."

Her rejection left Trent reeling. She must have seen his shock, for she reached over and hugged him in a way that was disturbingly platonic, as if she'd decided to forget those kisses.

He wouldn't let her forget.

He tightened the hug, bent his head to her neck and kissed

the soft skin, exulting when he felt the leap of her heart against his chest. He moved up, found her lips.

She twisted away. "This has to stop, Trent. Not because of what I just said or because I don't want to. Because of the race."

This was getting worse and worse. "What the hell is that supposed to mean?"

She said seriously, "We have no idea how kissing me—kissing anyone—might affect your racing. Even if…even if it doesn't mean anything."

He ran a hand through his hair. "A kiss?" he said skeptically. "You think a kiss can be that dangerous?"

She looked him in the eye. "Some kisses can."

TRENT FOUND HIS ZONE the moment before he pulled onto the Talladega track the next day. He relayed the good news to Kelly, in her usual place next to Rod. Despite several cautions that kept the traffic bunched up for a lot of the race, he was able to pull ahead of the pack when it counted. He finished second behind Danny Cruise.

He'd stayed focused on the track throughout the race, but the moment he climbed out of the car, his focus switched. He had to find Kelly. She owed him a kiss.

Then she was right in front of him, her brown eyes shining, pride and happiness glowing in her face, her mouth curved enticingly. "You were incredible," she said.

"I was, wasn't I?"

She laughed, and he wanted to merge her joy with his. He caught her in his arms, planted what he intended to be a quick, hard kiss on her mouth. It turned into something different altogether, making up for last night, now that there was no danger he might jeopardize his performance on the track.

The only thing in jeopardy was his heart.

Where did that come from? Panicked, he released her. He turned to Chad, began an overenthusiastic analysis of the race.

Chad was more than happy to rehash every glorious moment. But when Trent got onto the subject of how effective his key words had been, Chad turned to Kelly and said, "You did an incredible job, Kelly." His smile was warm, way more intimate than Trent would have liked. Chad had a nerve. Just because he hadn't had a girlfriend of his own in a while he thought he could muscle in on Kelly.

Trent slung an arm across Kelly's shoulders. "Yep, that's my girl."

Chad picked up on the challenge. "Kelly, you're an asset to the entire team. We *all* appreciate what you've done." He was giving Kelly that lady-killer look that Trent hadn't seen him flashing around in months. Did he seriously like Kelly, or was he just trying to bug Trent?

Unable to resist rising to the bait, Trent tightened his grip on her shoulder. "Kelly and I sure do work well together."

"I'm so glad I had the good sense to hire you," Chad told Kelly, "even when Trent wanted to throw you out on your—"

"Will you two grow up?" Angry, Kelly twisted out of Trent's grip. Damn the man! Last night, he'd been so tender, so genuine, she'd almost believed they could have a relationship. Not a permanent one, but by Trent's standards a long one. It had taken all her willpower to refuse to date him. Now, he was using her in some stupid game of one-upmanship with his brother.

And it hurt so badly, it could only mean one thing.

Kelly managed to throw a disgusted look at Trent and Chad before she stalked away. Fast, so Trent wouldn't see the realization in her eyes.

She'd fallen in love with Trent Matheson.

I love him. With all my heart. She wobbled as she walked, had to work to steady herself again.

How unoriginal.

She was a card-carrying member of Planet Belly Button.

What do I do now? Number one: don't tell Trent. Number two: get over it.

TRENT KNEW Danny Cruise wasn't a big fan of his right now, having just been relegated to fifth in the standings, one spot behind Trent.

So when Cruise turned up in Matheson Racing's reception area on Monday morning asking to see him, Trent was naturally wary. No matter that Cruise gave him an affable smile and said "Hey, Matheson, how goes it?" with evident friendliness. Trent confined his response to a noncommittal sound.

"That was some race yesterday," Cruise said. Trent made the noise again. "Guess that shrink of yours got your head in the right place at last."

Trent sensed an agenda being set out. Okay, he'd play along. He shrugged. "I'm the one driving the car."

Cruise's smile widened. "Just as well."

He'd lost Trent. "I don't think Kelly would make much of a racer."

Cruise chuckled, but it wasn't a friendly sound. "Yeah, she's even less reliable than you are."

Ah, so that's what this was about. Undermining Trent's faith in his advisers. Trent relaxed. He didn't blame Cruise for trying. He'd do the same thing himself if their positions were reversed. But having a go at Kelly wouldn't work. She was the best thing that had happened to him in a long time.

Cruise continued, "After that disaster in New Zealand, she's lucky to have any job at all."

Trent willed the muscles of his face not to tauten. "You think?" he said mildly.

"Some would say she's dangerous."

Kelly? Dangerous? Trent exhaled in relief. Cruise had definitely gotten this wrong. "They'd be liars," he said, annoyed at the shortness in his voice.

"She was lucky it happened in New Zealand and not in the U.S.A.," Cruise said. "I mean, if you broke your neck as a result of following her advice, you'd sue her for millions, wouldn't you? But down there, you can't sue quacks like her—all you can do is pay them to leave the country." His voice rang with the confidence of truth.

Trent forced out a response. "Get. Out."

A slow smile spread across Cruise's face. "Good luck for Sunday—mind your neck," he said, dropping all pretense of this being a social chat, and sauntering out.

Trent only just restrained himself from running after him and wiping that smug grin off his face. It couldn't be true. Kelly couldn't have caused a client to break his neck, she would have told Trent. But she hadn't said much about her time in New Zealand—that night they'd dined with her family, she'd been downright evasive. Chad had checked the reference she supplied, a sprint car racer in Auckland. The guy had been glowing in his recommendation. But what about the rugby team she'd worked with?

Trent needed air. He strode out to the parking lot. Despite the coolness of the gray day, perspiration broke out on his brow. He could feel the elation of Sunday's race, the invincibility, slipping away. He tried to cling to it, but it was gone, hovering just beyond his reach, tantalizing in its nearness.

He took a deep breath. He could get it back. He would talk to Kelly.

As if his intention had conjured her, she drove into the parking lot in her Toyota. She hadn't seen him, and he watched as she gathered her papers and files off the passenger seat, stacking them so they looked neater than he knew they were.

She tugged her skirt down over her trim little backside, and Trent averted his eyes.

"Hey." She caught sight of him; gladness lifted her voice and she picked up her pace. When she saw his face, she faltered.

"Tell me about New Zealand," he said.

Color drained from her skin, making her brown eyes look darker than normal. "Who told you?"

Dammit, that meant Cruise was right. Trent realized he'd been holding on to the hope that his rival's mischief-making was just that. "I want *you* to tell me."

Kelly looked around, as if some escape route might miraculously appear. She wished beyond wishing she'd found the courage to confess to Trent earlier. "Can we go inside?" she asked, her voice reedy.

He shook his head. "We'll go out." He pulled his keys from his pocket, pressed the button that unlocked the Lamborghini.

She guessed it was sheer habit that had him opening her door for her, snicking it shut without force when surely he would have preferred to slam it. He drove fast, expertly, through the midmorning traffic.

"Where are we going?" Kelly dared to say.

"My place."

She was tempted to ask if they could go to hers. Being on her own territory might shore up her courage.

But if she possessed even a scrap of courage, she'd have told Trent the truth before now.

They drove through the black wrought-iron automatic gates and stopped outside Trent's house. Kelly scrambled out before he could get around to her door. She followed him inside. A few months ago she'd have speculated she was the only young woman in Charlotte who hadn't been here, but now she knew better.

She surveyed the home of the man she loved. Two huge, squashy yellow couches flanked a stone fireplace in the living room. The open-plan room also held a dining area, with ten chairs drawn up to a long oak table. Beyond that, Kelly glimpsed the kitchen, granite and stainless steel. From where she stood, she could see pictures of Trent, hung in no apparent order, on most of the walls. Trent holding up the NASCAR Busch Series trophy. Trent borne on the shoulders of his crew. Trent signing autographs for a couple of kids. On one wall, Kelly saw a picture of a younger Trent, probably only twelve or thirteen, sitting in a go-cart. She recognized an old photo of Brady in his racing uniform, looking more like Chad than ever. Then there was a picture of Trent with his two brothers, all three of them wearing uniforms, helmets tucked under their arms.

Trophies crowded the living room shelves and mantelpiece. Some of them sat askew; all of them could have done with a good dusting. Trent's home was messy, with stuff everywhere, but it had a nice feel about it.

"Sit." He pointed her at a couch. He took a blue-and-white checked armchair for himself and watched her, expectant.

"I worked with a rugby player, a rising star who had some consistency problems."

His eyes narrowed in recognition of the commonality between the rugby player and himself.

"With my help, he became more reliable, and he was selected for the New Zealand national team." She said defensively. "His coach and his family gave me the credit."

Trent nodded, and she wondered if there was a chance she could come out of this okay.

"In his first international game, he didn't go in hard enough on a tackle that would have prevented a winning try—that's like a touchdown. He was furious with himself, and he lost a lot of confidence."

Trent nodded, and she could see he understood.

"I worked with him to rebuild his confidence, got him to do some easy tackles during practice, then build up to some more aggressive moves during his games for his home team.

But when the next international game came around, the stress got to him again. He had the chance to make a tackle—it wasn't even a crucial moment—and he overcompensated. He went in too hard, things got messy with a couple of other players, and he broke his neck."

Trent's hand went involuntarily to his own neck.

"He recovered fully," Kelly assured him, "but the accident ended his career. He blamed me, so did his parents, so did his coach. I'd pretty much kept to myself, and I didn't have anyone who could take my side or help me get another job. So I came home."

She waited for Trent's reaction.

He blew out a long breath. "Was the accident your fault?"

She shook her head. "Not unless you think I should have total control over my client's decisions. He chose to go against my advice."

"Maybe you should have taught him the judgment skills to determine the aggression he'd need at that level of play."

Others had said the same.

"I did everything I could. I couldn't build toughness in him, I could only advise him how to build it himself. Whether he achieved that or not came down to his own efforts." She thought about the times she'd suggested to her client he use his judgment to vary the strength of his tackles, but he'd refused. But that was normal. No client ever did exactly what you advised, Trent included.

"There must be something else," he said. "Something you're not telling me. What you've told me isn't enough for them to blame you."

She lifted her chin. "There's nothing else, I give you my word."

He made a *pfff* sound that might have been disbelief. "Why didn't you tell me this at the start? Did Chad know?"

She felt herself coloring. "I knew I hadn't done anything

wrong, but that kind of admission isn't the way to start a job interview. You'd have had me out of there in five seconds."

He didn't deny it. "You lied then, how do I know you're not lying now? That there isn't more to it?"

"I didn't lie. I chose not to tell you something that couldn't easily be explained but which I knew had no impact on my ability to work with you. I realized almost immediately I'd done the wrong thing, and I've been looking for the right opportunity to tell you ever since." She willed him to believe it.

"What did your family say?"

She froze. "They, uh…"

"You didn't tell them?" he said, incredulous.

Kelly knotted her fingers. "You know what they're like."

"A little quick to condemn," he said, "but nice folks who love you."

"They think nothing of me." Kelly saw recognition in his eyes, and pushed her point home. "I couldn't tell them I'd failed yet again, just as I had with chess."

"They love you," he reminded her.

"They do," she agreed. "But I want more. I wanted to get this job, to do a brilliant job for you—which I've done— and show them how good I am before telling them about… the other."

Trent raked a hand through his hair, uncertain how to respond. On one level he wanted to take Kelly into his arms, kiss away the hurt that darkened her eyes and put that quiver in her lips.

But on a practical level he had to wonder, what did this mean for his racing? He'd come to rely on her, and he was only just beginning to realize how much. Could Trent trust her when she said it wasn't her fault? It didn't *sound* as if it was her fault—but then she'd already concealed the truth from him once. Twice, if he counted the chess thing.

Maybe she hadn't even admitted her culpability to herself. Maybe she'd built that guy up to believe he could win, without underpinning that with real skills. Maybe that's what she'd done to Trent, with her key words and her routines.

Of course, this was exactly what Danny Cruise wanted Trent to think. But, hell, sometimes what you see is what you get.

Trent stood, paced the floor, more rattled than he'd felt since the day Kelly had first shown up in his office. So much had happened between them since then. He'd trusted her.

He longed to trust her still. But there was too much at stake. The NASCAR NEXTEL Cup Series, the business, his relationship with his father and Chad. His heart.

He stood, paced to the other side of the room and looked back at her, still and hunched on the couch.

"You don't believe me." The wounded look in her eyes almost undid him.

He raked a hand through his hair again. "I don't know what to believe. You haven't been straight with me."

"All the work we've done together has been straight," she said. "That's real."

He shook his head.

"If you've lost confidence in me—" her voice cracked and she paused "—I can't work with you." The rise at the end of the sentence made it a question.

There was only one answer Trent could give. He told himself she would be expecting it. She knew that in the end, Trent Matheson was all about Trent Matheson. "I'm sorry, Kelly. I won't risk the Cup."

She flinched as if he'd hit her. Dammit, he felt like a heel, when she was the one who'd lied. "I'll go back to the office and collect my things," she said.

"I'll take you." He grabbed his keys off the coffee table, but she shook her head.

"Please, Trent, I'd rather go alone. If you could call a

cab, I'll wait outside." She pulled out her wallet and leafed through it, maybe to check she had enough money to pay for a cab, but mainly, Trent figured, to avoid his eyes. "Race well on Sunday." Her lips barely moved as she spoke—she looked frozen.

She walked out of his home with a dignity that kicked at Trent's conscience.

CHAPTER THIRTEEN

TRENT DIDN'T PUT too much thought into the reason for the summons to his father's office the next day. He'd been too shattered by the encounter with Kelly to care about much else.

Yet there was no reason for him to feel guilty, to feel as if he'd somehow failed her. Even Chad, when he'd heard the truth, had agreed it would be difficult for Trent to trust her advice now.

Julie-Anne wasn't in the outer office when Trent arrived. But Brady's door was ajar. Trent heard the murmur of voices, so he went on in.

He found Julie-Anne in Brady's arms. The embrace was loose, but their foreheads touched, and the warm, teasing, intimate tone of Julie-Anne's voice made Trent think of Kelly.

He cleared his throat, and the two sprang apart. Trent almost laughed at the flush that spread up Brady's neck and over his face.

"Hi, Trent." Julie-Anne pushed her hair back behind her ears and spoke with a casual friendliness at odds with Brady's discomfort. Brady gave a growl that might have been hello.

Julie-Anne shot Trent a mischievous grin as she walked past him. He smiled back. Good for her. She'd managed to get past Dad's crusty exterior.

"Heard you got rid of Kelly," Brady barked, probably to overcome his embarrassment.

"Yep." Trent pulled out a chair and sat down. He wanted

to talk about Kelly even less than he suspected his father wanted to talk about Julie-Anne.

"Was that wise?" Brady asked.

Trent sighed. So much for subjects best left undiscussed. He explained the circumstances behind Kelly's departure.

"She should have told you," Brady said.

"She should," Trent said, relieved.

"But you shouldn't have let her go."

Dad was starting to sound like Kelly, adding these little riders every time he said something approving. "Why not?" He figured Dad would tell him anyway.

"I like her," Brady said. "She's good for you. Not just for your racing."

"What?" Surely Dad didn't mean—

"You care about her. I could see it when Chad and I met with you two after the race at Chicago."

"Dad."

Brady put his hands up in mock self-defense. "Sorry, son, but that's what spending too much time with Julie-Anne does to a guy."

"Turns his brain?" Trent asked.

"Sets him thinking about feelings." Brady frowned. "Mind you, I'm not saying that's a good thing."

"Absolutely not," Trent said emphatically. "Dad, what did you want to see me about?"

Brady looked as relieved as Trent to end that too-personal conversation. He resumed his normal gruff demeanor as he said, "I've been thinking about what you said, about wanting to run this place when I retire." His large hand made a sweeping gesture that encompassed all of Matheson Performance Industries.

It wasn't want Trent had expected. "Uh-huh," he said cautiously.

"I like what you're doing, going to those college classes."

Another surprise. Then Brady added, "Though you should have said something and we could have fitted it around your racing. Then maybe you wouldn't have been so distracted."

Once again, Brady was starting to sound like Kelly. "You're right," Trent said. Though they both knew he wouldn't have found a sympathetic ear in his father or Chad.

Brady looked mollified. "I respect your intentions," he said. "I respect *you*."

"Really?" Shock had Trent blurting the word. Dad had never, ever indicated that he respected Trent for anything more than his ability as a race car driver.

"Of course." Irritation shadowed Brady's face. But Trent saw guilt, as well, and realized his father was annoyed at himself. "I asked you here to tell you I'll take a look at whatever ideas you've got for the business."

"You mean…I'm in the running for the job?"

"I didn't say that. All I'm saying is, I won't be too hasty in dismissing what you have to say."

Trent couldn't tell exactly what that meant. But he figured it had to be progress over Dad's earlier outright refusal to think of him as anything other than a driver. Brady got to his feet and Trent knew the meeting was over.

He stood. "What changed your mind, Dad? Last time we discussed this, you said no way."

Brady frowned and said defensively, "A man can think things over, can't he?"

Maybe, but Brady Matheson didn't. Trent waited. Brady reddened again. "Julie-Anne gave me a shove in the right direction," he mumbled.

Against all odds, Trent kept a straight face. "Okay," he said, as if it was the most normal thing in the world for the immovable Brady Matheson to have his head turned by a woman.

He stuck out a hand and Brady shook it. Trent had the craziest urge to give his father a hug. He almost thought he saw the same impulse in Brady's eyes. He contented himself with tightening his grip on his father's hand, and put his appreciation into that firm handshake.

On his way out, he stopped beside the photocopier, where Julie-Anne was stapling memos. She gave him her usual bright smile, not the least bit embarrassed at having been caught kissing her boss.

"Thanks," Trent said. He kissed her cheek. Unlike him or his father, she had no hesitation in wrapping her arms around him and hugging him.

"Everyone deserves a shot at what they want," she said.

Trent hoped that if Brady was what she wanted, she would get him.

"Now," she said, "you just need to fix things up with Kelly."

He detached himself from her embrace. "That's not going to happen." He meant it, even though without Kelly to share it with, Dad's change of heart felt like a hollow victory.

AT CHARLOTTE, he raced like a rookie. His key words didn't get him into the zone, then he rode his tires too hard and found himself struggling to control the car well short of the first pit stop. The race didn't get any better, and he finished twenty-eighth, after starting seventh on the grid.

"What the hell were you doing? The way you were sliding on that track, you could qualify for the Olympic ice-skating team," Chad said when Trent got of the car.

It was fair criticism. He'd driven appallingly. Now, all he wanted was to call Kelly and—

No. Rewind that. All he wanted was go home, have a beer.

He would do better at Martinsville next week. Without Kelly.

KELLY SAT IN FRONT of the TV and willed Trent to race better at Martinsville than he had at Charlotte. She'd wept for him, literally, when she'd seen his ashen face last week, the pain in his eyes. Even though he'd smiled at the reporters and done his usual dumb driver act, she could see his failure was tearing him to pieces.

She wanted to tell him to relax, to control his breathing, to keep focused on his key words no matter what anyone else did on the track. Most of all, she wanted to tell him she would love him just as much if he never won another race. Not what any driver wanted to hear from anyone. Least of all Trent, from her.

Now he was doing a prerace interview, which wasn't allowed in his prerace routine. The idiot. Couldn't he at least give today his best shot?

"Did your poor performance last week have anything to do with the departure of Kelly Greenwood from the Matheson Racing team?" the journalist asked. "Why did she leave?"

Kelly shot upright. If he told, she'd be ruined.

Trent gave the man a vacuous smile. "Kelly and I worked well together, and that helped me qualify for the Chase. But we reached a stage where we agreed she'd done all she could."

She put a hand to her chest to calm her pounding heart. Nothing Trent had said would jeopardize the interview she had lined up with SouthMax Racing next week for a job on their driver development program.

Back in the studio, the sportscaster said, "Since Richmond, Trent Matheson's been demonstrating some pretty impressive driving. But now he's looking like he did in his worst moments. Can he find that magic again?"

The answer, it seemed, was no. Passing was always difficult on the Martinsville track, and Trent had qualified far enough back that there just weren't enough opportunities to get any higher than the eleventh place he eventually finished.

TRENT WATCHED the interview on tape on Monday.

The question about whether he'd find the magic again resonated inside him, knotting the tension in his gut into a convolution no Boy Scout would be able to unravel. He hadn't managed to get in the zone the last two races. The more he thought about it, the less likely it seemed that his loss of confidence in Kelly could bear all the blame for his abysmal performance. There had to be some other factor, something he was missing in his routine.

He pulled his notebook toward him, the one Kelly had used for logging his routines. She'd mailed it to him a couple of days after he'd said he couldn't work with her again, which was pretty generous.

He ran his finger down the "night before the race" list, checking each item with his finger. He'd had a light dinner, spent the evening with Chad and Rod, keeping them up until 2:00 a.m. despite their protests. He'd slept five hours, had Shreddies for breakfast. He hadn't returned his father's call, confining his conversation to Chad and Rod. He'd kept his breathing even and cleared his mind of thoughts of anything other than the race.

He'd started the race with his key word *smooth*. The start hadn't gone quite as well as he'd have liked, but he'd regained the places he'd lost by the end of the first quarter.

He remembered the moment he'd shot past Danny Cruise, Rod's shout of elation over the radio. For half a second, Trent had anticipated Kelly's gleeful comment. Then he'd remembered she wasn't there, wasn't standing beside Rod the way she'd been during all his best races.

The way she'd been during all his best races.

That was it! The truth was so obvious, Trent couldn't believe it hadn't smacked him in the face before.

Kelly was the missing X-factor. Not her key words or her routines or Shreddies for breakfast. The fact was, Trent raced best when she was standing next to Rod in the pits.

Kelly brought Trent luck. The pure, dumb luck that often as not was the X-factor that made the difference between a bad race and a good one.

And he'd forced her to quit.

Panic rose in Trent, choking him, making him tug at the neck of his T-shirt. He tried to convince himself he was wrong. But he'd been in this business long enough to know the luck principle worked, no matter how unscientific.

He had to get Kelly back, had to have her next to Rod for the race in Atlanta. And the one in Texas. Every damned race from here to Miami.

If he didn't, he was doomed.

JULIE-ANNE walked into Brady's office—she'd given up knocking weeks ago. Besides, if he was doing anything he shouldn't behind that door, it would be with her. They'd been dating for the last month—if you counted grabbing a burger after a late night at the office as dating. Which you did, when each evening ended with increasingly heated kisses.

Julie-Anne just wished she knew how Brady felt about her. Maybe it was too soon to talk about love—too soon for him. But if he would just give her some hint as to where he saw their relationship going…

Be patient, she told herself.

Despite the fatigue that etched lines at the side of his mouth and darkened his eyes, Brady smiled when she came in. "Hey, gorgeous."

She raised an eyebrow. "You're in a good mood."

"Comes from seeing you," he quipped. She knew that really it stemmed from his relief they were almost done with this proposal for his potential investor in MPI. But she didn't contradict him, and she didn't argue when he stood up, came around his desk and took her into his arms.

This was her favorite place in the whole world. He might not love her yet, but she had fallen for Brady Matheson lock, stock and barrel.

She lifted her mouth for his kiss, reveled in the hands he

ran through her hair, the closeness of his hard, masculine body, the moan of need that escaped him.

"How do you do this to me?" he muttered, before he moved his lips down to her neck.

"Just lucky, I guess." The words came out a breathless, girlish mess. That was how he made her feel—like a girl in love.

"I'm the lucky one," he growled.

Julie-Anne pulled back. She absorbed the pallor of his face. "It's past six, you should go home. You were here till midnight last night."

He smiled at her concern. "No time, Gypsy." He'd adopted the nickname a few days ago, and Julie-Anne found she liked it. "Besides, you stayed late yesterday, too, and you're still here."

"I'm younger than you." She added mischievously, "A *lot* younger."

He swatted her behind.

"I'll tell you a secret," she said. "I have a thing about older guys."

Brady tugged her into his arms. She'd been here once today already, but it wasn't enough for him. Hungry, he devoured her. She responded, every inch of her warm, soft body pressed against him, those curves melding against his chest. He wanted her more than he could remember wanting anyone since Rosie.

Damned if there wasn't a tightness in his chest when he thought about Julie-Anne's easy affection, her generous spirit. She made him feel ten years younger. Twenty years younger. But as he leaned into her, he felt a faint tremor that told him however young he felt inside, his body knew exactly how old it was. Julie-Anne was right, he was exhausted.

The only bright spot about all this pressure was the amount of time he got to spend with her. He could hardly bear to leave her each night.

He murmured against her ear, "Come home with me." He'd

never asked before, but they'd been building up to this for weeks. For too long.

Her answer was a sigh of longing, a renewed energy in her response to his kisses until he thought he might explode. "Please," he groaned.

She broke off the kiss, breathing as heavily as he was. "If I come home with you tonight," she said seriously, "where does that leave us tomorrow?"

That was why he hadn't asked her sooner. Brady slackened his grip, put a few inches of space between them. Without meeting her eyes, he pushed a strand of hair back behind her ear. "I'm very fond of you, Gypsy."

He chanced a glance at her. Her eyes shone with disappointment. Didn't she know by now he wasn't given to flowery overstatement? That fondness was a big deal? That he couldn't in all honesty promise more?

"But I'm too old to start over," he said. She moved out of his embrace and he realized he'd messed up totally. But now he'd started, he might as well go all the way. "I'm busy with the company, with the boys."

"You're not busy with the boys," she broke in. "You do your thing, they do theirs, and once a week you get together to slap each other on the back before you go your separate ways again. You don't know the first thing about having a real relationship with your kids. Do you know why Trent wants to run the business? Why Zack doesn't speak to you more than once a month? Why Chad's so unhappy?"

Dammit, he didn't even know Chad *was* unhappy—though now he thought about it, his oldest son's sense of humor had gone AWOL a while back and never returned. Nor did Brady know the answers to Julie-Anne's other questions. In self-defense he snapped, "That's rich coming from a woman who hasn't lived with her daughter for seventeen years." He'd hurt her, the redness in her cheeks told him that. But she'd been out of line.

"I'm not just looking for sex, Brady," she said. As if he

hadn't figured that out in the last two minutes. "I want someone who loves me enough to share his whole life with me."

"You mean marriage?" he said, aghast.

"Yes, I mean marriage. But more importantly, I mean your heart, your thoughts, your feelings, your…everything."

Her words terrified him. If he married her, there would be no holding back. Every emotion would be up for grabs. He hadn't done that since Rosie. Back then he'd been young, he'd relished the ups and downs of being in love. Now, he had his life organized the way it suited him. He didn't want to feel that all-consuming love for a woman.

"I'll take that as a no," she said in a small voice.

Had she been proposing?

She blinked rapidly, then she ran her hands through her hair in a smoothing gesture, as if she could ever tame its thickness.

"I think," she said, "we'd better stop seeing each other."

By which, no doubt, she meant stop kissing each other, stop taking a break for coffee together, stop sharing all the little details of their days.

It sounded lonely.

"Let's not be hasty," he said, selfish to the last. "Maybe we could just carry on as we are, and see how things go?"

As he expected, his offer didn't cut much ice. Julie-Anne shook her head. She left the room without a word. Brady heard her gathering her things up in the outer office. There was still time to call out to her, to get her back in here, to tell her he wanted to try doing things her way.

He stayed silent.

KELLY'S CELL PHONE rang as she entered the reception at SouthMax Racing. She glanced at the display, intending to turn off the phone. Then she saw who was calling.

She shouldn't answer it, not when she was on the verge of an important job interview.

She smiled an apology at the receptionist who'd just phoned through to the team owner to announce her arrival, and turned away as she answered the call. "What do you want?"

"Missing me, sugar?" Trent's voice disturbed a bunch of butterflies in her stomach, made her feel fluttery all over.

"No," she said.

"I'm thinking about giving you another chance."

She almost dropped the phone, fumbled it with both hands in her attempt to hold on to it. She got it back up to her ear. "Let me guess." She wasn't about to show him how her spirits had leapt at his words. "Because you drove so badly the last two weeks?"

For a moment, he was silent. Then he said, "Something like that," with a meekness that made her suspicious.

"You're too late," she told him in a low voice. "I'm at SouthMax—I have an interview right now."

"No!" The alarm in his voice was genuine. "You have a contract with Matheson Racing."

"Which you terminated."

He tutted. "Chad never confirmed that with you, I checked. You're still being paid."

"I assumed that was severance."

"Come back here and we can argue over the details," he said. "Hell, you can have a pay raise if you want."

"What's going on?" she demanded. "What are you up to?"

Silence again. So long, she thought he'd hung up. The swing doors behind the reception opened, and the owner of the SouthMax team emerged, hand outstretched in welcome.

Kelly fumbled for her phone's off button.

As Trent said, "I need you, Kelly."

SHOW KELLY the woman who could resist a plea like that from the man she loved, and she'd show you a woman made of granite. She stayed at SouthMax just long enough to explain her change of circumstances, then hotfooted over to Matheson Racing.

It felt like coming home.

Trent was unmistakably relieved to see her. So were Chad and Rod. Kelly didn't waste time asking questions about Trent's change of heart. Right away she had him debrief her about the last two races, trying to figure out where things had gone wrong.

"So you couldn't find the zone, and 'smooth' wasn't working as well as it has in previous races?" she clarified at one point.

"Yeah, I said that." Trent glanced at his watch, as if he was impatient to be somewhere else. Kelly decided to overlook it. No doubt it had been difficult for him to admit he needed her—he might even have some resentment about having her back. She didn't care.

"Right," she said briskly. "We might need to consider refining our key words."

"Uh-huh," Trent replied.

Kelly told her hackles not to rise. "We need to do that before the race in Atlanta."

His gaze sharpened. "You'll be there, won't you?"

She detected an undertone of anxiety. A tender warmth spread through her. He really wanted her there, and she could tell it wasn't just about her skills as a psychologist. In some way or other, Trent cared.

She smiled what felt like the goofiest smile in history. "Of course I'll be there."

"And you won't leave?"

Maybe he cared even more than she dared think. "I won't leave," she said, blinking away tears.

His shoulders relaxed. "That's great, sugar," he drawled.

CHAPTER FOURTEEN

ATLANTA WAS ONE of the best days of Kelly's life. Trent had a dream race, right after a dream practice and dream qualifying. In the seventh of the ten races in the Chase for the NASCAR NEXTEL Cup, Trent shone like a star.

"Kelly, sugar, are you there?" he asked, as he took the lead on lap 280. It was the fifth time he'd been out in front today, more than any other driver.

"Present and correct," she said. He'd been in regular radio contact with her right through the race. Not so often that he'd get distracted, but enough to make her feel the work they'd done was key to today's improved performance. "You're doing great," she said, "just keep those words going."

"Sure thing, sugar."

Kelly strained to see him across the far side of the track. He'd be back around this side in a few seconds, but she wanted to see him as far as she could. She slid down off the pit box.

Rod's hand clamped on her shoulder. "Where are you off to?"

Kelly blinked. "I thought I'd watch from the wall."

"Stay here, Trent'll be pitting soon."

She thought they'd agreed Trent would pit on lap 300, but she didn't argue. Tensions were high, even with Trent doing so well, and after the last couple of weeks she wasn't about to rock the boat.

The one other time she tried to move, after Trent had pitted and gone back out again, one of the over-the-wall guys shepherded her back to Rod, a look of alarm on his face. Kelly wondered if the team didn't trust her. It wasn't a pleasant thought. She recalled her first weeks at Matheson Racing, when they'd been so resentful of her after she'd labeled Trent an airhead. Maybe her temporary departure had made them doubt her loyalty.

When Trent floored it past the checkered flag in third place, which put him fifth in the standings, Kelly's heart almost burst with joy. The team's distrust was the last thing on her mind.

THE MOOD AMONG the Matheson Racing crew fizzed with excited anticipation that, in Texas, Trent would once again deliver a result that would bring him back into contention for the series win.

Kelly had worked with him all week, alternately pleased by his interest in her advice, then frustrated by his habit of going off into a space in his head that she couldn't reach. Sometimes, she'd swear he wasn't listening to a word she said.

On Sunday afternoon, she took up her usual position next to Rod.

Trent started on the front row, next to pole-sitter Tony Stevens. When the green flag fell, both drivers flew into Turn One. Kelly knew Trent wanted the low groove—during practice he'd found his car stuck better there than anywhere else. No doubt Stevens wanted it, too.

She whooped when Trent passed Stevens on lap ten. But she knew better than to get excited at this early stage. She chewed on the edge of one thumbnail as Stevens got so close to Trent it looked as if he might bump him.

Was it her imagination, or had Trent lost speed? She stepped away from the pit box toward the wall. Yes, he was definitely—

"Uh, Kelly?" It was Tim, the jackman. "You need to stay over by Rod."

Unbelievable. After all she'd done for Trent the last two weeks, these guys still didn't trust her. "I won't get in the way," she said shortly.

"You really have to go back to Rod." He sounded flustered but determined. Kelly felt her cheeks heating.

"Quit telling me where I can stand," she snapped.

Now he looked panicky, which made no sense at all. "Trent said you have to stand next to Rod or—" He clamped his mouth shut.

"*Trent* said that? Why?"

The kid shook his head, pressing his lips together as if she might try to pry a secret out of him.

Kelly folded her arms. "If you don't tell me, I won't go back to Rod. I'll stand right here for the rest of the race."

To her surprise, the threat worked. He paled, darted a quick look around to check no one else was in earshot, and said, "Trent reckons you bring him good luck when you stand next to Rod."

"*What?*"

"Please, could you just go back there?" The boy sounded really worried now.

Kelly returned to Rod on leaden feet. She registered the relief on the crew chief's face as she joined him. He was in on this, too—they all were. She remembered how Trent had been so anxious to check where she was during last Sunday's race. Sickened, she realized the only reason he'd asked her back onto the team was not because he respected her expertise, not because he'd forgiven her. It was because he thought she was some kind of...of lucky charm. Like Danny Cruise's girlfriend, with the belly button ring that Danny rubbed ahead of each race.

The rest of the race passed in a blur, punctuated by Kelly's curt responses to Trent's occasional queries as to her whereabouts. He came third—a brilliant result—but she didn't hang around to celebrate.

KELLY HAD SPENT YEARS shrugging off the unintentional insults of people she loved but who didn't respect her. She wasn't about to let Trent get away with this deliberate demeaning of her talents. He'd taught her she was worth more than that.

In the run-up to Phoenix, she didn't bother to make any suggestions to Trent—and he didn't ask her for any. His not asking was all the proof she needed that she was here to bring him luck, not skill.

Instead, she went shopping. At the team store, she bought a tight red T-shirt with a deep V neck and a pair of black pants that sat low on her hips, fitted to her knees then flared outward. She already owned a pair of high-heeled red cowboy boots.

On race day, she got dressed in her hotel room. She left her hair down, applied more makeup than usual, and, the pièce de résistance, carefully attached a fake belly button ring to her spray-tanned midriff. *Let's give Trent something to rub.*

The burst of bravado evaporated, and she quailed at the thought of confronting him before the race. She delayed her entry to the pits until he'd joined the lineup out on the track.

Kelly held her head high as she headed for Rod. She heard the beginning of a catcall, quickly stifled, then a few murmurs of approval. Rod turned to see the cause of the commotion. His jaw dropped, and several seconds elapsed before he remembered to close his mouth again. She sent him a serene smile, as she took her assigned position. "Has Trent been asking for me?"

Rod made a strangled sound, then shut his mouth, swallowed, and tried again. "Yeah, I told him you were on your way."

Kelly clipped on her headphone. "Trent, I'm here," she said, her voice saccharine sweet.

"You okay?" She heard the hesitation in his voice.

"Just fine, cutie pie," she said.

Snickers erupted behind her.

"What's going on, Kelly?" Now he sounded worried, and she realized she risked jolting him out of the zone. No matter how mad she was, she didn't want to do that.

"Just kidding around." She reverted to her usual matter-of-factness, and thought she heard a breath of relief in her ear.

Trent's performance was polished and close to perfect. Even when his second pit stop turned costly—an eagle-eyed NASCAR inspector noticed a loose lug nut and forced the crew to return to the right side of the car, extending the pit stop out to nineteen seconds—Trent didn't lose focus. He finished fifth, having started the race in fourteenth.

TRENT COASTED into the pits and climbed out of the car. Immediately, he got caught up in the back-slapping and the high-fiving, but at the first opportunity, he looked around for Kelly. Dammit, he couldn't see her, and he wanted more than anything to share the triumph that had elevated him to third in the series standings.

He scanned the crowd, but there was no sign of her in the crisp shirt and staid pants he'd come to consider one of the most welcome sights in the world. His gaze skimmed past a particularly attractive, tight-clad derriere that belonged to a woman who was talking to Chad. Blond hair hung flirty down her back, and when she stretched, her tight red look-at-me T-shirt lifted from her black pants to give a moment's peek at a tanned midriff and the glint of gold in her navel. As Trent moved on, the woman turned to face him and he got an eyeful of cleavage.

A couple of male onlookers, tourists with garage passes, were practically drooling as they looked at—*Kelly!*

"What the—?" Trent strode forward.

She turned ever-so-briefly from her conversation with Chad and said with a sunny smile, "Great race." Then she resumed talking to Trent's brother.

Trent paused only to yank on the Energy Oil banner that hung suspended above the work area. He ignored the ripping of fabric, focused only on Kelly. Alarm widened her eyes as he got close enough for her to register his anger.

He wrapped the flag around her, protecting her from the frank appreciation of the men standing around gawping.

"Show's over," he announced, with enough menace in his tone that the drooling visitors turned away with remarkable speed.

"Have you gone crazy?" Kelly squirmed underneath the protective cover, her arms pinned to her sides.

"No, I haven't, despite your best efforts to drive me that way," he snapped. "What the hell are you wearing?"

Her tawny eyes blazed an unexpected, angry heat that turned him on more than he could have imagined. "I'm dressing the part," she hissed.

"What part?"

"Your good luck charm. The one who stays right by Rod throughout every race."

Uh-oh. Trent wondered fleetingly how she'd found out. But that wasn't his biggest problem. His biggest problem was that his lucky charm looked fit to combust—and he needed her for next week's final race.

Yeah, he felt a little guilty about using her the way he had. But the NASCAR NEXTEL Cup Series Championship was way more important.

"Calm down, sugar," he placated her. "I admit I should have told you. But you're not exactly Snow White in the 'should have told you' department, so I figured you'd understand."

"You figured wrong," she said coldly. "But here's something *you* can understand. I. Quit."

She somehow managed to fight her way out of her wrapping, and now Trent had a full view of the bosom that heaved with outrage. He longed, ached with the longing, to put his hands to her waist, to haul her to him and take her mouth in a kiss she'd never forget. But even he could see she was too mad for that. Besides, the guys were back to their ogling.

He picked the banner up off the floor, with the intention of dressing her in it again, maybe a little less restrictively. But she took advantage of his movement to step away, and before he could stop her, she was stalking through the crowd.

"Kelly, come back," Trent called after her. Around him, crew members stopped what they were doing and looked after her, at the sway of her derriere. Then they looked at him, standing there like an idiot, begging a woman who'd been nothing but trouble to him—when she wasn't bringing him luck—to come back. Trent caught Chad's pitying smile, saw the smirks some of the younger guys couldn't suppress.

He was damned if he was going to run after Kelly. Next thing, she'd be expecting him to go down on his knees and beg. It wasn't going to happen.

JULIE-ANNE had passed the last two weeks alternately mortified and furious. Mortified at her own stupidity in mistaking Brady's attraction to her for love. But her fury was directed at Brady. Couldn't that mule-headed man recognize a good thing when it was right in front of him?

Today, the day of their presentation to Rieger Investment, he looked even worse than she did, his shirt only adequately ironed, the knot in his tie crooked. Two weeks ago, she'd have straightened it for him. Now she said politely, "You need to check your tie in the mirror."

He did as she said, fixed it up. They were ready to leave. She ordered the taxi that would take them into uptown Charlotte. Brady questioned her decision, as always, but she told him they didn't want to fuss with parking ahead of such an important meeting. He grunted his acceptance.

As he got into the cab beside her, he sighed heavily. He looked gray. "Are you okay?" she said.

He didn't meet her eyes—he'd been avoiding eye contact ever since they'd broken up. "Bad sleep."

Served him right. The fifteen-minute cab ride passed in silence. Brady's lips moved occasionally, and Julie-Anne guessed he was rehearsing his pitch. He rubbed at his chest. "Indigestion," he growled when he caught her looking at him.

Good. She hoped he choked on his lunch, too. *After* he'd done a great presentation.

They arrived at the Rieger Investment offices, where Brady's lawyer and accountant were waiting for them in the lobby. The receptionist phoned through the news of their arrival.

"Go on up," she told them. "I'm afraid the elevator is out of order—we're waiting for the technician. You'll have to take the stairs to the fourth floor."

"What's the bet Rieger's making us walk up just for the hell of it?" Brady said to Julie-Anne out of the corner of his mouth. It was the friendliest thing he'd said in days, and she smiled, willing to break the ice.

By the time they got to the fourth floor, Julie-Anne was regretting wearing her high-heeled pumps. She was out of breath—though not as out of breath as Brady, who was puffing in a way she could see annoyed him. Sweat stood out on his brow.

She was about to ask again if he was okay when she caught his glare. Pressing her lips together, she followed him into the meeting room.

Rieger stood up to greet them, as did the posse of lawyers and accountants seated at the far side of the boardroom table. The Matheson team took the near side, Brady at the end closest to the projection screen, Julie-Anne next to him so she could hand him what he needed at the right moments. She and Rieger's secretary were the only women there. The room so pulsed with testosterone, Julie-Anne could almost see it.

Some of her worry eased when Brady started to talk. He did a great job of presenting the proposal they'd worked on so hard. He was articulate, persuasive, even charming in his gruff way. Through his exhaustion, he shone. Julie-Anne knew from what he'd told her that Rieger was a nervous investor—surely Brady's performance today would reassure even the most jittery.

He'd been talking for about fifteen minutes when Julie-Anne noticed his tiny grimace. He rubbed at his chest. That indigestion must be playing up again.

Not indigestion.

A heart attack.

Realization and memory assailed her, making the floor drop out from under her so that she clutched the edge of the table. Her sudden movement jerked the audience's attention toward her. Brady frowned, but kept going.

Julie-Anne forced her nerveless fingers to pick up a pen. Silently, she pulled a piece of paper out of the stack in front of her. A page of their carefully prepared contract. Too bad. She turned it over. What should she write? Brady would only have a second to read it, so she couldn't give a long explanation of how the symptoms he'd displayed this morning— shortness of breath, perspiring, chest pain, the grayness of his complexion—were an exact replica of the symptoms of her brother's coronary. The doctors had said that if they'd reacted faster, Tom might have lived.

In dark, block capitals she scrawled, YOU'RE HAVING A HEART ATTACK. HOSPITAL NOW.

She slid it along the table to Brady, saw the flicker of his eyes as he registered its presence. But he didn't look down. She could have screamed.

Half a minute later, there was a natural pause while he shut down the PowerPoint presentation and prepared to answer questions. At last, he scanned her note. His brows drew together and he sent her a disbelieving glance. She gave him a barely discernible nod. His negative shake of the head was equally subtle. But its message wasn't. He didn't believe her, and he wasn't about to go to the hospital.

Damn Brady Matheson and every stubborn bone in his beautiful body! Damn him for always thinking he knew best, for always taking hours and days to be convinced otherwise. Hours and days he might not have.

He sat down, pushed the paper back to her, then looked around the table. "Any questions, gentlemen?" He sounded relaxed and confident. The presentation had gone well and everyone around that table knew it.

It seemed there were plenty of questions, for several people spoke at once. Brady put up a hand to quiet them, then directed Rieger's head lawyer to take first turn.

"I have some concerns about these profit projections," the man said. "They rise dramatically between years three and four."

It was a question they'd anticipated. But Julie-Anne didn't give Brady the chance to launch into his prepared answer.

"I'm sorry, Mr. Green," she said. Everyone's eyes swiveled toward her. "Brady's having a heart attack and I need to get him to the hospital."

There was a moment's stunned silence. Then pandemonium broke out, with questions being hurled in all directions. Above it all, Rieger's voice rang out. "What kind of stunt is this, Matheson?"

Brady looked mad enough to spit. "I apologize for Ms. Blake, gentlemen. She's been under a lot of stress getting ready for today. I assure you I'm in perfect health and I'm ready to answer your questions."

Loudly and deliberately, Julie-Anne said, "You are having a heart attack. You must go to the hospital." She thumped her fist down onto the table, rattling coffee cups and making several people jump. "Now."

"If there's any chance she's right, it wouldn't be legally

safe for us to continue these negotiations," one of Rieger's lawyers opined.

Julie-Anne saw red. "*Legally* safe? This man could die today, and you're worried about legalities?" She leaped to her feet, and he flinched.

Brady stood, too. He rounded on Julie-Anne, his face puce with fury. "You're fired," he said. "Get out of here."

Julie-Anne picked up her purse. She grabbed the stack of papers in front of Brady, piled them on top of her own stack, then scooped the whole lot up in her arms and headed out the door.

CHAPTER FIFTEEN

"BRING THAT BACK," Brady roared. She ignored him, raced to the elevator, jabbed the button. Then she remembered it wasn't working and sprinted for the stairs. Brady almost grabbed hold of her, but she slipped past him and ran downstairs, praying all the way that she wouldn't fall and break her neck in these heels, that when she got outside there would be a taxi, and that Brady wouldn't expend so much energy racing after her that he died before they got to the hospital.

God was listening on all counts. She made it to the reception in one piece, having lost a few pieces of paper on the way down. Someone was alighting from a taxi right outside the building, and when Brady threw himself into the back of the cab behind her, he was still alive. And enraged.

"To Presbyterian Hospital, he's having a heart attack," she shrieked at the driver, even as Brady began to grapple with her for the files. She knew from experience the hospital offered the best cardiac treatment.

"You sure you don't want an ambulance?" The guy pulled out into the traffic with a suddenness that sent Julie-Anne's head crashing against the window.

The thud, and her yelp of pain, ended the struggle. She was clutching the papers in a death grip, Brady sprawled half on top of her.

"Are you nuts?" His words came out a rasping croak.

Julie-Anne didn't answer. He knew why she'd done this.

She shut her eyes, kept praying he would be okay. Brady was panting heavily, trying to regain his breath. She wondered if he realized how terrible he sounded.

The drive to Presbyterian Hospital took a little over five minutes. Julie-Anne didn't realize the taxi driver had radioed ahead until staff—nurses, an orderly—came running to meet them. Someone hauled open the door of the taxi, and a burly guy grabbed Brady and pushed him into a wheelchair so fast, Brady didn't have time to protest. He was wheeled inside, out of Julie-Anne's sight, before she could even get out of the cab.

Now, she burst into tears. Sobs of gratitude that they were here, that he was in good hands. Tears of panic that she might lose him. With shaking fingers, she fumbled with the catch of her wallet and drew out a twenty-dollar bill. She looked at it so long, wondering why on earth she had it in her hand, that the taxi driver gently took it from her.

"You need some help getting in there?" He jerked his head toward the hospital as he handed over her change.

Julie-Anne shook her head. She got out of the taxi and stood for a moment on legs that might give way. Knowing she still had a lot to do, she let strength seep back into her.

The emergency room staff directed her to the chest pain emergency department. "I'm with Brady Matheson," she told a nurse there. "The heart attack."

Things moved so fast they were a blur. As soon as the doctors confirmed it was a heart attack, they whisked Brady into the operating room.

All Julie-Anne could do was make the necessary phone calls, then wait.

SOMETIME LATER—probably not much later—Trent arrived. He hugged her tight. "What happened?"

She told him every detail—about the meeting, how well it

had gone, how she'd guessed about the heart attack and tried to warn Brady, how he'd ignored her. Trent made a sound of frustration at that, and she surprised herself by smiling. "You know what he's like."

Trent's gaze sharpened and she realized the tenderness in her tone had given away the depth of her feelings. Oh, well, it couldn't be that much of a shock.

"Where did you leave things with Rieger?" Trent asked.

He was listening to Julie-Anne's description of the chaos that had ensued after her announcement when he saw Kelly.

She hurried into the waiting area, slowed when she saw him. She must have seen his frown, for she said, "Julie-Anne called me. I wanted to come."

Trent nodded to tell her it was okay.

"How is he?"

"Still in surgery." He searched Kelly's face for a sign of softening toward him. But though worry for Brady clouded her face, she kept her distance from Trent, physically and with her refusal to maintain eye contact. She was still mad.

Julie-Anne said, "I guess I'd better call Rieger, tell him what's happened. It'll kill Brady if that guy backs out over this." She flinched when she realized what she'd said, and Kelly squeezed her hand.

"Chad's on his way here. Maybe I should call him on his cell, tell him to go see Rieger," Trent said.

"That's a good idea. Rieger needs lots of reassurance," Julie-Anne said. "Brady says he's a real worrywart."

Kelly spoke up unexpectedly. "If he's short on confidence, then you should be the one to visit him, Trent."

Surprised, he shook his head. "I know next to nothing about this deal."

"You know more than anyone about the kind of confidence that gets people on your side," Kelly said.

Julie-Anne managed a shaky chuckle. "She's right."

"You really think I'm the right person?" he asked Kelly.

"You're the best."

TRENT'S ANXIETY fired him with determination. He was surprised to find it was only an hour since Dad had left that
meeting. Thank God for Julie-Anne's instincts. He shuddered
at the thought of how close he'd come to losing his father.
Even now, who was to say he might not pull through?

Trent should have hugged Dad the other day, when he'd
thought about it.

When he got to Rieger's office, the man and his lawyers
and accountants were back in the boardroom, a result of the
call Trent had made en route. Trent had the receptionist
announce him, but he didn't wait to be admitted. He headed
straight for the fourth floor, taking the stairs, as Julie-Anne
had advised him.

He'd brought the documents she'd walked out with. She'd
briefed him on what they comprised, told him where Rieger's
anxieties lay.

Warned by the receptionist, the men were waiting when
Trent entered.

"Gentlemen." He approached the table, took the seat
opposite Rieger, where he guessed Dad had been sitting.

"How is your father?" Rieger asked, sounding more suspicious than concerned, as if Brady might fake a heart attack
to gain some commercial advantage.

"Having bypass surgery as we speak," Trent said. "The
doctors are confident he'll make a full and swift recovery."
He had no idea if that was the case, but he knew for certain it
was what Dad would want him to say.

"In the meantime," he continued, "I'm here to answer any
questions I can and to assure you of our determination to
proceed with this investment. Our people will be here any

minute." He'd phoned the accountant and the lawyer from his car.

"This is somewhat irregular," Rieger said, his dry voice grating on Trent's tautened nerves.

"This is NASCAR," Trent told him. "It's a business, but it's also a passion. It doesn't work like other businesses."

The conviction in his voice arrested the other man's protest. He steepled his fingers and waited.

Trent's mind blanked. On his way here he'd rehearsed what he would say, but now the words had fled. Panic rose. Swiftly, he collected himself. This couldn't be any harder than a race. What would he do if he was in his car, passing the green flag?

Smooth, he told himself. He said it again. He felt the fog clearing, could see his way ahead.

"Mr. Matheson?" Rieger said.

Trent said, "Winning a NASCAR NEXTEL Cup Series race is all about performance. The car, the driver, the team all have to perform with a synergy that, when you get it right, feels like nothing else on earth. What my father is asking is for you to invest in performance, in making that synergy happen every time."

As his mind cleared, his words came faster, smoother, just like a race car. He made his arguments with precision, overtook the obstacles the opposing team threw at him, even sideswiped a rookie who asked a dumb question. As his confidence grew, he switched key words. *Plenty of room.* He could do this.

At last, he sensed the checkered flag ahead. He couldn't afford to slow down. He kept up the pace to the end, answering questions, handling objections, then hitting a metaphorical finish line with a flourish that was the verbal equivalent of a victory doughnut.

He'd done great, he knew he had. He beamed around the

table. And was mildly surprised when no one gave him a standing ovation.

Instead, Rieger leaned back in his seat, regarding Trent through squinty eyes. His minions did the same in what surely had to be unconscious imitation.

"You present a compelling case," Rieger conceded. "We still have questions about the financials, which I suspect you're not the best person to answer. I'll look forward to reviewing them with you and your father upon his recovery. Which will be…?"

"Very soon," Trent said. Now he'd finished, thoughts of his father's surgery crowded out the exhilaration. He had to get back to the hospital.

THE DOCTORS REPORTED that Brady's quadruple bypass was a success. He would be in the hospital two, maybe three weeks, and it would take several months for a full recovery, but then he would be his old self.

Julie-Anne cried when she heard the news, not caring that Chad and Trent, and their brother Zack, who'd driven from Atlanta the moment he heard about the heart attack, were witnesses to her emotional display.

"Maybe you should go home," Chad told her, sounding worried. "We're grateful for what you did, but it's been a hell of a day for you. You must be shattered."

She stared at him, mute. Clearly Chad had no idea what was going on between her and Brady. Or did he, and did he know she meant nothing to Brady?

"Dad's going to want to see Julie-Anne, probably more than he'll want to see us," Trent told his brothers. "Why don't we go grab some dinner and come back later?"

"But she's—" Chad stopped, but the words "only his secretary" might as well have been splashed in scarlet paint across the lemon-yellow hospital walls.

"No," Trent said, "she's more."

Chad looked at Julie-Anne, and what he saw in her face turned him brick-red. "Sorry," he said awkwardly.

"Call us when he wakes up," Trent told her.

Zack, watchful and silent, nodded at Julie-Anne and followed his brothers out of the waiting room.

As soon as they were gone, she went to the nurses' station and asked if she could sit with Brady.

She perched on the edge of the green vinyl chair next to his bed, held his still hand in hers on the blanket. Every so often his eyelids flickered, and she thought he might wake. But each time he slept on. She was both comforted and frightened by the glowing, beeping monitors that measured his vital signs. The machines told her he was alive, reminded her he could so easily not be.

"Stubborn fool," she told him, with a little shake of his hand.

"I thought I fired you." The words were a rasping whisper, spoken with his eyes closed. A moment later he opened them, and looked at her with a kind of surprised tenderness that tugged at her heart.

"How are you feeling?" she asked stupidly.

"I'm o—" His eyes widened. "Gonna barf." His head lurched forward as he retched. Julie-Anne grabbed the plastic bowl next to the bed and held it under his chin while he vomited.

By the time the nurse responded to her frantic press on the buzzer, Brady was done. He subsided back into the pillows with a groan.

"Cheer up, Mr. Matheson, at least you're alive," the nurse said briskly as she helped clean up. "Nausea isn't uncommon after an anesthetic. We'll see about getting you some meds." She took the bowl and left.

Brady blew out an embarrassed breath. His voice was stronger when he said, "I'll bet that was attractive."

Julie-Anne shrugged. "It's not as if you and I are an item."

He frowned. "Oh, yeah, I broke up with you."

"You didn't break up with me," she said crossly. "*I* broke up with *you* because I wanted more than you can give."

"Yet you're still here," he said, so quietly she had to strain to hear. "You saved my life."

She smiled as she shook her head. "Does that mean you'll un-fire me?"

"No," he said. "But I'd like to un-break up with you."

She tamped down the flare of hope. He was desperately ill, grateful she'd saved him. He probably didn't mean it. Before she could probe further, he closed his eyes, and for one awful moment she thought he'd drifted back to sleep. Then he opened them again. "Maybe better to start over," he muttered.

"You mean, you and me?"

"Well, I don't mean me and Nurse Godzilla out there."

Julie-Anne laughed. She loved that he could make her laugh in the midst of her fears.

"Who's to say if we start over, we won't end up exactly where we did last time?" she asked. "I'm not about to change, Brady. I want a man who'll give of himself. I don't want to get down the track and find out you're never going to be that man." She added frankly, "It hurts too much."

His fingers closed around hers and he pulled her toward him. She smelled the drugs on his breath. "I thought we might fast-forward this time," he said. "To the part where I give you all of me." He looked down at his chest, bare but for the large dressing over the center, with disgust. "What's left of me, at any rate. If you still want it."

She couldn't think of anything she wanted more. But there was still the chance this was delirium. "Maybe we should wait until you have a clearer head."

He growled a low growl that told her he was going to be fine. His grip on her hand tightened. "Would 'Will you marry me?' make more sense?" he demanded.

She gasped.

"Dammit, Julie-Anne, don't make me wait," he said. "I've barely slept these past couple of weeks for worrying that I'd lost you, that I'd screwed up beyond recovery. Hell, worrying about you probably caused this damned heart attack, and if you don't marry me I'll probably have another one from the stress." He sighed. "It's not going to be easy for me to be the touchy-feely guy you want, but I'm damned well going to do it, and when I mess up, you can haul me back into line." His breath came faster, shallower, but he resisted her efforts to shush him. "I love you, woman, I love you so much I can't think straight, I can't sleep, and I've turned down dozens of perfectly good casseroles. Just say yes."

"Yes," she said.

Momentarily, she'd silenced him. Then he blustered, "You mean that, or are you just saying it to stop me having another heart attack?"

"Both," she said, laughing and crying. "But mainly because I mean it."

Satisfaction curved his mouth. "I should damn well think so."

KELLY VISITED Brady in the hospital on Wednesday morning, when she knew Trent would be at his class.

Brady was dozing, so Kelly spent a couple of minutes in whispered conversation with Julie-Anne. Eventually, their murmuring disturbed the patient. He opened his eyes, looked immediately at the empty chair next to his bed, then looked around in alarm.

"I'm here, baby," Julie-Anne said.

Baby? Kelly goggled as Julie-Anne approached the bed and bent over Brady to kiss him. Her eyes nearly fell out when Brady wrapped his arms around his secretary and turned the kiss into something that would likely disturb younger viewers.

*

Eventually, she cleared her throat. Brady relinquished Julie-Anne. The pair of them were somewhat red in the face.

"So…you guys are getting along okay?" she said.

Brady chuckled. "Could say that." He squeezed Julie-Anne's fingers. "Nice to see you, Kelly."

She'd barely finished handing over the motor sport magazine she'd brought him when male voices, raised in good-natured argument, sounded in the corridor.

Trent's voice hit her ears first—he must have cut class—then Chad's. She didn't recognize the third. Then they stood in the doorway—three incredible-looking guys—all tall, dark and unbearably handsome. But only one held Kelly's heart.

Kelly was intrigued to meet Zack Matheson. Despite the physical similarities between him and Trent, he didn't display his younger brother's surface charm. Yet she found his quiet assurance, his guarded smile, appealing.

"Kelly, great to see you." Chad grinned a genuine welcome, then enfolded her in a warm hug. She let herself enjoy a moment of closeness with this man she'd come to view as a friend. She'd missed their easy chats, their mutual enjoyment and frustration over Trent's antics.

"Break it up, you two," Trent snapped.

Chad tightened his grip on Kelly. "Calm down, little brother."

Uh-oh, why did Kelly have the feeling she was about to get caught up in the middle of one of the brothers' frequent arguments?

Zack folded his arms and looked on with interest as Trent took a step toward Chad. "I told you to let her go," Trent said.

Chad pulled away from Kelly so he could see her face, but he didn't relinquish her. "Am I bothering you…*sugar?*"

Kelly giggled at his borrowing of Trent's drawl, Trent's endearment. Before she could deny he was any bother, Trent physically shoved Chad aside.

"Get your own girlfriend, Chad," he said.

Right, that did it. Kelly pulled away from Chad, rammed her hands onto her hips and demanded, "What is your problem, Trent?"

Trent didn't know where to start answering that one. But he did know there was more to that "friendly embrace" than Kelly imagined. Chad was hot for Kelly—who wouldn't be? But that didn't justify this boiling rage, this desire to punch his brother in his self-satisfied, irresistible-to-women jaw.

He ignored Kelly's question and said to Chad, "I mean it, Chad, stay away from my—" Damn, what was she to him? "Kelly," he ended feebly.

"I am not *your* Kelly."

He might have known she'd have something to say about it. The day she took what he said without arguing would be the day some of the light left the world.

To Trent's horror, Chad looked worried, even pitying. He said, "Trent, I'm not flirting with Kelly, I promise."

Trent snorted. "You haven't looked at any woman since she joined the team." He sounded like a jealous idiot, but he couldn't help himself.

Chad took him seriously. "I hadn't paid attention to any woman for a long time before Kelly arrived," he said.

Trent was too mad to listen. "I don't care if she *is* gorgeous, and smart, and funny," he roared. "You'll break her heart."

Kelly gaped. That was rich coming from the only man who had the power to break her heart and who seemed determined to exercise that power on a regular basis.

"Trent, I am *not* after Kelly," Chad shouted. "For Pete's sake, I'm *married*."

A thunderous silence burst over the group. All heads turned toward Chad, whose mouth was clamped so tightly that he looked in danger of breaking his jaw. He backed toward the door, but Zack moved silently to block his exit.

"Married? Who to?" Brady demanded.

When Trent's horrified gaze darted in Kelly's direction, she rolled her eyes. "Not to me."

"No one you know," Chad said.

"When did you get married?" Brady sounded shocked, and hurt. Julie-Anne took his hand in hers.

Chad shook his head, as if he didn't want to talk about it. "Last year. After the race in Vegas."

"You've been married over a year?" Brady's voice rose, until Julie-Anne tapped him sharply on the hand, and he subsided again.

"That's when you took a week off, unplanned," Trent said. "We couldn't get hold of you."

Chad nodded, a curt, resentful movement of his head.

So Chad hadn't even planned to get married? Kelly couldn't imagine this man, a control freak of the finest order, marrying on a whim. He must have fallen hard and fast for his bride.

"So where's your wife?" Zack asked.

"Did I forget to introduce you?" Chad said sarcastically. "Obviously, we split up."

"Why didn't you tell us you got married?" Brady said. "When did you split? Are you getting a divorce?"

Chad shut his eyes. "We got married, we split up pretty soon after. I didn't tell you about it because—" his baleful look encompassed his father and both brothers "—the Brady Bunch doesn't have much time for failure." He folded his arms. "I'm not saying anything else about it right now. So someone better change the subject." He looked fierce, but Kelly heard the plea in his voice.

Brady must have, too, for, though clearly reluctant, he cleared his throat and said, "I have some news. Julie-Anne and I are getting married."

Both Julie-Anne and Kelly groaned at his tactlessness, but Chad pounced on the news with relief. "That's great, Dad." Though Kelly thought his enthusiasm didn't quite ring true.

"Congratulations." Trent shook his father's hand. Then he said, "What the heck," and hugged Brady. He kissed Julie-Anne, and Zack followed suit. In the ensuing discussion of when might be a good date for the wedding, Trent's childish, jealous outburst and Chad's shocking revelation were lost.

"I have more news," Brady said. Everyone looked at him warily, including Julie-Anne. "I already told Chad this yesterday," Brady said. Chad inclined his head.

Brady turned to Trent. "You did a great job with Rieger. My lawyer called. We're good to sign the contracts as soon as I've answered the rest of Rieger's questions."

Trent whooped.

"I decided I'm willing to give you equal consideration with Chad when I decide who takes over the business," Brady said.

"Dad, I—" Trent felt a heat around his eyes, a moistness that told him he was about to overreact in a way that would embarrass both him and Brady. He sucked in a deep breath and said a steady, "Thanks."

Brady nodded. "Whatever I discuss with Chad about the business, anything I teach him, I'll teach you, too. You boys will be on a level playing field."

Although it was what he'd wanted, Trent realized now he'd never believed he would get to this. Emotion threatened to choke him again, so he threw out a question. "What about Zack?"

Brady looked alarmed. "He wants to run the company, as well?"

Zack spoke up. "No, I don't. But I have some news, too." He folded his arms in a way that suggested he didn't want to hear any arguments. "I want to come back on the team."

Once again, stunned silence was the order of the day. Then Brady laughed and beckoned Zack for a hug, which the younger man returned awkwardly.

"You mean—?" Chad said.

Zack nodded. "I want to race in the Cup Series next year. I'm asking you to find a way to make it happen."

Trent noticed Chad looked as if he was biting back some pithy words. No matter that Zack had had to swallow a trailer-load of pride to say what he'd just said, it wouldn't be easy for him to make a comeback. Doubtless Chad was already stressing over where they'd find more sponsorship dollars this late in the day.

But no one was going to refuse Zack a place on the team, not after what had happened. Two years ago, Trent had usurped Zack's position as Matheson Racing's NASCAR NEXTEL Cup Series driver. Zack had quit Matheson Racing to drive for another team. He and Trent had been the final two contenders for the tenth spot in the Chase for the NEXTEL Cup, until Trent had bumped Zack in the closing laps of the deciding race, sending his brother flying into the wall and out of the competition. Zack had accused Trent of hitting him deliberately, and they'd barely spoken since. Things had gone downhill from there for Zack, and he'd quit racing.

So if Zack was holding out an olive branch, the rest of the family would grab it with both hands. But could Trent and Zack work together again?

Now wasn't the time to try to get his head around all that. Trying to confine everyone to a safer subject, Trent said to Brady, "I'll do my best to justify your change of heart, Dad."

"I know you will." Perhaps uncomfortable with the sentiment that hung heavy in the air, Brady made a shooing motion with his hands. "I'm tired, you all better leave." He grabbed hold of Julie-Anne. "Not you, Gypsy."

"I'm not going anywhere," she said.

Trent was glad when Zack decided to ride back to the office with Chad. He needed time alone to absorb what had happened this morning. He watched Kelly get into her car. Damn, he missed her. How much sweeter Dad's capitulation would have been if Trent could have shared it with her. It was thanks to her he'd known how to handle that meeting with Rieger. They should be celebrating. Together.

That wasn't all he wanted to celebrate. He wanted to celebrate Kelly's beauty and her brains, celebrate her gorgeous body by worshipping it with his, celebrate his successes, which without her meant nothing.

"Damn," he said in the face of dawning realization. "I love her."

No matter that Kelly drove him crazy with her refusal to fall for his obvious charms or to accept less than his best. No matter that he'd never wanted to be a one-woman guy.

He loved her.

What the hell was he supposed to do about it?

CHAPTER SIXTEEN

KELLY MADE HER OWN WAY to Miami for the final race of the NASCAR NEXTEL Cup Series. Chad had called to offer her a seat on the Matheson Racing plane, but she'd turned it down. She was on her own again, better get used to it.

She flew into Miami on Saturday morning and checked into the hotel near the track at Homestead, where her whole family was staying. It was, of course, the final of the NASCAR Busch Series tonight, too, and they all wanted to cheer Josh on.

She had a late lunch with them in the hotel restaurant, then they made their way to the track. Josh had given them garage passes, so they went straight there. Her brother was calm, focused, just the way he should be. No one wanted to distract him, so after a short chat, they headed out onto the infield.

"Kelly, Kelly Greenwood," a voice called as they left the building.

Kelly turned to see a camera crew following her. She looked at the signage on the microphone—a Miami TV station she hadn't heard of. They were probably too insignificant to qualify for an interview with anyone from Matheson Racing, and hoped they could get her views on Trent's performance.

She waited for them to catch her up, happy to talk up his chances to anyone who'd listen.

The guy shoved a microphone under her nose. "Kelly, is it true you lost your last job after a client blamed you for a broken neck he suffered during a rugby game?"

Shock robbed Kelly of speech. She closed her mouth, then opened it again.

"Is it true Trent Matheson fired you after he discovered the truth? Do your methods put competitors under undue stress?"

Kelly looked around wildly, saw the shocked faces of her family. None of them, she registered dully, looked as if they didn't believe the reporter. Why should they, when it was true? Behind them, Josh looked horrified. He'd never forgive her if this screwed up his race.

"I have nothing to say." She pushed out at the microphone with a shaking hand. "Leave me alone." It took several reiterations that she had nothing to say to convince the journalist she meant it. At last, the guy turned away in disgust.

Kelly's father said, "How could you screw up like that and not tell us about it?" And although her mother hugged Kelly, her first words were, "You'll never get another job in NASCAR."

Just this once, couldn't they support her? The way Trent had over Josh's wedding fiasco? Then, as now, they'd jumped to the conclusion she must be in the wrong.

It wasn't fair.

Trent had told her she shouldn't let them get away with that behavior and, dammit, he was right.

She rounded on them. "I'm having a tough time here, and the last thing I need is my family bailing on me. What are you guys for?" They looked back at her, identical blank expressions on their faces. Okay, she'd have to spell it out.

"I'm calling you on your lack of respect," she said. "It's time you guys got into line and realized I'm just as much a member of this family as the rest of you celebrities. I may not be famous, I may not be brilliant, but I'm your daughter, your sister, and you owe me your support and protection."

"Honey, of course we support you," Mom soothed her. She quailed under Kelly's fierce glare.

"Then show me," Kelly challenged her, challenged them all.

To her shock, her father wheeled around and strode after the reporter. He tapped him on the shoulder, and a heated debate ensued, which Kelly couldn't hear from here. Then she couldn't see it, either, because Josh enveloped her in a bear hug.

"Sorry, Kel," he said. "This is all my fault. Nikki found out from a friend of hers that you had trouble in New Zealand. She didn't tell me what it was and I told her I didn't want to know. Her dad works for that TV station, she must have given him the story."

"It's not your fault." Kelly sniffled.

He hugged her tighter. "Last night I worked through those questions you gave me. I figured out I do love Nikki and I want to marry her—if it's not too late. I was going to tell her after today's race."

Kelly pulled away. "Okay, now that *is* your fault," she said crossly. "If you'd told her last night, this wouldn't have happened."

He grimaced. "Yeah, I owe you—for getting my head straight and for this garbage." He indicated the camera crew. "Maybe I can—"

"It doesn't matter now," Kelly said. *It's too late.*

LATE SATURDAY NIGHT found Trent flicking between channels on the TV in his motor coach. One more race, and the NASCAR NEXTEL Cup Series would be over. He felt calm, at peace, thanks to his strict adherence to his prerace routine. He'd had an early dinner with Chad and Zack, then they'd gone to watch the NASCAR Busch Series race. It had been a struggle to keep the talk noncontroversial, given the news about Chad's marriage and Zack's intended comeback, the reasons for which Zack had been reticent to share. In the end, they'd agreed both topics were off-limits until after tomorrow's race. All three of them had been feeling their way—which came naturally to none of them—but somehow they'd made it work.

Chad and Zack had gone to buy beer. They'd be back any minute to keep Trent company until his 2:00 a.m. bedtime.

Trent would start tomorrow third in series points. The drivers below him were too far off to be a threat for the series win, but only five points separated him and Danny Cruise at number two. Tony Stevens topped the list, a hundred points ahead of Trent. Trent couldn't beat Stevens unless something went badly wrong for the other driver. Then he'd only have Cruise to worry about.

With such narrow margins involved, he wasn't about to risk a distraction by breaking his routine. He remembered how Kelly calling him an airhead had scuppered his race at Charlotte all those months ago. She'd said she would retract that on air if he won the series. Right now, it looked as if he was condemned to be an airhead.

He still hadn't figured out how he was going to repair things with Kelly, but that was off-limits tonight, too. He would tell her he loved her. Could she accept that, despite his ego, he was different from her family?

Sensing he might be about to shatter that inner peace he'd worked so hard to cultivate, Trent stabbed at the remote control. Nope, couldn't watch his usual station because it was running a preview of tomorrow's race. Kelly had forbidden him to watch any commentary about the upcoming race—together they'd worked out it was one of the things that distracted him.

The football on another network didn't hold Trent's interest for more than five minutes. He wished Chad and Zack would hurry up. He flicked through the local TV stations. The umpteenth rerun of *Golden Girls*—popular fare in this part of the world, he guessed—a high-school football game on some kind of alternative channel, and then a local news channel featuring…Kelly!

He'd flicked past it, so now he zapped back to Homestead

News. It was definitely her. She looked upset. "Go away," she was telling the journalist. "I have nothing to say to you." The scene changed to Kelly's father saying, "We love Kelly very much, and we'll be hearing her side of the story before coming to any conclusions. It would pay you guys to do the same."

Now the camera traveled to Kelly, being hugged by Josh. What the hell was going on? Cold, clammy fear gripped Trent.

Back in the studio, the announcer said, "Scenes of confusion and panic today as it was revealed that Kelly Greenwood, the sport psychologist credited with turning around Trent Matheson's recent performance, may have been responsible for a life-threatening injury suffered by a former client. Was Matheson aware of the scandal? Homestead News asks if our sports stars are taking the quest for victory too far, putting their mental and physical health in the hands of so-called experts who—"

Trent cursed as he switched off the TV.

This couldn't be worse for Kelly's fledgling career. No matter that Homestead News probably had a total audience of about two thousand people—this story would be picked up by all the networks. Soon.

He tried to imagine how Kelly must feel. Devastated. Alone. Even though family was there, she would withdraw into herself, try to sustain herself under her own steam, as always. Her family wouldn't understand how she needed them, they'd only see her fierce independence. Only Trent understood.

But he couldn't help her. Not without screwing up his prerace routine. If Trent missed so much as a beat tomorrow, Danny Cruise would finish ahead of him. *Not going to happen.* Trent had visualized winning the NASCAR NEXTEL Cup Series so many times, he could practically feel the cool silver in his hands.

In his visualizations, Kelly always stood beside him.

"Damn," he said. Because suddenly, when he pictured winning the Cup, it felt more like he'd lost what mattered most.

There was knock on the door of his motor home, then Chad and Zack came in. Chad dropped a six-pack of beer on the counter. "You look like you've seen a ghost."

"How do you know when you've met the right woman?" Trent demanded. "When you've met The One?"

Chad cocked an eyebrow. "You're asking me?"

"You're right, scratch that." Trent directed a disgusted look at Zack. "No point asking you, either, Ice Man." From the clues occasionally supplied by his taciturn brother, Trent had gleaned that Zack had some kind of perfect woman in mind who probably didn't exist.

"None at all," Zack agreed.

Okay, so his brothers were no help. Trent paced the living area while Chad opened the beers. He had to make this call on his own. And right then, he knew what it had to be.

He would be there for Kelly tonight. The way she'd been there for him through everything, through every effort he'd made to get rid of her, until finally he'd screwed up so badly he'd driven her away.

He stopped pacing. "I need to talk to the TV guys. The big ones. You guys can give me a lift."

He walked out with them, leaving behind his best shot at winning the Cup.

HER FAMILY had been wonderful, but now Kelly wanted to be left alone. She'd booted them all out of her hotel room as soon as the broadcast ended, not wanting them to see how bad she felt.

She lay on her bed, too drained to cry, contemplating the charred ruins of her career. This would be all over the TV by the late news. There could be no comeback.

She didn't know how long she lay there, the TV on mute, pictures flickering meaninglessly across the screen.

Then Trent's face flashed on the screen, the words *Breaking News* superimposed over him.

She sat up, scrambled to find the remote and eventually located it under her pillow. She turned up the sound in time to hear the announcer say, "Trent Matheson broke his habitual prerace silence tonight to defend the woman he says is single-handedly responsible for the transformation fans have seen in his driving this season."

"What?" Kelly squeaked.

The announcer summarized the story that had appeared on the local news earlier, then she handed over to an interviewer, outdoors at the track with Trent.

"Kelly Greenwood did an incredible job of identifying where I was going wrong in my racing," Trent said. "Without her, I wouldn't be in Miami this weekend with a chance of winning the NASCAR NEXTEL Cup Championship. She got me back on track."

It was so spookily like that dream she'd had soon after she met him, that Kelly blinked and rubbed her eyes.

"What about the client who broke his neck as a result of following Kelly's advice?" the interviewer asked.

"Kelly told me about that. It's clear what happened was an accident and in no way related to her work. It's tempting to blame someone else when things go wrong—hey, how often have I blamed Danny Cruise for one of my smashes?" he joked. The interviewer laughed. "One thing I learned from Kelly is that I'm responsible for my own mistakes," Trent said. "I can get the best advice, but it's up to me whether or not I follow it. I can tell you that following Kelly's advice is the best thing I ever did."

Kelly was crying too hard to hear any more. Trent had saved her reputation, her career. If it had been possible to love him any more than she already did, this would have swung it. He'd risked his entire no-stress, no-media prerace routine to come to her rescue. Who knew what impact that might have on his racing?

Just like that, her weepy delight turned to dry-eyed suspicion. *Trent Matheson doesn't do things like this.* Though Kelly loved him, she didn't harbor any illusions about who came first in his life.

She paced the room, trying to second-guess him. On her third circuit of the confined space, the answer hit her.

Trent wanted her back. He wanted her standing next to Rod Sutton tomorrow, bringing him luck. Kelly sagged onto the bed, knowing the truth. This wasn't about helping her, at least, not mostly. This was about him, about winning the NASCAR NEXTEL Cup Series.

A thumping sounded on her door. "Kelly, it's me, let me in," Trent called.

He'd come to collect on the debt she owed.

Kelly scrambled off the bed. She ran her hands through her hair, caught a glimpse of smudged makeup in the mirror. She opened the door.

His grin was elated. "Hey, sugar, did you see me on TV?" He grabbed her around the waist and waltzed her into the room.

"I will not come to tomorrow's race and stand next to Rod," she said.

He did a double take. "What?"

"You qualified tenth for tomorrow's race. You believe you can't win unless I'm there."

"The car was too tight," he said. "The crew fixed it, it'll be fine for tomorrow. I can win from tenth, you know I can."

"Not without your lucky charm."

He released her, stepped back. "I did not come here to ask you to bring me luck," he said, his voice going deadly cold.

For a moment, she wavered. "You're interrupting your pre-race routine. We both know you don't do anything that doesn't suit you. It didn't suit you to believe me when I told you what happened in New Zealand, it didn't suit you to tell me you were using me to bring you luck."

"I went on TV tonight because I love you," he said.

He couldn't have hurt her more if he'd tried.

"Your life is all about you," she said flatly. "You can't commit to one woman." She saw the flash of panic in his eyes at the word *commit.* She pushed home her point. "You're not here to ask me to marry you, are you?"

"*Marry* you?" He must have heard the alarm in his own voice, because he backpedaled. "I only just figured out that I love you. You haven't even said you love me back."

"You're here because you want me at the race." She moved away from him, forced herself not to yield to the angry tears. "I wish you well for tomorrow," she said, almost calmly, "but I won't be a part of it."

His mouth was flat, a hard line. "You are one sad woman. You've been fighting your own battles so long, you have no idea how to accept that someone else cares the way you want them to. Well, sugar, you'll find out." He grabbed her, crushed her lips in a kiss that held anger, resentment and something else. Then he left.

Kelly shut the door behind him. Then she opened it again. "Make sure you get five hours' sleep," she called after his retreating back.

CHAPTER SEVENTEEN

KELLY ONLY WISHED she could get five hours' sleep herself. At 3:00 a.m. she was still awake, feeling terrible about what she'd said to Trent. No matter what his reasons, he'd saved her career. She did owe him. If all he needed was for her to stand next to Rod Sutton for his final race, then she would do that.

She slept at last, waking at nine o'clock. Five hours to kill until the race. She watched the buildup on TV, and soon after midday she headed for the track, going straight to the garage. Only to find a security guard blocking her way.

"I have a pass." She held up the hard card Chad had given her.

"Are you Kelly Greenwood?"

She sighed. She'd been stopped three times on her way in by people wanting to talk about last night's TV interview. All of them had been positive, but she'd scarcely been able to talk to them. No way could she risk being late to see Trent before the race. "That's right."

"Sorry, ma'am, I can't allow you in here."

The words took a moment to hit her. "Excuse me?"

"Orders of Trent Matheson. He said you're not to be admitted."

"But he needs me there. I'm his— I bring him luck."

The man shrugged. "Looks like he doesn't want any luck today."

She argued until the people in the line behind her told her

to shut up and go away. Then she came back and tried again. To no avail.

Outraged, she paced outside the garage area. What was Trent up to? How could she possibly bring him good luck if she couldn't get to her place next to Rod?

Unless… She stopped, put a hand to her mouth.

Unless this wasn't about luck. Unless he'd helped her last night, put today's race at risk, with no thought of gaining her help. Purely with the thought of saving her.

It was the kind of thing a man would do for the woman he loved.

He told me but I didn't believe it.

"He does love me," she said out loud. Tears sprang to her eyes. Trent had risked everything, for her.

The idiot. Dear, sweet idiot.

She had to get to him. She ran back to the security guard, who groaned when he saw her coming.

"You have to let me in," she said. "I'm Trent Matheson's fiancée." Okay, so he hadn't proposed yet. But if he loved her, that would be next, once he got his head around the commitment thing.

The guard didn't even try to hide his laughter. "If you knew how many ladies have told me that today…"

"Forget it," Kelly snapped. She had to find somewhere where she could keep tabs on what was happening in Trent's car. That meant watching it on TV.

She raced to Trent's trailer, punched in the access code she'd seen him use. Soon she was ensconced in front of the large-screen TV.

She watched Trent climb into the car. The camera stayed on him while he put on his helmet. She thought she saw him take a deep breath. Was he in the zone?

Trent made swift work of his first four passes, earning the vocal approval of the crowd. Then he stuck like glue to the five front-runners, none of whom seemed in any hurry to give up their place. But quick work by the crew in Trent's first pit stop lifted him one place to fourth.

He more or less stayed there, occasionally changing places with the car behind or in front of him, until his third pit stop, when he was penalized for speeding on pit road and had to pass through again on his next lap.

Kelly moaned when he dropped back to tenth. But he soon began to work his way up again.

"You can do it," she urged him when the Number 186 car got up to fifth. "You can win."

ON LAP 200, Trent still felt great. He'd just missed getting caught up in a two-car smash near the bottom of the track and was still cursing the drivers who'd nearly ended his race when his spotter said, "Number 53's out."

Trent circled the track slowly under the yellow caution flag. It was true: unlike Trent, Tony Stevens hadn't been able to avoid the mess, and his car was now a tangled wreck.

The leader was out.

And that left only Danny Cruise for Trent to beat.

Trent set his sights on Cruise, who was running second, three places ahead. A new determination propelled him past the two cars between him and Cruise. When Cruise surged forward, Trent knew Danny's spotter had told him Trent was on his tail.

"You can run, but you can't hide," he muttered. Then he added his key words, "Plenty of room." He wondered if Kelly was watching, if she'd tried to come to the track, if she'd realized yet that he meant what he said. After he'd left her last night, Trent had finally figured out what to do about loving her. He wanted—

Win the race first.

By lap 300, Cruise was running first, Trent second. Trent

had tried several times to pass his rival, but Danny wasn't letting go. If Cruise kept going the way he was, he would win.

"Pitting now," Rod told Trent with twelve laps to go.

Trent made an instant decision. "Two tires and a splash," he told Rod as he started down pit road.

"We agreed four," his crew chief said. "This is no time to change our strategy."

"Two," Trent insisted. "It's the only way I can win." He heard Rod's grunt of reluctant agreement at the same moment as he saw the Energy Oil flag waving on a pole extended ahead of him. He pulled into his pit box.

Putting on only two new tires, when most teams would seek the extra grip that came with four, was a risk. So was taking only a splash of fuel. But Trent could see no other way to gain the seconds he needed to beat Cruise.

As he came out of the pits, he knew he'd made the right call. The two new tires were sticking just fine, and Trent felt as if the car had a new lease of life. He surged onto the straightaway.

WHEN TRENT CAME OUT of his final pit stop ahead of Danny Cruise, Kelly jumped to her feet and screamed, along with the crowd in the stands. She couldn't sit down again. She paced back and forth, back and forth, as he dueled with Cruise over those last crucial laps. Twice, Cruise got out in front. Twice, Trent regained the lead.

The last lap loomed.

Trent came into the lap ahead. The crowd went wild, cheering the red car. Cruise was agonizingly close. The two cars went into Turn Three side by side, so close Kelly would have sworn they'd touched. Coming out of Turn Four, both drivers ran high, and this time they did clash. There was an audible thump as they hit and veered away from each other. For a fraction of a second, Cruise lost control of his car. Then he was back, focused as ever.

But that lapse had cost him the race. Trent streaked down the last straightaway in the lead, to pass the checkered flag half a car-length ahead of Cruise.

"He did it," Kelly yelled. She whooped, hollered, jumped up on Trent's leather couch and danced.

Trent must have spun a dozen doughnuts down the front stretch, to the delight of the crowd.

Kelly suddenly realized where she was—and where she wasn't. She had to be there when Trent got out of that car.

She sprinted back to the garage.

"Not you again," the guard said wearily.

But she was already past him. This time she didn't stop to argue, and the surprise factor got her through.

"Hey!"

She heard him running after her, and picked up her pace. She made it to Victory Lane just as Trent climbed out of the car. He looked past the microphones and cameras, past the officials holding the magnificent sterling silver trophy he'd earned today, and scanned the crowd.

Looking for her.

Which made no sense, Kelly thought acerbically, when he'd done his best to keep her out of there.

Then he saw her, and had someone open the gate to let her in. "I knew you'd get here."

Something in his voice caused a hush to descend on the crowd, which parted to let Kelly through.

She walked toward him, not hurrying now, feeling oddly shy. Then she tripped over a camera bag, and had to right herself. She ignored the chuckles of the bystanders. At last, she reached him.

He took her hands in his. "I need you, Kelly." His voice shook with the strength of his emotion. "I need you by my side. Not for luck. For love."

"I need you, too," she said.

"I want to marry you." The light in his eyes turned tender. "I've done some dumb things, but I do love you. I want to be with you for the rest of my life."

Kelly blinked away tears, struggled to speak without dissolving. Someone elbowed her in the side, a hard jab. "Tell him you love him," the elderly mother of the president of Energy Oil said.

Kelly giggled. She said to Trent, "You're talking about a one-woman commitment, right?"

"You're the only woman for me, sugar." He tugged her into his arms. "Now, are you going to marry me?"

"First I need to keep a promise I made you a while back." She pulled out of his embrace and addressed the waiting media. "I want to make one thing quite clear," she announced.

Cameras snapped and the journalists waited, microphones and pens poised.

"Trent Matheson is *not* an airhead." She turned back to Trent and said conversationally, "Obviously I couldn't marry you if you were."

"Obviously." He chuckled, but there was an edge of frustration to it. "Sugar, I sure hope you're getting around to answering my question."

"I love you, Trent," she said. "Of course I'll marry you."

He claimed her in a kiss that silenced the crowd and left Kelly breathless. When at last he pulled away, she gloried in the promise of forever that blazed in his blue eyes.

"Now that," he said, with the self-satisfaction Kelly adored, "is what I call a win."

* * * * *

Mediterranean Nights

Join the guests and crew of Alexandra's Dream, *the newest
luxury ship to set sail on the romantic Mediterranean,
as they experience the glamorous world of cruising.*

*A new Harlequin continuity series
begins in June 2007 with
FROM RUSSIA, WITH LOVE
by Ingrid Weaver*

Marina Artamova books a cabin on the luxurious cruise ship
Alexandra's Dream, *when she finds out that her orphaned
nephew and his adoptive father are aboard. She's determined
to be reunited with the boy…but the romantic ambience
of the ship and her undeniable attraction to a man
she considers her enemy are about to interfere
with her quest!*

Turn the page for a sneak preview!

Piraeus, Greece

"THERE SHE IS, Stefan. *Alexandra's Dream.*" David Anderson squatted beside his new son and pointed at the dark blue hull that towered above the pier. The cruise ship was a majestic sight, twelve decks high and as long as a city block. A circle of silver and gold stars, the logo of the Liberty Cruise Line, gleamed from the swept-back smokestack. Like some legendary sea creature born for the water, the ship emanated power from every sleek curve—even at rest it held the promise of motion. "That's going to be our home for the next ten days."

The child beside him remained silent, his cheeks working in and out as he sucked furiously on his thumb. Hair so blond it appeared white ruffled against his forehead in the harbor breeze. The baby-sweet scent unique to the very young mingled with the tang of the sea.

"Ship," David said. "Uh, *parakhod.*"

From beneath his bangs, Stefan looked at the *Alexandra's Dream.* Although he didn't release his thumb, the corners of his mouth tightened with the beginning of a smile.

David grinned. That was Stefan's first smile this afternoon, one of only two since they had left the orphanage yesterday. It was probably because of the boat—according to the orphanage staff, the boy loved boats, which was the main reason David had decided to book this cruise. Then again, there was a strong possibility the smile could have been a reaction to David's attempt at pocket-dictionary Russian. Whatever the cause, it was a good start.

The liaison from the adoption agency had claimed that Stefan had been taught some English, but David had yet to see evidence of it. David continued to speak, positive his son would understand his tone even if he couldn't grasp the words. "This is her maiden voyage. Her first trip, just like this is our first trip, and that makes it special." He motioned toward the stage that had been set up on the pier beneath the ship's bow. "That's why everyone's celebrating."

The ship's official christening ceremony had been held the day before and had been a closed affair, with only the cruise-line executives and VIP guests invited, but the stage hadn't yet been disassembled. Banners bearing the blue and white of the Greek flag of the ship's owner, as well as the Liberty circle of stars logo, draped the edges of the platform. In the center, a group of musicians and a dance troupe dressed in traditional white folk costumes performed for the benefit of the *Alexandra's Dream*'s first passengers. Their audience was in a festive mood, snapping their fingers in time to the music while the dancers twirled and wove through their steps.

David bobbed his head to the rhythm of the mandolins. They were playing a folk tune that seemed vaguely familiar, possibly from a movie he'd seen. He hummed a few notes. "Catchy melody, isn't it?"

Stefan turned his gaze on David. His eyes were a striking shade of blue, as cool and pale as a winter horizon and far too solemn for a child not yet five. Still, the smile that hovered at the corners of his mouth persisted. He moved his head with the music, mirroring David's motion.

David gave a silent cheer at the interaction. Hopefully, this cruise would provide countless opportunities for more. "Hey, good for you," he said. "Do you like the music?"

The child's eyes sparked. He withdrew his thumb with a pop. *"Moozika!"*

"Music. Right!" David held out his hand. "Come on, let's go closer so we can watch the dancers."

Stefan grasped David's hand quickly, as if he feared it would be withdrawn. In an instant his budding smile was replaced by a look close to panic.

Did he remember the car accident that had killed his parents? It would be a mercy if he didn't. As far as David knew, Stefan had never spoken of it to anyone. Whatever he had seen had made him run so far from the crash that the police hadn't found him until the next day. The event had traumatized him to the extent that he hadn't uttered a word until his fifth week at the orphanage. Even now he seldom talked.

David sat back on his heels and brushed the hair from Stefan's forehead. That solemn, too-old gaze locked with his, and for an instant, David felt as if he looked back in time at an image of himself thirty years ago.

He didn't need to speak the same language to understand exactly how this boy felt. He knew what it meant to be alone and powerless among strangers, trying to be brave and tough but wishing with every fiber of his being for a place to belong, to be safe, and most of all for someone to love him....

He knew in his heart he would be a good parent to Stefan. It was why he had never considered halting the adoption process after Ellie had left him. He hadn't balked when he'd learned of the recent claim by Stefan's spinster aunt, either; the absentee relative had shown up too late for her case to be considered. The adoption was meant to be. He and this child already shared a bond that went deeper than paperwork or legalities.

A seagull screeched overhead, making Stefan start and press closer to David.

"That's my boy," David murmured. He swallowed hard, struck by the simple truth of what he had just said.

That's my *boy.*

"I CAN'T BE PATIENT, RUDOLPH. I'm not going to stand by and watch my nephew get ripped from his country and his roots to live on the other side of the world."

Rudolph hissed out a slow breath. "Marina, I don't like the sound of that. What are you planning?"

"I'm going to talk some sense into this American kidnapper."

"No. Absolutely not. No offence, but diplomacy is not your strong suit."

"Diplomacy be damned. Their ship's due to sail at five o'clock."

"Then you wouldn't have an opportunity to speak with him even if his lawyer agreed to a meeting."

"I'll have ten days of opportunities, Rudolph, since I plan to be on board that ship."

* * * * *

Follow Marina and David as they join forces to uncover the reason behind little Stefan's unusual silence, and the secret behind the death of his parents....

Look for From Russia, With Love *by Ingrid Weaver in stores June 2007.*

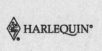

Mediterranean
NIGHTS™

Tycoon Elias Stamos is launching his newest luxury cruise
ship from his home port in Greece. But someone from his
past is eager to expose old secrets and to see the Stamos
empire crumble.

Mediterranean Nights
launches in June 2007 with...

FROM RUSSIA,
WITH LOVE
by *Ingrid Weaver*

Join the guests
and crew of
Alexandra's Dream
as they are drawn
into a world of
glamour, romance
and intrigue
in this new
12-book series.

REQUEST YOUR FREE BOOKS!
2 FREE NOVELS PLUS 2 FREE GIFTS!

SPECIAL EDITION®
Life, Love and Family!

YES! Please send me 2 FREE Silhouette Special Edition® novels and my 2 FREE gifts. After receiving them, if I don't wish to receive any more books, I can return the shipping statement marked "cancel." If I don't cancel, I will receive 6 brand-new novels every month and be billed just $4.24 per book in the U.S., or $4.99 per book in Canada, plus 25¢ shipping and handling per book and applicable taxes, if any*. That's a savings of at least 15% off the cover price! I understand that accepting the 2 free books and gifts places me under no obligation to buy anything. I can always return a shipment and cancel at any time. Even if I never buy another book from Silhouette, the two free books and gifts are mine to keep forever.   235 SDN EEYU 335 SDN EEY6

Name	(PLEASE PRINT)	
Address		Apt.
City	State/Prov.	Zip/Postal Code

Signature (if under 18, a parent or guardian must sign)

Mail to the **Silhouette Reader Service**™:
IN U.S.A.: P.O. Box 1867, Buffalo, NY 14240-1867
IN CANADA: P.O. Box 609, Fort Erie, Ontario L2A 5X3

Not valid to current Silhouette Special Edition subscribers.

Want to try two free books from another line?
Call 1-800-873-8635 or visit www.morefreebooks.com.

* Terms and prices subject to change without notice. NY residents add applicable sales tax. Canadian residents will be charged applicable provincial taxes and GST. This offer is limited to one order per household. All orders subject to approval. Credit or debit balances in a customer's account(s) may be offset by any other outstanding balance owed by or to the customer. Please allow 4 to 6 weeks for delivery.

Your Privacy: Silhouette is committed to protecting your privacy. Our Privacy Policy is available online at www.eHarlequin.com or upon request from the Reader Service. From time to time we make our lists of customers available to reputable firms who may have a product or service of interest to you. If you would prefer we not share your name and address, please check here. ☐

SSE07

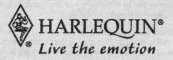